*Un*RAVELED

Guzzi Duet, Book One

BETHANY-KRIS

Published by Bethany-Kris

BK

www.bethanykris.com

eISBN 13: 978-1-988197-31-9
Print ISBN 13: 978-1-988197-32-6

Cover Art © Mignon Mykel at Oh, So Novel Designs
Editor: Nina S. Gooden

Dedication

For Gian. Break hearts, my French-Italian boy.

Contents

BETHANY-KRIS

Chapter 1

The most devastating emotion was grief.

All-consuming.

Suffocating.

A horrible, monster of an emotion that embedded its very poison into a person's soul, and didn't let go. Instead of eventually freeing its victim from the never-ending torment, to allow them to step back and breathe, the grief continued to spread and infect like a disease.

There was no healing. There was supposed to be. The stages of grief were eventually supposed to move on to a point where a person could go forward, away from the constant struggle, and begin to heal.

Cara Rossi had yet to find that stage.

She didn't think she would ever reach it.

Her grief had gone far beyond the instant devastation, and straight into a hellish non-existence where no one could possible understand how bereft she was, left in her little world.

There were those people who believed that when a person lost someone they loved, a piece of their soul went with them. Cara wasn't sure how she was supposed to take that statement every time someone offered their well-intentioned, yet incredibly hurtful, advice.

She hadn't just *lost* someone she loved.

Her best friend. The identical face she stared at for everyday of her life since birth. Someone she hadn't spent more than a few hours away from at a time for two and a half decades.

It wasn't a piece of her that was missing. It was an entire *half* ripped away. Twenty-five years together and then ... *gone.*

Her identical twin was dead.

Just like that.

But, *it's been four months, Cara.* And, *look at the beautiful day outside, sweetheart.* More of, *she would want you to smile, and to be happy.* A few, *can't you try a little more?*

Four months was a long time to be missing something so incredibly important to Cara's everyday life. It was a long time to be walking around out of control of her emotions, incomplete, alone, and lost.

She had a hard time closing her eyes.

She could see that day.

Perfectly.

Clearly.

Painfully.

When gun fire rang out …

When white marble steps turned red with blood …

When her twin died.

How was Cara ever supposed to move on, when every time she closed her eyes, she was standing back on the steps of that mansion, staring at her sister's blood on her hands, and listening to Lea gasp for help?

She couldn't.

She never would.

"You could always come back to Chicago," Tommas said, posing the suggestion quietly. "I could get you a ticket tonight, Cara."

Cara rubbed at the tension headache beginning to form at the base of her skull, and focused on the words her older brother was saying over the phone. She wasn't sure how to answer without hurting his feelings. The siblings had already been separated by countries for years, only occasionally coming together for family events. Tommas, in Chicago. And Cara, in Toronto, studying at the university.

"The break might be good for you," Tommas continued, when Cara stayed silent. "Chicago isn't Toronto. Things might feel familiar here."

"Chicago isn't home," Cara snapped.

Tommas took a sharp inhale. Cara was even surprised at her outburst, colored heavily with anger. Her brother's silent response was answer enough. Cara wished that she could check her temper toward her brother, but she didn't have anything to give him, but for her anger.

Her brother—more than anyone left living that she loved—knew how she felt about Chicago. Or … her parents.

Or rather, the remaining parent she had left.

Addiction, hate, and pain. That was all their childhood had ever been. It was all that was left in Chicago.

"Ma would like to see—"

Cara stopped her brother before he could even attempt to say more. "I don't give a shit about Ma, Tommas."

Tommas cleared his throat. "She lost her husband. Give her a break, Cara."

"A man she hated. A man she only pretended to love and only when she was drunk. A man she beat on. A man she put first before her children. So, her husband is dead, big fucking deal. I doubt she feels even an ounce of the hell that *I've* been living with for *four months*."

"We don't know what goes on inside Ma's head."

"I don't need to know. Her soul is black. Her heart is black. She should be dead like he is. We would *all* be far better off without them both."

"*Cara.*"

The truth hurt, but it was better than a blissful lie. Those hurt worse in the end.

Cara and Lea had been eighteen years old when they'd left. Dual Canadian citizenship and the family ties they had in Ontario got them away from their abusive, alcoholic parents. Tommas, however, had been long gone from the house by the time the twins left.

Tommas also had ties to the Chicago Outfit—a criminal organization that had been bred deep into their family's blood and name for decades— like their father. It was all he knew. Leaving Chicago, and the Outfit, had never been a thought in her brother's mind.

Now, seven years later, Cara was twenty-five, their sister was dead, and nothing was going to ever be the same again. Tommas thought going back where she hated the most, to the people of the Outfit that he called family *and* the place that had taken Lea from her, would fix this.

It never would.

"I'm not going back to Chicago," Cara said after a long stretch of silence.

"Ever?" Tommas asked.

There was no judgement in his tone. He'd asked it with very little emotion, as though he already knew exactly what her answer would be.

"Not if I can help it, Tommas."

Cara waited for those words to sink in, hoping that her brother finally got the point. She loved Tommas, even if their relationship was strained from years of separation and the past. She knew that Tommas loved her, too.

"I don't think you understand how difficult it is to get up in the morning. I pass her bedroom and try not to breakdown. I still have *all* of Lea's things. They litter this apartment from top to bottom." Cara couldn't bear the thought of getting rid of any of it. But she could barely stand to look at it all, either. "The apartment—and even Toronto—is basically the same thing. I struggle daily, to even leave the apartment and get done what I need to do. Every place I visit, all the sights I see, are touched by a memory of Lea. And that *hurts*," Cara said quietly.

There was a lot she didn't say, too.

Her college marks were suffering, her dream of becoming a therapist diminishing with missed classes. Frankly, *she* needed to be the one talking to a therapist, but that meant opening the front door and *going outside*.

It felt like her heart was ripping apart at the seams, the second her hand touched the front doorknob. She was leaving behind the only tangible ties to her sister that were not merely memories.

She was so useless like this.

Broken.

Incomplete.

Without.

"Cara," Tommas said.

The softer tone her brother used brought Cara from the black abyss that was her thoughts. Her new constant companion.

"Yeah, Tommy?"

"I know it's hard—"

"Harder, actually," Cara interrupted.

"I'm sorry. I want to do something to help, but I need you to give me some kind of direction here, Cara. Or *how* to help. What do you need me to do?"

Leave me alone, she thought. *Stop making me remember. It hurts.*

Cara would never say those things to her brother, as they would hurt him.

It had been *his* people who had taken her sister away, even if it hadn't been him, directly, who had pulled the trigger. It was still *the Outfit*. Tommas was an Outfit man. Cara didn't know how to separate Tommas from the organization.

It was dirty money, bad blood, stained histories, and pain.

"Cara?" Tommas asked again.

She took a deep breath and rolled from her side to her back on the bed. A comforting place that she rarely left, now. Slinging her arm over her face, she blocked out the light that filtered in through the blinds.

"Just give me some time," Cara settled on saying.

"Is more time actually going to help, Cara?"

"I don't know."

Cara stumbled from her bed. The persistent knocking—the bitch of a thing that had woken her up in the first place—continued to echo throughout the quiet apartment.

She'd made it perfectly clear to everyone that she wanted to be alone. She wasn't without family in Toronto. She had her aunt and uncle, a couple of cousins, and a few friends from school.

As for the family side, Cara tried to stay away from their business as much as possible. Unless it was for something she couldn't excuse her way out of, Cara tried not to intrude on their lives. And usually, they didn't intrude too much on hers.

Well, before Lea died. She had seen more of her aunt and uncle since Lea's death than she wanted to admit. She wished they would all go back to the polite greetings and occasional meet ups.

For good reason … It didn't seem to matter where Cara lived, Canada or the USA, she couldn't escape her family's legacy.

The Rossi family—from the Canadian side, all the way to the American—was marked by *crime*. The mafia had weaved itself through her family tree from the very distant members, to her closest relatives. Cara needed distance from her family, and all the rest of the shit that they were involved in, as she always had. Now, though, since Lea's murder *because* of the mafia, she needed that distance even more.

"*Cristo*," Cara swore in Italian as she neared the front door to the apartment. The knocking had yet to cease, and that only kicked her irritation up to another level. "I'm fucking coming, relax."

Cara flicked the deadbolt lock, and yanked open the door with more force than was necessary. She didn't even bother to wipe the scowl off her face. She was not expecting who she found waiting.

Bambi Emmi.

For a long while, Cara simply stared at the young woman until Bambi's usual wide smile faded a bit. In a tight, red dress that fell at her mid-thigh, and complimented her ruby lips and dark hair, Bambi was an exceptionally beautiful woman. Cara, with her crazy, red, curly hair and blue eyes, had never quite felt inferior when standing next to Bambi, though.

Their previous meetings had been passing, brief moments when Bambi's friendship with Lea had managed to involve Cara as well, and politeness was expected.

"Hi," Bambi said, shifting the diamond-studded clutch she held from one hand to another.

Cara said nothing.

She didn't know *what* to say, truthfully.

While she would consider Bambi a friend of sorts, the girl had been much closer to Lea. Despite being close, and twins, the girls hadn't always shared the same likes, dislikes, or behaviors.

Lea had been out-going, making friends wherever she went. Cara preferred to stand off in the shadows and watch people interact in all sorts of situation. To her, that was fascinating. To Lea, interacting and growing her circle had been the interesting part of life.

"So …" Bambi said, drawing the word out for much longer than what was necessary.

Awkward.

Finally, Cara's mouth decided to play catch-up with her brain, and work. All she managed to say was a confused, "So."

Bambi didn't look offended over Cara's lack of response to her presence, never mind her lack of enthusiasm at conversing like a normal human being. No, if anything, Bambi looked happier, her smile growing all over again.

And then Cara had to go and open her mouth to ruin it with, "What exactly are you doing here?"

Bambi's smile vanished instantly, replaced by a hurt dancing over her pretty features. "I'm sorry. Am I not allowed to visit a friend?"

First, Bambi had always been more of a friend to Lea than Cara, for the most obvious reason ... being Bambi's lifestyle. *For lack of a better word,* Cara thought.

She could be brutally honest—Bambi liked her *made* men. Mafia men were just her thing. But the second reason why Bambi should not be knocking on Cara's door?

Cara looked at the clock on the wall. "It's eleven-thirty at night."

Jesus. Was it really *that* late already? Hadn't she been talking to her brother that afternoon?

Well, shit.

Cara had literally slept her day away. She'd missed another round of classes. An exam. An assignment that was due. A lecture.

And she needed groceries.

Fuck.

She was a *mess.*

She didn't even know how to go about fixing it. Or even if she wanted to.

Bambi only stared at Cara as though she had suddenly grown a second head in the span of seconds. "What are you talking about?"

Cara pointed at the clock. "It's late."

"Yeah, if you're fifty."

"I have school in the morning."

Bambi cocked an eyebrow. "Tomorrow is Saturday, and I remember Lea saying once that you don't have classes on Saturdays."

Was tomorrow Saturday?

What was happening to her life?

Cara rubbed a hand over her face. "What do you want?"

"I was in the neighborhood. I thought you might like to see a familiar face."

"You thought wrong."

Cara could have softened that blow, but she didn't have the patience to. Bambi didn't seem all that offended. In fact, she looked as though she had expected that.

"Yeah, seems I'm not the first person you've chased off with your nasty attitude lately. People talk, and others tend to take notice and listen. I know we're not the greatest friends, but your sister looked out for me a lot, and I'd like to think that Lea would be super pissed at me if I didn't offer the same to you."

Cara cleared her throat, more uncomfortable than ever. "I'm fine."

"Well, that's a lie."

"Bambi—"

"You look like shit just came over and took *another* shit on your head."

Ouch.

"Okay, that's enough," Cara said, grabbing the door to close it in the woman's face. "It's time for you to go."

"Wait." Bambi put her body into the doorway, effectively stopping Cara from closing her out. "One night, Cara. You can take *one* night to get out of this apartment, away from this …" Bambi waved at the darkness behind Cara. "Whatever this mess is, and do something. Maybe it'll be fun. Maybe you won't have to think for a while. Maybe you'll even smile. What would it hurt to *try?*"

It could hurt *a lot.*

"I'm not even dressed or done up," Cara said weakly.

Bambi smiled slyly, gesturing at herself. "That is why you have *me.*"

"I can dress and do my own makeup, thanks."

"And I will be right here to make sure you actually do it. A new club opened up three blocks away, last week. I happen to know the owner is a great guy, and throws an awesome fucking party. Give it a chance."

Cara was too mentally tired to argue. Or maybe it was that she *wanted* to feel normal for a minute. Even if that meant using alcohol and deafening music to do it.

That was that.

"All right," Cara said. "Give me fifteen minutes."

Bambi looked her over. "Twenty, at least."

"You could be nicer."

"You could look less dead."

Bitch.

Chapter 2

"You're looking terribly *miaou* tonight."

Gian Guzzi gave his mother a kiss on her head. "*Mamma*, it's not appropriate to catcall your son. Even when you're doing it in French."

"Am I the first woman to tell you that this evening?"

"I came here from the penthouse. Where would I find a *femme* to catcall me?"

"Well, one would think in your *penthouse*, considering."

Gian chose to ignore that jab, if only because Celeste Guzzi meant no harm. She wished for better things for her two sons and one daughter—happier things. At the moment, Gian was the only one of her adult children that she felt was *not* happy, for a multitude of reasons. Especially at his twenty-nine years of life, she wanted to see more from him.

He could only give what he had.

"I have a club opening," Gian explained. "New suit, one of several, since the season is going to change."

"Armani, I think."

His mother knew her brands well.

Gian smiled. "*Oui*, Armani."

"Give me another kiss before you run off to find your father and grandfather," Celeste ordered, pointing to her cheek, but never looking up from her magazine.

He indulged his mother, bending down to kiss her again before straightening to his full six-foot, four-inch height again. Something else he had taken from the male, Italian side of his family, and not the short, pale-skinned genetics of his mother's Acadian *Français* side.

"And show off that new suit!" his mother shouted at his back.

Gian waved a hand over his shoulder, offering nothing else.

He loved his mother dearly. As a child, he had been enamored with her ability to never fail, never falter. She always wore a smile, and she had loved her husband, unwaveringly, through his many faults. If possible, he would prefer to have a woman like that. Silent strength and steadfast love.

Wishes, however, were not for made men whose lifestyle—one governed by the rules of *Mafioso*—was meant to benefit *la famiglia*, not the individual man. Especially not one like Gian.

As it were, he had been given too much privilege being born with his last name. According to some, anyway.

Gian navigated the halls of the mansion, heading up to the second level where he knew he would find his father and grandfather. Usually, he would meet his grandfather—the boss of their Cosa Nostra *famiglia*—at his home across the city, but tonight had been a change in scenery, for whatever reason.

From all the way down the hall, Gian could already hear the Italian murmurings between a father and son in the office. It never failed to amuse him—or confuse the fuck out of people he brought around as a younger man—that depending on which part of the house a person was in, the language could change. From French, to Italian, to English. Some, like he and his siblings, or his parents, could easily navigate between the three languages without issue in both reading, writing, and conversing.

His half Italian, half French, but fully Canadian family was certainly … colorful.

In more ways than one.

Well, considering the men were criminals and the women were wives of those same criminals, he supposed that led a little credence to the color.

Gian's presence was instantly noticed when he stepped foot in the opened doorway of the office. His grandfather—Corrado—sat in one of the many chairs, while Gian's father stood next to the windows, peering out over the darkness that had settled outside on the massive, private property.

"*Il mio ragazzo!*" his grandfather greeted.

"*Ciao*, boss."

Corrado made a face. "No boss nonsense tonight."

Gian nodded. "All right. I interrupted a conversion, didn't I? The Raptors game, I think. Someone thinks they're going to lose the next one."

Corrado passed Frederic a look. "They've been on a streak. Every time that damn team goes on a streak, they choke."

"Oh, they do not, Dad," Frederic argued. "They're the best basketball team in—"

"*Merda!* You only believe that nonsense because you're attached to the team."

Maybe Gian should have left the conversation lie with his arrival. "Argue about sports on a night when I don't have somewhere to be, huh?"

His grandfather's sharp, dark gaze skipped to him in the doorway, but the irritation was quickly replaced with the sort of mirth only an eighty-five-year-old man could have. Perhaps had it been another made man, and had Gian's tone not been so playful when he spoke, his grandfather might have gotten up from his chair, ready to discipline his subordinate as only a Guzzi Don could.

But it was Gian.

And this was his *Grandpapa*.

He often got away with more than he should.

Gian tried not to abuse his grandfather's affections. Corrado only looked old on the outside, as his mind was still as sharp, volatile, and prone to violence as it had ever been. He didn't let Gian get away with very much when *others* were around.

Others not including Frederic, of course. Gian's father was not a made man like he and his grandfather. Those rules of respect did not apply.

"You're late tonight, Gian. You almost missed me, I was going to head home and go to bed. It's been a long day." Corrado pushed up from the large leather chair, wincing a bit as he stood. "My bones are getting too old to be up this late."

"You will not, Dad." Frederic jumped into the conversation from his spot at the windows. "It's late, you don't need to be driving all the way across the city tonight. You can sleep in the room you like upstairs. The one with the terrace overlooking the backyard."

"I like that room in the spring, when the birds are back from wherever the hell they go for the winter."

"You'll stay here," Frederic said firmly, shooting his father a look. Then, he gave his son a smile. "Did you say hello to your mother?"

"Would she recognize me as her son, otherwise?" Gian asked back.

"Point taken." Frederic finished the last of the whiskey in his glass, and set it on the corner of his desk. "I'll leave you two alone, then. Keep it at a dull roar, Dad. The room upstairs will be waiting when you're done."

"Yes, yes." Corrado waited until his son was gone from the office, and the door was shut, before he spoke to Gian again. "The new club is opening tonight, *sì*?"

"Opened a while back, actually. This is the first night I'm going in to see the place in action. It's fashionable to be late, or so I'm told."

His grandfather chuckled. "Only when a boss is not involved, or …?"

Gian smirked. "Or you are the boss. I know, Grandpapa."

"You have to learn, Gian, even the stupid, small things. Someday, I won't be here to repeat this same, old shit to you every day of your life, and then who will? How will you remember when the time is most important?"

"You're going to be here forever," Gian said, "so what in the hell do you mean?"

"Not forever." Corrado sighed, turning to face the window. "I'm as old as dirt, and you know it. There are too many people who continue to remind me of how old I am, Gian, and how it would be better if I stepped down for—"

"Fuck those people."

A dark laugh escaped his grandfather as he turned back around. "Yes, what you said."

Unfortunately, what his grandfather said had a lot of merit. Most Cosa Nostra bosses did not live long enough to see eighty-five. Never mind the fact that Corrado had already held his position for forty-five years. Bosses usually retired their seats before their age started to become too prevalent, as no good made man wanted to be seen as weak or senile to his men.

And now, their *famiglia* had gotten to a point where there were, at times, three generations sitting around the table with a voice wanting to be heard. His grandfather's generation, men of his father's age, and then their sons, too. Younger made men who didn't get much of a voice.

Gian didn't fall entirely into the *young* Capo category, considering he was his grandfather's underboss with his own seat at the table, but he understood and sympathized with their frustrations.

"Well, I'll send you off then, since there's nothing to chat about that can't wait until morning," his grandfather said, passing him by with a clap on the shoulder.

"My evening is never as important as you are. I can wait."

"It's fine, just the usual nonsense with the men. I was thinking maybe we could work to erase some of the lines between the generations if we sat down and talked about it, but it can wait until tomorrow. Enjoy your evening, Gian, and *behave*."

Gian scoffed. "I behave."

"Define that word, and then we'll talk."

Corrado was already leaving the office. Gian followed behind his grandfather, only separating at the stairs, where Corrado went up, and he went down to the bottom level of the wing. He expected to leave, as his visit was over, but he found his father waiting at the front door, and nursing another glass of whiskey.

Frederic didn't see his oldest son approach, and for a moment, Gian was struck at how young his father looked in the dim light of the hallway. It was almost like looking into a mirror, although an older one.

All the men in his family shared the same dominant traits—a strong, squared jaw, brown eyes with gold flecks, a nose with a straight, sharp slope, and lips that, even when not smiling, almost seemed to be pulling into a grin of some sort, just from their shape alone. Even their hair was the same dark brown, from his youngest brother Domenic, to their grandfather. Gian wore his hair slightly longer, leaving a bit at the top to be styled if he wanted, while keeping the sides sheared short.

"He didn't keep you up there long," Frederic noted.

"You know how he is."

"I do."

Something in the lilt of his father's tone caught his attention, and not in a good way.

"What is it?" Gian asked.

"Corrado needs to slow down, Gian."

"I'm aware. Tell him that."

"I have, and so have his doctors."

Gian's brow knotted together. "Pardon? He won't go to his doctors for more than a checkup or a flu shot."

Frederic glanced down the hall, behind Gian, as though he were looking for someone to be standing there. No one was. "He's not going to tell you, if he didn't tonight."

"Tell me what?"

"That he's not well. Some strange results showed up in his bloodwork. He went in a month ago to have another round of tests."

"He didn't tell me about any tests."

His father sighed, tipping his glass higher for another sip. "I think he tells no one. I know because I'm the surviving son, I *need* to know."

Gian didn't like where this was going. "What is it, then? What's wrong?"

"Colon cancer, it seems. Aggressive. He's supposed to start treatment within the week, but you know how he is."

Corrado wouldn't put himself in any situation that would give another made man in the organization a chance to point at him and call him weak—*unable*. This would do that, entirely. But not getting aggressive treatment would mean certain death, wouldn't it? If the cancer was already at an aggressive stage ...

"Does it matter if he gets treatment?" Gian asked quietly.

Frederic's gaze dropped to the floor. "It'll give him a bit more time."

"Be specific."

"A year or two, with treatment. Six months, maybe, without."

Fuck.

Fuck.

Gian grimaced as pain shot its way through his whole body all at once.

"I'm sorry, Gian," Frederic murmured.

He loved his family. It was what Italians *did*.

But his grandfather?

It was far more than love. It was respect, and an adoration that had followed Gian since he had been a young boy under his grandfather's feet. His relationship with his grandfather had always been different. Sometimes difficult, always strong, and never wavering.

"I ... don't know what to do," Gian said lamely. "Do I bring it up to him or no?"

"It's up to him, either way. He's eighty-five; he's old and wise enough to make this choice. Don't ask him, or tell him you know, if he doesn't bring it up to you first."

"Yeah, I got it."

He didn't like it, but he understood. Apparently, like his grandfather, Gian was supposed to simply pretend nothing was wrong. And in six months, when it all went to shit, where would that leave him?

Gian didn't know.

"Try to forget about it for the night. You're young, Gian, and he knows that, which is probably why he didn't want to upset you tonight. I'm not like him, though, and the longer you were made to wait before being told, the angrier you would be. Enjoy your time, deal with the rest another day."

His father's words seemed simple enough. That didn't mean they would be easy to follow.

Gian bypassed the line at the front door of the new club—*Danza*—and went in through a back entrance where he had a man standing guard. He nodded a greeting to the enforcer as the man stepped aside, and held the metal door open.

"Busy, Raul?"

"Packed full, boss."

Always respectful.

Always appropriate.

It was the little things, like calling an underboss "boss" whenever the actual boss wasn't around, instead of his name. Made men appreciated those things *and* remembered when it was time to give a man his *in* to the family. Although, Raul had been given his button years ago.

Gian clapped the guy on the shoulder. "Good. I won't be long, and then you're free to do what you want for the rest of the night."

"Thanks, boss."

Gian moved through the back hallways that were used for storage, and then up the spiral staircase that led to the offices. One for the manager, and one for his personal use. He didn't run the club full-time, but it was nice to have a place to hide away if the need arose.

Waiting papers rested on his desk, and Gian quickly flipped through what the manager had left for him. He tossed the papers aside again before moving toward the one-way mirrored windows that covered a whole portion of one office wall. He surveyed the people down below, looking for faces he recognized in the crowd.

Only a couple stood out.

But it was a couple of faces he gave a shit about, too.

Stephan Zito and Constantino Rossi sat in the sectioned off VIP area of the club at a circular booth that allowed their backs to be at the wall, while their fronts faced the crowd. Both were Capos for the Guzzi Cosa Nostra, though Constantino was closer to Gian's age, while Stephan was nearing his mid-thirties.

Gian put up with Stephan for the sake of respect, but otherwise, he didn't have a lot of patience for the guy. Constantino, however, had been one of the few men Gian had grown up with—a friend from childhood. Those were hard to find *and* keep in their world.

It was too damn bad that Constantino enjoyed Stephan's company a lot more than Gian did.

Gian brushed off the irritation at seeing Stephan in his club, his gaze passing over the other people sitting in the booth with the two men. An enforcer for both Capos sat opposite to them at the booth, and a familiar woman sat beside Stephan.

Bambi, Gian thought her name was. Stephan's *goomah*.

The guy was not very quiet about the mistress he had, not that it was exactly required for him to be so. Made men were a lot of things, but faithful didn't have to be one of them. Especially, if their wives didn't make too much of an issue out of it.

Gian's gaze skipped to the woman sitting on the other side of Constantino, her red hair—a fiery ruby shade that was almost shocking under the lights of the club—set in perfectly-managed curls fell halfway down her back. That was all he could see of the woman, but guessing by the way she kept her body angled *away* from Constantino, she was not his date.

Gian wondered who she was, or rather, how she had gotten into his VIP section with made men. He planned to find out.

Five minutes later, the bouncer at the roped-off section of the VIP area stepped back to allow Gian through. On the way, Gian had grabbed a glass of whiskey at the bar, the one drink he would allow himself for the evening. It didn't look good for a man to be drunk and acting foolish, even in a place he owned that was meant for drunken foolishness.

"Gian!"

A smile split Gian's lips at his oldest friend's shout. Constantino was already pushing his way out of the booth, offering little more than a fast apology to the redhead sitting beside him.

"You're late," said his friend.

"The boss called. I sent you a text and said I had to run over to Ma's."

That was all he gave as an explanation.

20

Constantino didn't ask for more.

"Well, you're here now and—" Constantino's words cut off as his gaze fell on someone in the crowd over Gian's shoulder. His eyes narrowed, and Gian knew then that whoever his friend had recognized was about to wish that Constantino hadn't seen him. "He owes me a grand, that fucking cocksucker."

"All right, try not to break anything while you're in here, huh? Keep any blood spills to a minimum."

Constantino flashed a grin. "For you, always."

"Yeah, yeah. Play nice."

"Whatever you say."

He smacked Constantino hard in the back of the head as the guy walked past him, dark laughter escaping him as he ducked an incoming swing from his friend.

"You're getting slow, *cafone*," Gian taunted, his back now facing the booth that Constantino had come from. "You're supposed to be the young one here."

"Give me fifteen minutes," his friend shot back. "We'll see how slow I am."

Then, Constantino was gone, disappearing from the VIP section and off into the swelling crowd of people.

"I see you finally climbed off your grandfather's dick long enough to show your face around here, Gian," came a voice from behind him.

Gian stiffened, his teeth grinding. Reason number *too-many-to-count* why he hated Stephan Zito.

Turning slowly, Gian faced the grinning Capo at the booth, paying no mind to the other people at the table. "Do you want to try that again, Stephan?"

"No, I think I got it right the first time."

"Do you? Think really hard, now. You've got some time."

"Well—"

"Because I'm pretty fucking sure that to you, his name is *boss*, and nothing else. And if we're going to be talking about climbing on dicks, I'll let you take the lead on that one, since you seem to have quite a grasp on which man likes which dick the best. You're the only one speaking up about it, anyhow."

Stephan's face reddened.

Gian only smiled.

"Stephan, grab me another one of these, would you? They're delicious."

Bambi's high voice broke the staring contest between the two men, making Stephan look to his *goomah's* hand, where she held out an empty martini glass. The girl was smart; Gian had to give her that. It was not the first time she had stepped in to divert her man's attention and kept him from getting his face broken.

Made men didn't fight. It was against every rule Gian knew. He'd break that one for Stephan, if pushed the wrong way.

"Yeah, sure, babe," Stephan said, grabbing the glass. "Pretty sure that's what the fucking servers are for in this place, though."

Stephan was pushing out of the booth and heading past Gian without a look back.

Gian couldn't help himself.

"Grab me another drink, too, Stephan," Gian said at the man's back.

Stephan's steps hesitated, and Gian could almost hear the man's refusal trying to force its way out. The guy wasn't entirely stupid, and kept walking. Underbosses trumped Capos, after all. Stephan didn't have to like Gian when the rules came into play.

"You could try not to antagonize him as much," Bambi said quietly.

Gian turned to face the woman again. "Like he does for me?"

"That's just Stephan's ways."

"And those ways will eventually get him killed."

Bambi frowned, but wisely chose not to respond. Then, she turned and said something to the woman at her side but a couple of seats away in the booth, drawing Gian's attention there.

To the redhead.

A woman he *thought* he hadn't known from Adam. She had been so quiet at the table, her attention on the few people at a booth across the way from theirs, and not making a spectacle of herself as Stephan had done for him and Bambi. It suddenly made sense then why Constantino had not been treating the girl as a disinterested date.

It was his cousin, or rather, one of them.

At first, Gian thought *Lea Rossi*. But his mind quickly corrected that, as Lea Rossi's death—an event that had been widely publicized, due to the nature of the murder—had happened months ago. He only knew *of* the Rossi twins, as their uncle was an older Capo for the Guzzi *famiglia*.

Gian had met Lea Rossi on a scarce few occasions when their paths crossed for different events or whatever, but he had never sat down and had an actual conversation with the girl. He had been told by Constantino—the twins' cousin—that the twins lived in Toronto.

He knew Lea had a twin. He did not realize her twin was *identical*.

That red hair of hers that had been so striking under the club lights from up above, was even more stunning close up. A shade that a woman couldn't buy in a bottle, and couldn't quite be duplicated in a salon.

A black double-wrapped velvet choker rested around her throat, showcasing tanned skin and the delicate line of her neck. A simple bow was tied at the middle, making Gian wonder what she would look like with the choker on, looking up from her knees.

He wasn't quite sure where that idea came from, but it was a good one.

Cara, he thought her name was. Wasn't that what Constantino had said before about his cousins—Lea and Cara.

Gian didn't pay attention to names, unless it served him some purpose to.

Her ice-blue eyes looked him over, and Gian was taken aback by the lack of makeup on her pixie-like features. Most woman put too much makeup on instead of too little, determined to make a man focus on attributes instead of imperfections. But all she wore was just enough to shape her wide eyes, and a red tint on her full lips that matched the color of her hair.

From what he could see, her tight black dress fit to her curves perfectly, and guessing by the way she crossed her legs out to the side, she was not a short woman.

Beautiful.

Natural.

Sexy.

All of that and more came to mind.

"You stare a lot, don't you?" the woman asked.

Gian came out of the daze with a bang. "Am I not allowed to stare?"

Bambi glanced away from the two, hiding her smile. "I think I'll go find Stephan and see what's taking him so long."

Do that, Gian wanted to say.

He said nothing until Bambi was gone. The two men left at the booth, quickly followed her lead, leaving Gian alone with the beautiful redhead. He didn't sit, though, simply stayed where he was.

"It's Cara, right?"

She glanced up, her blue eyes widening further. "How do you know my name?"

Gian smirked. "Family friends."

"Right." Cara flashed him one of her own smiles. "It's Gian, right? Gian *Guzzi*."

He lifted a single brow. "My name is well-known around this place."

"The owner—I know. Constantino told me."

"Oh?"

"And Guzzi isn't exactly a ... little name, either."

"Would you like a drink, Cara?"

She didn't even think about it before saying, "No."

"A dance?"

"No."

"Then why are you here?" Gian lifted a hand, waving at the club

23

behind him. "That's sort of what you do in a club, *bella donna*."

"I do speak some Italian."

"Good, then you know what I think of you. A very beautiful woman."

She did manage a smile that was slightly truer than her first. "You're terribly arrogant. Flash a smile, say a few pretty words, and I bet most women eat out of the palm of your hand."

"The men of my family like to say it's a learned talent, actually." He grinned, and didn't miss how for a moment that Cara was silenced by the sight. "And as of right now, I'm not trying any of those things on you."

"How do you hold all that cockiness and those damn grins in then?"

"I don't."

"And everyone melts."

"I'm not looking at everyone. I'm looking at you."

Cara laughed lightly, a sweet sound that helped to light up her pretty features. "Smooth, Gian."

"That was nothing, only the truth. But seriously, if you don't want a drink, you don't want to dance, and you don't have a date ..." Gian left that one hanging for Cara to finish for him.

"No date, either."

"Then what are you doing here?"

"I wanted to feel normal for a night. Not so suffocated, I guess, or out of control. Also, someone showed up at my place and wouldn't take no for an answer."

Had someone else said those words, Gian might have been confused. He thought, considering this woman had recently lost someone important in her life, that her statement made a hell of a lot of sense.

"Your sister—your twin." Her lips turned into a frown, a question in her stare. He quickly added, "Her face was all over the news, and Constantino is a very old, and good friend of mine."

"Huh."

"That's what you meant, though, isn't it?"

Cara shrugged. "I'm supposed to be having fun, not being sad tonight."

Gian knew better than to engage Cara in any more conversation than what he already had done. He certainly didn't have the time to invest to be interested in the woman, never mind struck by her unassuming beauty. It would be different, if he wanted nothing more than a quick ride and little else from a woman, but in that moment, he wasn't looking for that, either.

He *was*, of course, but not right then. Cara was still sitting, staring at him, and waiting. He wouldn't usually bother to talk at all.

"Are you going to sit?" Cara asked.

He knew better.

Gian took a seat in the booth when Cara moved in farther.

Knowing better meant *nothing* to Gian.

Chapter 3

Cara wasn't entirely sure how she had gotten tucked into a booth at a club with a man that she had no business talking to.

It wasn't that Gian Guzzi was off-putting. In fact, he was the exact opposite. Cara was sure the man knew exactly how he came across to those around him, and had no qualms about using it to his advantage.

Charming.

Gorgeous.

Sharp lines, dark eyes, a chiseled jaw, carefully styled hair, and that was only the *surface*. That was what he greeted a person with at first glance. It was the second glance, and then the third, that Cara was sure won a woman over. He brought out the Italian pet names, and then murmured a quick line in French with such perfect precision that it was simply shocking. Tan skinned, a three-piece, fitted suit that showcased his athletic form, a smile that surely made most women weep, and an attitude that begged for attention.

Cocky, even, with his smirks and fast replies that took Cara off guard.

Confident.

As his brown gaze had turned on her, the rest of the club had ceased to exist to Gian. He talked to *her*. He looked at *her*. He interested *her*.

Cara wasn't quite sure what to make of that.

She had been so stuck in her own head for four months, that for the first time when she decided to pop back out of it and say hello to the world, it happened to be Gian Guzzi waiting there to greet her.

Gian with his fucking suit.

Gian with his goddamn grins.

Gian looking at only her in a club full of beautiful women.

Cara wouldn't deny that it was something she liked.

There was something she liked about Gian. She didn't know what to make of it all.

Cara was not stupid. She recognized the surname Gian sported—Guzzi—and knew exactly what it meant, even if she didn't know him personally.

She knew enough, like the fact that having that last name meant Gian was no doubt involved in things she avoided. In her efforts to stay away from the mafia, she could blame her success for the reason why she didn't know anything about Gian.

She didn't know what to blame for her attraction.

"You're staring," Gian said.

Cara's gaze moved up from the slight scruff on Gian's throat to the pleased curve of his lips, and then to his eyes. "So are you, apparently."

His grin only widened. "I'm not trying to hide mine, though."

"Fair enough."

"Still can't interest you in a drink, can I?"

"I try not to drink socially, and only on very special occasions. I do like a good beer or glass of wine, occasionally, but I don't indulge often."

Gian lifted a brow high. "Why's that?"

"Alcoholic parents."

She usually wouldn't offer too much information about her history or childhood under the feet of her drunken, neglectful parents, but she found it easy to say to Gian.

Gian took the information in stride, saying, "That's a good reason, then."

"I thought so."

"I could order something ... virgin," Gian suggested.

"Kind of a waste, isn't it?"

Gian laughed, leaning into the booth and tossing an arm over the back, behind Cara. Normally, she would have moved, seeing the gesture for what it was—a move to get closer to her, nothing more—and that would have shut down any further advances.

Cara didn't do that.

She rather liked how relaxed and confident Gian looked at her side, his arm resting behind her, and his gaze never leaving her.

"I'm *not* the only woman in this club, Gian," Cara said.

"I'm aware."

"You keep looking at me like I am."

"Is that a bad thing?"

No. "Unsettling, maybe."

"Unsettling, or gratifying?" he asked. "Because I've come to learn that things we find unsettling can often end up being quite gratifying, too."

Cara wet her lips, and didn't miss how Gian's gaze dropped to watch her do that, either. "How thick are you rolling out the charm right now?"

"Not even a little bit, but I doubt you would believe me on that end."

"I do find it hard to believe."

He learned forward, close enough for Cara to get another whiff of whatever spicy cologne he wore, and his grin disappeared. Seriousness clouded his features, and suddenly, the interest she had thought he hadn't been hiding, bloomed in his eyes. It told her that as much as she thought Gian was showing all his cards, he was keeping a few hidden.

"My charm gets me immediate results, and I use it when that's what I'm looking for." Gian's fingers lightly grazed the bare skin of Cara's shoulder, and she damn near jumped at the touch, shocked at the jolt of heat that flooded her. "I didn't have any intentions of leaving with someone when I came into the club tonight, and I still don't. That doesn't mean I don't want to, especially with you, it just wasn't in my intentions."

Cara sucked in a quiet breath at his candor. "So, I don't get the charm, then?"

"Oh, no, you've got the charm. And then some. I may have lied a bit there. But I'm still sitting here, and so are you, because at the moment, this seems far more interesting than sending you off with a smile. Although, you *are* smiling, and I wonder how long it has been since you did that ... considering?"

She glanced away, the dull ache of her lingering grief settling deep into her heart again. Whatever smile she had been wearing quickly fled, and Cara felt the weight of her pain come down to sit on her shoulders again.

Gian's fingers slipped under her chin, and Cara found herself looking back in his eyes. "Sorry, I didn't mean to make you sad."

Cara laughed weakly. "I'm always sad, now."

"Actually, earlier, you said out of control, if I remember correctly."

"That, too."

"I'm sure it feels like that, but trust me when I say, feeling out of control should not leave you sad."

"No?"

"That's not what being out of control is, *bella*. Losing control is ... a freedom, something you can't get with any other experience because it's one of a kind, Cara. Grief is a weight that you can't get rid of, not right away. Freedom is weightless."

She liked the way he said her name. His interesting inflection to his words—likely caused by his ability to speak Italian and French—made her name sound far more interesting than it actually was.

Like him, she thought, *one of a kind*.

"One of a kind" fit Gian, given what he seemed like, in those moments with her. A man who was more interested in talking and being near her, than getting her to the closest flat surface simply because he liked the way she looked. She assumed that, if given the chance, he would probably take an offer to fuck, but she didn't think for even a second that it was first on his mind.

Then, he glanced to the side, his gaze narrowing at the sight of a couple returning to the VIP section and heading toward their table.

"That," Gian murmured, "is my goodbye for now, unfortunately."

Cara tried to hide her frown, but failed.

Bambi and Stephan were returning, it seemed.

She didn't know where in the hell Constantino had gone to.

"Here, your drink." Stephan set the whiskey glass down forcefully, spilling a good tablespoon of the spirit on the table. Gian offered Cara another brilliant smile. "I've decided I'm not in the mood for it, now."

"You asked for—"

"Cara," Gian said, "I know that it's a no on the drink, but my other offer is still open, if you're interested. My interest here, however, is fading fast."

It took Cara a minute, long enough for Gian to stand and leave the booth, before she realized what offer he meant. She watched him disappear into the crowd, trying to decide if she wanted to take him up on it.

"What offer was that?" Bambi asked.

Stephan grunted something under his breath as he sat down at the booth again.

Cara ignored them both, and decided to go for it.

What would it hurt?

Maybe Gian had a point.

Maybe being out of control—or even refusing to be swallowed whole by her grief for a short while—was actually meant to be a *good* thing.

"Cara?" Bambi asked. "Are you leaving, or ...?"

"A dance," Cara replied, grabbing her coat. Gian had been *far* more interesting than what she was leaving behind. "I think I'd like to dance."

That had been Gian's offer, after all. A drink or a dance. Whatever came of those things—or after—had not been talked about really. She only needed to find him.

Cara figured the rest might be worth it.

The club was far bigger than Cara first realized when she'd come in with Bambi, and she was starting to think, after ten minutes of walking around, that she wouldn't be able to find Gian.

"You look lost, *mon ange*."

Cara had gotten lost in the swell of people in her effort to find Gian. It seemed she hadn't needed to look hard, because he had found her.

"What does that mean?" Cara asked, spinning around to face a grinning Gian. "My French is non-existent, and my Italian can be a bit rusty."

"It sounded good, didn't it?"

Cara cocked a brow. "That isn't what I asked."

"No, but it *is* what matters. Do you want that dance, Cara?"

"I came to find you, didn't I?"

"You did."

And just like that, Cara found herself pulled closer into Gian's body and at the same time the loud, fast music changed to something slower. Not quite slow enough that it required a waltz of any sort, but rather, a grinding, deep bass that vibrated the floors under her heels.

Gian led them into the dance, his hands slipping under Cara's jaw to tilt her head up while her body moved instinctively closer to his. She wasn't much of a dancer, but she knew how to move her body, and it wasn't all that hard to match the rhythm of his dancing. With her face in his hands, she was forced to stare at him, taking in all of those lines and gorgeous features, under flashing lights as he kept watching her.

Cara hadn't drunk a drop, but she still felt light on her feet.

Dazed, even.

It was strange and wonderful at the same time.

She had never been quite so attracted—never so fast or easily—as she found herself to be with Gian, for whatever reason. He made it easy. She forgot about the people.

Cara only saw Gian.

He didn't look away from her, either.

"I want you to leave," Gian said, "and spend the night with me."

He didn't even *ask*.

Cara liked that he was of the type to simply state his desires, not dance around them until the truth spilled out. He clearly didn't play games. Maybe he was the kind of man who always won, no matter what.

"Cara," he pressed.

"I don't usually do that sort of thing."

She had before; she didn't make it a habit, though.

"But will you, Cara? If you really want to know what it feels like to be out of control, you've met the right man to get you there, but you have to say yes."

Let go for a night, her mind demanded.

"Yes," she said before thinking better of it. "I will."

"Just so we're clear on something, before we get to my place," Gian said from the driver's seat.

Cara hadn't entirely heard him, as she was too busy watching the street pass her by.

"Huh?"

Cara glanced over at Gian as the Lexus slowed for a red light. His gaze caught hers, he flashed a grin, and then he was leaning over before Cara even knew what happened. The kiss came fast, stunning Cara momentarily. Something wicked, sweet, and hot curled in her stomach and shot down between her thighs.

She forgot they were at a red light as Gian's lips moved against hers, slow and languid, yet still rough and demanding at the same time. She wasn't quite sure how he did that, kiss her softly, yet managing to take her breath away with the gentle nip of his teeth to her bottom lip. The slight stubble on his jaw left the best sensation on her softer skin. His tongue warred with hers, a lingering taste of whiskey blooming over her taste buds before it too was gone, and so was his kiss.

The car lurched forward as Gian leaned back into his seat, that grin of his still firmly in place. The light had turned green again. "Pay attention to me now."

Cara swallowed hard. "You're very good at distractions."

"So I've been told."

"What was that you were saying—about knowing something before we got to your place?" Cara glanced out the window, thinking it would help to clear the haze. "Let me guess, don't snoop, and be out before morning. I can do that."

Gian laughed, drawing Cara's attention back in an instant. "Not even close."

"Oh?"

His gloved hand—covered with black leather driving gloves—found her thigh, slipped high enough to disappear under the skirt of her body-con dress, and then grabbed tight. Cara's muscles jumped at the sudden touch, but somehow, she didn't move otherwise. It had grounded her.

Then, his hand moved higher, his pinky stroking over the lace covering her sex.

Cara needed air.

Badly.

"You can leave whenever the hell you want, but while you're with me, there's only one thing that matters. This is mine for the night," Gian said, his pinky stroking along the seam of her lace-covered pussy again. She shuddered under the pressure of the touch, surprised at how her body reacted to such a simple thing. "It's mine. When and how I fuck it, and how many times I make you come tonight—that's all mine. Understood?"

His grin had turned sexier under the dash lights.

"Cara?" he pressed.

God, she really needed that air.

"Understood."

Or, she'd figure it out.

Apparently, Gian intended to start teaching her *right fucking then*. His hand came back out from between her thighs, and he flipped his palm up on her lap. "Unclasp the wrist for me and pull the glove off, would you?"

"Why?"

"You'll see."

Cara did as he wanted, setting the driving glove aside. Once the item was out of his way, Gian's hand was back up under her skirt, his fingers slipping under her panties, while his other hand stayed firmly on the wheel. His gaze stayed on the road, too.

First it was a simple stroke of his fingers—testing and feeling along her folds. Then, it was two of his fingers sliding fast into her pussy, the sound of her wetness sucking his fingers in deeper as her inner walls clenched around the intrusion.

How was she *that* wet already?

"Damn," Gian said, the edges of his lips curling with satisfaction, "you're soft like silk, *Tesoro*. And soaked, too. Tight as fuck." His fingers slipped out of Cara's sex with a slowness that damn near killed her, before the very tips found her clit and started working the nub with quick, rough circles. Cara let out a hard breath at the change in sensation, her legs tightening to his hand. Never once did Gian look away from the road. "Has it been a while?"

She did not want to answer that question.

Her mouth worked before her brain did.

"Too long."

"Has anyone ever made you come in a car, going twenty over the limit, in the dark, on the highway, Cara?"

Were they on the highway, now?

Cara's eyes flew to the windshield, finding, *yes*, they were, and she had somehow missed them turning off onto it. She checked the dash, too, noting the speed—twenty over the limit.

His fingertips pressed harder against her clit, making it throb, and Cara stuttered on her next breath. "Holy fuck."

"I quite like hearing my name on your mouth, so try again." As he spoke, he stopped working her clit, and filled her with two fingers instead, widening the digits as he thrust them in. Those wet sounds echoed as he fucked her with slow, measured strokes, each time widening his fingers, dragging them against her walls. "*Try again, Cara.*"

"You're trying to kill me, Gian."

"No, I'm just taking away what you think is your control."

He flashed her with a wicked smile.

His fingers curled against her G-spot on the next thrust.

She came harder than ever.

Cara's head tilted back as an orgasm raced through her bloodstream and the elevator dinged, the doors opening. Gian's hand slipped out from the back of her skirt like he hadn't been doing a thing to her the entire ride up to what he said was his penthouse.

Her legs were weak.

Her pussy was wet, sensitive, and *needy*.

Her body was hot as fuck.

She took a couple deep breaths as Gian stepped forward, leaving the elevator with a wink over his shoulder. "You're so wet that you left a spot on the arm of my jacket." He lifted his hand, waving the two fingers he'd had stuffed up her pussy as they rode the elevator up to his penthouse. "Not that I mind. It was kind of my fault."

Jesus.

That was damn dirty.

And he'd said it without even a *grin*.

"Are you coming in?" he asked.

Cara nodded, stepped out of the elevator, and kicked her heels off as she looked up. Vaulted ceilings and a beautiful brass and crystal chandelier stared back at her. It was a stunning sight, as most penthouses didn't have cathedral-style ceilings, never mind a bachelor's place. The place was very white—the floor, the walls, and the decoration. All white, yet it made it bright, open, and inviting.

"Wow," she said to herself.

Gian chuckled, hitting a button on the wall that forced the elevator to close. "Admire in the morning. It's my turn tonight."

"Your turn, huh?"

Gian took his time removing his shoes and suit jacket, putting the items away, along with Cara's things. She toyed with the velvet choker at her throat as he checked his cell phone, then put it away with his other things as well.

Then, his attention was back on her.

Entirely.

Fully.

Unwaveringly.

Cara was frozen in place while Gian moved closer, taking his steps slow until he was close enough to pull her in the rest of the way. His one hand slid under her jaw, tilting her head up to look at him while his other slipped lower. She sucked in a sharp breath when his hand skipped under her skirt for the *third* time, only, instead of fucking her with his fingers until she came, he pulled the panties down around her thighs. The article fell the rest of the way to the floor on its own.

"You don't need these, sweetheart."

The second time he kissed her was nothing like the first had been in the car. It wasn't slow or languid, but rough and demanding. Cara barely registered the zipper on the back of her dress being pulled down, not with how Gian's tongue seemed to tangle with hers in a way that made her wish it was working between her thighs. He had quite a talent with that tongue of his, and she wondered what it would take to get him to put it to use.

He made quick work of pulling her dress down, letting the top half pool around her waist as he exposed more skin. The penthouse was warm, as far as that went, but Cara still shivered.

His fingertips dragged down her flesh. His palms flattered to her toned stomach. He stroked his digits softly over her lines and curves, like he was taking time to commit them to memory. Each time, she *shivered*.

The sensation raced over her skin.

"You can't help that, can you?" Gian asked.

"What?"

His fingertips traced invisible lines over her naked breasts—the dress looked better without a bra underneath. "When I touch you, you can't help what happens."

"I don't know if it's *you*."

Gian smirked. "I do. You wouldn't be so shocked if it wasn't a new thing, Cara."

Goddammit, he was too cocky for his own good.

"I'm going to take you hard in this hallway, fuck you until you feel like you can't breathe, and then I'll take you to my bedroom, strip you down, and do it *again*. I like that little spot you left on my jacket, Cara, but I really want to see what you can leave on my slacks before I have to take them off completely. How does that sound?"

"That sounds filthy."

"Really?" Surprise lit up his rugged features. "I would think filthy would be wearing them tomorrow with a new jacket to hide the stains because it gets me off."

Yeah, that was worse.

"I need you to give me a yes or a no," he urged huskily.

Cara smiled as his thumb stroked over her reddened lips. "You make it hard to say no."

"Still not a yes."

"Yes, Gian."

He tipped his chin up, teasingly. "And …"

"And, what?"

"And that sounds …"

Cara let out a groan. "That sounds fucking great."

"Well, one of us will be sounding very fucking great in a few minutes."

He wasn't lying.

Cara had thought he meant he would bend her over in the hallway, that she might use the table for support as he fucked her from behind.

Instead, he had been the one to lean his backside against the edge of the table, and undo his slacks. He didn't say a word, simply reached for her and drew her in closer as he pulled his cock from his pants and boxer-briefs.

Cara watched him fist his length, before she dropped to her knees, and took his cock deep into her throat for no other reason than she wondered what he felt like. Silky smooth and hot on her tongue, that's what. Gian hadn't even asked, and he only stopped her long enough to tug on her hair, bring her up for a kiss, and then he pulled a condom out of his pocket. He rolled the latex down his length, and pulled her in for another bruising kiss.

"Turn around," he demanded against her mouth.

She did as she was told, her dress was pushed up, and he pulled her into his lap. Cara didn't get much of a warning before she felt his cock at her sex, and then he was pulling her down his length with such strength that it took her breath *and* words away.

His fingers had been good.

So fucking good.

But they were a tease.

She hadn't realized how big he was until he was filling every inch of her pussy, and it took her more than a few seconds to adjust to that new sensation, and his size.

"Breathe," came his voice in her head.

His fingertips glided over her skin, her neck, back, and then one hand tangled into her hair. His fingers tightened, tugging hard on her hair with enough strength to make her scalp tingle.

Cara let out a soft gasp.

"What's mine tonight, Cara?" Gian asked roughly, his hips flexing forward to settle just a bit deeper into her pussy. "Tell me, *bella*."

"My pussy."

"And what does that mean?"

Cara took a second or two too long to respond, as Gian grabbed hold of her wrists, pinned them behind her back, moved her forward and took her with another brutal thrust. "*Cara*. I want to hear you use your words to tell me what it means that your cunt is *mine*."

She had never been fucked quite like this before.

Never been used.

Never been manhandled or roughly treated.

It stunned her how hot she was, how breathless, and weak, and *ready* she was.

"It's yours to fuck when and how you want," she managed to murmur.

"Good girl."

Those words felt like a softer caress than even his hands had been, earlier on her skin. Like an approval, his pleasure and satisfaction, all rolled into one, over her simple response.

He fucked her like that—hard, long and brutal thrusts with her arms pinned at her lower back and her hair tangled up in his fist. He urged her on with dark whispers in her ear, until all she could hear was his cock driving into her body, and his voice in her head.

"Ride that cock, Cara."

"Oh, my God."

Gian didn't hold back in the slightest, pulling Cara even harder onto his cock, making her toe a thin line between pleasure and pain.

"My pretty little slut tonight, aren't you?" he murmured in her ear.

She hadn't heard that before, either. Certainly not in the way he said it, like it was a compliment, as though he *liked* it, and not the slur that most used it for.

It didn't sound bad coming from his mouth at all. It sounded rather beautiful. Or he made it sound that way.

It was only when his finger hooked the back of her choker, tugged hard enough to take her breath away for long enough to make her shudder, that she *really* understood what he had meant.

"Come," Gian ordered in her ear.

She didn't think she had a choice. She came as her choker broke, as the air and the relief crashed through her body at the same time.

He touched.

He demanded.

Her body *reacted.*

Cara awoke with a *shiver.* She wasn't sure what had caused it, but the sensation had started in her toes and ended in her shoulders. She knew she wasn't at home, given the white walls, white sheets, and fluffy white pillows.

White everywhere.

Then, his voice came. The same as it had been the night before. Dark, heady, commanding, pleased, rough, and sinful.

Like sex made in to a *sound*.

"I'm not going to be able to forget that," Gian murmured.

Cara knew exactly why she shivered when he spoke, because she did it again at the same time his finger traced a soft, slow line from her lower back, up her spine, to the nape of her neck.

He touched her, and she reacted.

Simple as that.

"And there it is again," he said, satisfaction curling his tone with a gruff edge. "It's like you can't help it, *donna*. I touch, you take a breath, and I can watch it race right down your skin."

"Stop touching me, and I will help it."

"I think that defeats the purpose, Cara. Besides, I quite like it."

So did she.

That was part of the problem.

It was morning, the night had ended, and that meant it was time for Cara to get back to life. She had taken the night to do something stupid; something wild, crazy, and reckless.

"No, no," Gian said, his fingers trailing pathways over her neck with gentle strokes. "I'm not sure what exactly turned you stiff, but knock it off. I like you where you are right now. You could at least stay for breakfast or coffee before you run off."

"You are too smart for your own good."

"I like to think of it as that I'm *quick*."

"Whatever." Cara rolled to her back, only to find a very naked and pleased Gian lying beside her, his head propped up on his hand. He didn't hide his wandering gaze for a second, his eyes drifting down over her bare skin, her breasts, and then lower. "I still need to head out, Gian."

He didn't react to her statement.

"You look good in white."

Cara laughed, earning her another one of his grins. "Are you going to keep deflecting what I say if it doesn't fit what you want?"

"Will it get me what I want, *dolcezza*?"

Cara thought, *now or never*. A part of her wanted to stay right where she was. Another part knew it wasn't wise.

"Don't be offended, Gian, but I know enough about your last name and your family to make a quick exit. It's not *you*, not really. But it is, at the same time—you're everything I try to stay away from, that's all."

His brown eyes darkened with something unknown, but he hid it by looking away. "I see."

"But you make it really hard," Cara added after a moment, "and you should know that, too. You make it hard for me to not want to stay, or talk again like we did last night, or even fuck again. You make it *really* hard to say no, Gian."

His laughter came out rumbling and thick. Another one of his sexy sounds. "Do I?"

"Yeah," Cara admitted.

"Could I convince you on breakfast and coffee? Nothing more, I promise."

Cara didn't believe him, but still said, "Maybe."

His hand twisted into her curls, and Cara sighed with a smile before Gian pressed a quick kiss to her temple. Just the heat of his body, and the glimpse of his fit form leaning over hers, was enough to send her spinning right back to memories of the night before. Then, his kiss to her temple moved to the tip of her nose, soft and sweet, before dropping down to her mouth. She could plainly feel the hard length of his erection pressing into her thigh, but as fast as he had rolled onto her to kiss her, he moved away.

"No convincing needed—breakfast and coffee it is, and then you can go, Cara."

She nodded from the sea of white heaven that was his bed. "You really do make it hard."

Gian smirked. "Clearly not hard enough, unfortunately."

If only he knew …

"Your clothes are … somewhere," Gian muttered, rolling over and sliding out of the bed with ease. "Sorry about that."

Cara snorted. "Probably the hallway."

"I'll have the coffee ready by the time you find it all and get dressed."

She could manage that.

Surely.

Gian moved easily through his bedroom, picking up a dress shirt and slacks as he went. He didn't even bother to put them on, staying naked like he didn't have a single fuck to give in the world. Not that he had to cover up, Cara mused, as his body was a work of art that needed to be appreciated in the light of day.

Once he was gone, Cara went in search of her clothes. Like she thought, she found most of it in the hallway, but her heels and panties were *very* close to the front door.

God.

It had been worth it, though.

Cara headed for the kitchen once she had made herself decent, only to find Gian wasn't there, and no coffee or food was in the works. But as quickly as she realized Gian was not in the kitchen, she heard his footsteps approach from behind her.

She turned fast on her heel, thinking he was up to his tricks again.

Cara came face to face with *heartache*. Gian looked like heartache.

"Gian?" she asked.

He stared at her for a moment, running a hand through the slightly-longer bit of dark hair at the top of his head. In his other hand, he held a cell phone.

"Rain check on the coffee, at least?" He tried to smile, but he ended up with a frown, anyway. "I know that's not what you agreed to."

"A rain check?" Cara asked faintly.

"I'll call you a cab, if that's all right. I have to head out."

"Is something wrong?"

Cara knew better than to ask.

She should have taken this saving grace for what it was, and run with it. Whatever happened, it would get her out of Gian's penthouse quicker than before, and maybe she could leave her strange feelings behind with it. A part of her didn't really want that, though.

"My grandfather," Gian said, glancing down at the phone in his hand, "was murdered this morning, when he stood in front of the terrace windows of the room he uses at my parents' mansion. Sniper shot to the head—dead before he hit the ground—and he didn't see it coming."

Cara's body grew cold all over. "I'm sorry."

What else could she say?

She knew far too well how this life took and took and took, but rarely ever gave back.

"Rain check," Gian repeated.

Cara nodded. "Rain check."

Someday.

"A shame, that's what it is. *Dio.* Rest his soul."

Cara tried to brush off the mutterings of her uncle, but given the way her aunt passed her a false smile and rolled her eyes, this clearly wasn't a first-time thing.

"It's good to see you, dear," Daniele said, taking Cara's coat.

Constantino came into the house behind her, not even bothering to say hello. He passed his suit jacket off to his mother before she asked for it, and he disappeared down the hallway, likely heading for his father.

"Don't mind the men this week—they're a bit off," her aunt muttered, shooting a glare in the direction her son had gone.

It had been three days since Cara spent the night with Gian Guzzi, and she had not heard a single word from him, about him, or his family. She had come home from school to find a message on her voice mail from her aunt, asking her over for dinner.

She knew what Daniele wanted, and while it irritated Cara to feed into the whims of others, she went. Her aunt meant no harm, she only wanted to check up on Cara and likely make sure she was still amongst the living.

"Food is nearly ready," her aunt said, "so I hope you're hungry."

Cara almost asked if her aunt was going to report her state back to her mother, or even her brother, but thought better of it. No need to be rude to the only family she had left around, even if she would rather keep a distance, given her uncle and cousin's involvement with the mafia.

"Sure, *Zia*," Cara replied, "I'm starved."

Then, her uncle's voice boomed through the house again, making her aunt sigh heavily.

"But, Dad—"

"No one is saying anything, Constantino," Claud complained. "No one knows who killed the boss, or who would even want to. No matter, Edmond and Gian will figure it out, and make whoever it was answer for what they've done."

Gian.

It was the first time in three days that Cara heard his name.

Like his touch, it still made her shiver.

Chapter 4

Edmond Portella's calls and demands were not ones that Gian typically put in high priority, given both men's status in the Guzzi Cosa Nostra. Gian, as the underboss, and Edmond, as the consigliere to a now-deceased Corrado put them on an equal playing field. Well, to a point. It also put them on very different scopes, regarding *la famiglia* and what their duties were to both the men, and the boss.

Most, if not all, of Gian's control and duty came down to the men, but more specifically, the Capos of the family. He dealt with their issues, kept an eye on them, and if needed, stepped in to handle any problem that came up when his grandfather hadn't wanted to bother.

Edmond, on the other hand, had been Corrado's left-hand to Gian being his right. What Gian didn't step in to handle, like the more personal side of business, Edmond was there to do whatever was needed.

Gian was the business hand of the boss.

Edmond was the personal.

Therefore, whenever Edmond had an issue or demanded someone's presence, it was rarely ever Gian's. Their respective positions neither depended on, nor required, the other.

And yet, ever since Corrado's murder the week before, Gian found himself on the opposite end of Edmond's calls more often than he liked. Sure, the Guzzi Cosa Nostra was facing an upset of sorts, with their long-reigning boss dead, and no one to immediately take the open seat readily available. A murder that, for all purposes, had been done in cold-blood, and for no apparent reason other than to kill the boss.

It was more than that, too.

More, because Edmond had made demands. More, because he made no qualms about hiding the fact that perhaps it would be him who would best fill the open position in the family.

The *highest* position.

Gian was the messenger for the Capos of the family. Whenever Edmond wanted the men to know something or do something, it was left to Gian to deliver the orders.

It was easy to attribute the murder of his grandfather—Corrado had always been more than *just* the boss to him—as to why Gian didn't immediately step in to take control of the family. It was also not that simple.

Maybe he felt he wasn't ready. His grandfather had never told him that he was, after all. Maybe he felt that at his age—twenty-nine—someone older might fill the position with more experience and a stronger hand than he could. That reasoning, too, was a born and bred respect that had been pounded into Gian over the years where Cosa Nostra and made men were concerned.

It was also a major reason why there was so much unrest in the family. He was not the *only* young Guzzi man, a made man of a generation that was often overlooked or dismissed because of their age, which felt it was time for the older men to step aside.

That particular unrest had been brewing long before Corrado's murder, and Gian didn't think it would lessen anytime soon.

However, it was that born and bred respect of Gian's that got him out of his bed at twelve at night on a fucking Thursday, when Edmond called and asked him to come over. Edmond lived outside of Toronto's city limits, in the outer suburbs of a gated community. The large property cost far more than any Canadian would ever hope to make in their lifetime. It took Gian a good hour and a half to get to Edmond's home, and all the while, he still couldn't figure out what the hell the man wanted.

Edmond hadn't offered any hints.

Gian disliked *that* even more.

It was as if Edmond felt he could simply demand, and Gian should answer, no questions asked.

"Ma called today, going on like she does," Domenic said, his voice echoing through the speakers of the Lexus. Gian had been so caught up in his own thoughts that he'd forgotten about being in mid-conversation with his younger brother. "I think she's overwhelmed with what's coming up next week, and all that shit."

"Probably," Gian agreed.

The massive funeral arrangements had been mostly left up to Gian's father, who had passed the task onto his wife.

"You sound off, man."

Gian kept his eyes on the suburb streets, not wanting to get lost in the catacombs of his mind again. "Thinking."

"I could have come with you tonight, if—"

"No, you couldn't."

"Well, I *could.*"

"You're not a made man; you can't attend meetings, Dom."

His brother grunted under his breath. "Not for lack of trying, Gian."

"You'll get the button, eventually. It takes time, but until then, you can't attend this kind of thing. Whatever it is," he tacked on at the end, still irritated at being left out of a very important loop.

Finally, the long driveway leading up to the massive house belonging to Edmond came into view, and Gian turned off the road. "I'll call you when it's over, Dom."

"All right. And hey?"

"What?"

"Be careful," his brother said. "A lot of people you don't get to talk to that *I* get to talk to on the streets aren't happy right now. You only chat with made men, I get the word from the soldiers, too. I think they might get to hear some shit being said from their Capos that you aren't getting to hear at all."

"Go on."

"I told you—people aren't happy, Gian."

"That's not news, Dom."

"No, I don't mean the usual younger guys having rifts with the older guys. I mean they're looking for some kind of stability here, and coming up with nothing. That's not good on the streets. It makes people fight about stupid shit to have something to do."

Gian scowled. "Yeah, I got it."

"So yeah … maybe be careful."

He didn't need his younger brother lecturing him on how Cosa Nostra—or the made men within the family—worked, but he let Domenic have his moment. If nothing else, to let his brother feel like he had done something useful.

"I'll call you when I'm done," Gian repeated.

He hung up the call through the Bluetooth before Domenic could reply. Soon, he had driven the long length of the Portella driveway, and parked his car, cutting the engine as he surveyed the circular entrance.

Gian did not like what he saw.

Cars.

Several cars.

Yet, not enough for it to be a formal family meeting.

Of course, he recognized the vehicles, and could name the men to whom they belonged. A significant portion, if not all, of the older generation of Guzzi made men. Not one younger man, or one closer to Gian's age.

Except for him.

Gian stepped out of his car, not bothering to lock it as he headed for the front entrance of the large home. Edmond's wife let him in with a quiet greeting, and pointed in the direction of the upstairs.

"You'll find him in his office," she told Gian.

"*Grazie*," he thanked her.

Sure enough, Gian walked into an office that wasn't entirely filled with made men, but held a significant number to pull weight. All of them, with their graying hair, slightly rounded bodies, and older features, barely spared him a glance as he entered.

Edmond sat behind his large desk, a glass of scotch in his hand, and a lit cigar in the other. "Took you long enough, Gian."

Gian shrugged, stuffing his hands into the pockets of his suit jacket. "Seems everyone else that you wanted to be here must have gotten a call before me, Edmond."

"Oh, it isn't that, now. I made a call to Matthew and he called a few more."

Matthew, the older Capo in question, tipped his glass at Gian in greeting.

Gian offered nothing in response.

His attention was back on Edmond instead. "We both know that there are a lot of issues right now within the family, between the generations of men, and this isn't going to help, Edmond."

"I'm not sure I get what you mean."

Really?

That was likely half of the damn problem.

"You've called a meet for the men—clearly, look around—but not *all* of them. It's not good for the divide between the generations to add fuel to a fire when half of them already feel dismissed or overlooked in their positions. This will do exactly that, once they hear about it."

Edmond sighed, using two fingers to massage his forehead while his cigar dangled dangerously between his lips. "It won't matter after tonight, anyway. I called in the men who make a difference, the only ones whose voices need to be heard in this case."

Gian didn't like what he was hearing.

Nor what Edmond suggested.

"And what case is this?" Gian asked, not bothering to hide the edge of irritation sharpening his tone.

"It's time to fill the seat, Gian. We've gone a week without a boss, now, and that's not how it works in *la famiglia*. We'll do the nomination tonight, and take a vote. By morning, the Guzzi family will have a new boss, and we can all move forward."

"Except that's not how it works, Edmond."

"Why not?"

"Because *every* made man gets a voice in that vote, not a select few that *you* picked to be here for it."

Edmond smiled, a sight cold enough to make Gian stand a bit

straighter. "As I said, once the boss is the boss, there is nothing to argue about. Your grandfather would have understood, given the current atmosphere of the family, that this is the best way to go about stabilizing the ground floor of this *famiglia*."

"Not to the detriment of more possible problems," Gian argued.

"Right now, you're the only one causing a problem, Gian."

"Or is that how you want it to look, Edmond?"

Gian had hit the nail directly on the head, and he knew it in that moment. The old consigliere to his grandfather was not even bothering to hide the sneaky way he intended to go about taking the boss's seat. He was not going to even allow the majority of younger made men in the family to speak.

Perhaps because they wouldn't choose Edmond.

Perhaps because they would pick someone like Gian.

That pissed Gian off.

But what could he do?

Gian was acutely aware of his current situation, and how dangerous it could be for him. In a room full of made men, he would likely be the only one on his side. He could be killed, though, it was technically forbidden without proper reasoning, and no one would speak up and say why. Not when the older men felt as though they were getting what they wanted.

This was not a good situation for Gian.

Suspicion weaved through Gian's bloodstream, and he disliked how it left him feeling. A distasteful sentiment stuck heavily on his tongue as he looked to Edmond, and was forced to wonder … had he found the hand that ordered the gun on his grandfather?

He had no real reason to believe that, and the friendship between Corrado and Edmond was a long one. Far longer than both men's marriages, even.

It could be that Edmond was a fucking upstart, and this had been his chance to take control. Something that was entirely unrelated to Corrado's murder, but rather, a happy by-product.

Gian didn't particularly like either of those ideas.

But here he was.

Fucked.

"I know you're unhappy about this," Edmond started to say.

"That's an understatement."

"But it is for the best, Gian." The older man rested back in his chair, steepling his fingers in front of his face before he spoke again. "And consider that once the men have proper stability again to fall back on, we can begin to work on other things."

"Like what?"

"Corrado's killer, for one."

Gian's jaw ached from clenching so hard. "I see."

"It's time to let the men nominate, and take their vote to fill the seat. Don't you think so?"

No.

Absolutely not.

It would not help the unrest within the family ranks to allow a boss to be chosen without every man's voice being involved.

He still didn't have a choice.

"I guess it is," Gian said quietly.

"*Any* other day would have been far better than today for this," Gian muttered.

His attempt to complain quietly to his father without his mother overhearing had not been missed, unfortunately. Celeste glared over her shoulder, effectively quieting her son and whatever else he might say.

With his mother's attention back on the speaking lawyer, Gian glanced up at the ceiling.

"A funeral would have been enough, I agree," his father said softly. "But apparently, Corrado wanted his Last Will and Testament read before burial, and this was the only time the lawyer had available this week to do this. It's extensive."

Obviously.

They had already been stuck in the reading for two hours.

Once it finished, they had to be at the church for the ceremony and subsequent entombment of Corrado's casket until the thaw came in the spring. The mid-February ground was still far too frozen to dig.

"To my eldest grandson, Gian ..."

Gian's head lifted at his name being called out by the lawyer. It was the only time that Gian had shown any interest in the reading of his grandfather's Will, and not because he didn't care. He simply wished that it could be done one thing at a time. He didn't want to watch the things and legacy his grandfather worked so hard for be handed off and divided up on the same day they had to say goodbye.

The lawyer continued speaking, explaining the details of the things Corrado had left to Gian, including a trust, two antique roadsters that had been stored in the city, and other family heirlooms.

"And the building, including the two-level penthouse, in Ottawa," the lawyer said, looking over the rim of his large glasses to stare at Gian. "You're aware of that property, correct?"

Gian stiffened as the room quieted.

Of course, he knew the property. Everyone in their fucking family knew it. And what his grandfather had used it for, three decades ago.

At his side, Gian's father cleared his throat uncomfortably, spurring him to talk.

"Yeah," Gian answered quickly, "I know it."

"Good," the lawyer said, glancing back down at the papers. "All that's left in regard to you, Gian, is a few words your grandfather wanted you to hear. *Duty, legacy, and only then, love—always in that order. Always.*"

Those words were not new to Gian. He had heard them spoken from his grandfather's very mouth more times than he cared to count. He figured Corrado wanted the chance to say them one last time, to remind Gian.

It wasn't like he could forget.

He certainly couldn't forget what Corrado had left unwritten in his final note, either. *For when a man fails at duty, Gian, his legacy becomes nameless, and his love, hopeless.*

It seemed for a time, the usually bustling streets of Toronto where Corrado Guzzi had spent his life building an empire suddenly quieted. As if the shopkeepers knew what the gray skies meant, and the constantly moving people felt the need to step aside, away from the grief.

It was the only day, in a string of many days, where the men of the Guzzi Cosa Nostra quieted their grumblings, put aside their misgivings, and settled in to pay respects to a boss unlike any other.

Gian had expected sadness.

He'd prepared for it.

He found his grief was different for the funeral than it had been leading up to it. Not lessened, but rather, softened. He had done well to keep his emotions buried when he needed to, but as he traveled behind the hearse in a black town car, the grief was not as striking.

It still ached.

It still hurt.

It had simply softened for a moment.

Gian surveyed the familiar faces as the vehicles parked in a long line along the church, and then began to empty of people. He stood alongside his mother, father, brother, and sister as the hearse backed up to the entrance of the church, stopping at the steps.

Despite all the people, Gian still felt singular. Above, perhaps, looking down. Not entirely there, as the back of the hearse was opened to showcase the shined, black casket with gold-plated bars and leaf designs along the corners and sides. The casket matched the one his grandmother had been buried in two years before, after her heart had finally given out.

The whole day felt familiar.

Except for the fact that the men who pulled their caps off and bowed their heads, were not doing so for respect of their boss's grief, but rather, the loss of that very same man. He had not been expecting that second of distant familiarity.

"Let's go," Domenic said, his hand landing hard on Gian's shoulder.

Gian stepped forward with his brother as another six men filed in behind them. Six familiar faces to help carry the casket in, before they would help to carry it out, too.

One of those men happened to be Claud Rossi.

Gian had known that Claud would be one of the pallbearers for his grandfather, chosen by Edmond and several others in the family. Still, he looked around for the man's family, only finding Claud's wife and son. His oldest friend, Constantino, nodded at Gian as he passed, but oddly, that wasn't the face of a Rossi he had wanted to see.

He'd wondered if Cara might show up.

She certainly had no reason to, and no connection to his grandfather.

Gian had a million and one other things to let consume his mind lately, but more often than not, his thoughts drifted back to the redheaded Cara, and the coffee she had promised him.

He was going to need a break from his life after today.

Something to let him breathe.

Cara just might do …

Gian simply had to figure out *when*.

"Whiskey, neat," Gian ordered.

His grin deepened as Cara's head popped up at the sound of his voice. From behind the bar, her eyes widened.

"Gian."

He leaned over the top of the bar, pointing at the specific brand of whiskey he wanted. "That one, please."

Cara didn't make a move to reach for the bottle. "What are you doing here?"

"I could ask you the same thing."

"I asked first."

So she did.

"I have a meeting with your uncle and cousin. I'm a bit early—better that than late, I suppose. I figured I would get a drink while I wait, and here you are."

Under the specialty lights of the restaurant's bar, Cara's red hair seemed darker. Her blue eyes surveyed him with barely-hidden interest, and curiosity. Gian had the strangest urge to reach out and tug on one of the curls, to feel the softness under his fingertips, but he managed to hold back. Somehow.

"My uncle had a server that took sick, and his back up is gone for the week on vacation. I happen to know how to mix drinks," Cara explained. "Plus, my aunt thinks if someone doesn't force me out of the apartment every once in a while, I will likely die in there."

Gian chose not to comment on the second part of her statement, instead focusing on the first. "Yet, you don't drink them."

"A dichotomy, I'm aware."

"In a way," Gian agreed.

Cara reached for the bottle behind the bar, and a clean glass to go along with it. She poured Gian's drink with a smile that he returned.

Soon, her smile faded.

"I'm sorry about your grandfather," she said quietly.

Gian let out a sigh. "Thanks."

"The funeral was a couple of days ago, right?"

"It was. I didn't see you there."

Cara shrugged as she slid the drink across the counter. "Don't take offense, but I try to stay away from family business, you know."

"So you told me in bed."

At the mention of their hookup, Cara's cheeks flooded with a pretty red. It wasn't quite the same shade as her hair, but it was damn close.

Gian chuckled. "How—after that—can you be shy with me?"

She shot him a look, her lips curving with amusement. "A gift, I guess."

"Well, speaking of that night," Gian started to say, reaching for an item he had in his pocket. "I have something for you."

Cara's brow lifted. "Oh?"

"You forgot it. Or I broke it and you probably didn't think much about it after that."

Gian pulled the thin, double-wrapped choker with a small bow from his pocket. He had taken it to a jeweller to have the velvet fixed, and the small piece of the chain that had broken repaired as well.

"Here," he said, holding it out and letting it dangle on two fingers. "Ready for you to wear again."

Carefully, Cara plucked the item from his grasp. "You didn't have to—"

"Of course, I did. I broke it; it's only right that I fix it."

"It's just a cheap necklace, Gian."

"Maybe. I liked the way it looked around your throat. I might like to see it on you another time."

All over again, Cara's cheeks reddened.

"Huh," she said quietly.

"You do still owe me coffee, *mon ange.*"

"I figured you would have forgotten about that by now," she admitted, glancing up at him.

"Why?"

Why on earth would he have forgotten about her? She was not easily forgotten, even with the sudden craziness his life had become. Gian fully intended on learning more about Cara Rossi, even if he knew that he had zero business doing so.

"For starters," Cara said, "because we hooked up and that's all it needs to be."

"Tell me that's all it is, though, and then and *only* then, will that be all it needs to be, Cara."

Cara didn't get the chance to answer.

"Gian, you're early!"

He spun on his heel, whiskey in hand, only to come face to face with a stone-faced Claud Rossi. Constantino stood at his father's side, his hands shoved in his pockets.

Claud passed a look between Gian, and Cara. "Busy night, Cara?"

"Busy enough, *Zio.*"

"Good, good." Claud turned his gaze back on Gian. "Thanks for agreeing to meet with me. Constantino says he's sure we can work something out about the little problems the guys have been having on the streets, if you're involved."

Gian nodded. "Sure."

He hated to end his conversation with Cara short, but …

"That coffee," he told her over his shoulder, "is happening soon."

He didn't even leave it open to question.

It was no longer an offer.

Cara nodded, but quickly headed to the other side of the bar.

Then, as Gian turned back to discuss the business at hand with the father and son Capo-duo, Claud was still watching him. It was a pensive sort of stare that put Gian on edge.

"What?" Gian asked.

"Should I be asking you that, Gian?" Claud asked.

Constantino cleared his throat. "Dad—"

"Did I see you give my niece a gift like you're friendly with her?"

Gian resisted the urge to tell Claud to mind his business, though he had every right. "And if I did?"

"What in the hell are you doing, Gian?"

That was the million-dollar question, wasn't it?

Even Gian didn't have the answer.

Chapter 5

Cara tried to listen to the lecturer at the front of the hall, but her gaze kept drifting back to the time on her laptop. It wasn't that the lecture was boring—the effects of mental health driven on or exacerbated by addiction and the statistics for the children growing up in those situations, was a particular subject Cara had great interest in. If for no other reason, to help better understand her own childhood and parents.

For whatever reason, she couldn't concentrate long enough on the lecturer's words to keep track of where the guy was, or what he was currently discussing. That was probably caused by the fact this was her last thing to get done at school, and then she had the weekend free.

Cara had been doing well.

Two weeks, no missed days.

She hadn't even missed study halls or the specific lectures that were not considered required attendance for her grades.

Given her track record over the last few months of missing more time than she actually attended, Cara was going to take that as a win. It was one lecture—the current one—that she probably could have afforded to give herself off to relax, but she had refused. Seems she should have skipped it and downloaded it later off the university's online portal, because she wasn't getting a damn thing out of it anyway.

While it wasn't good form on a student to leave a closed lecture hall, Cara considered doing just that and grabbing a bite to eat on her way to the bus stop. She ended up pushing through those last ten minutes or so, taking the time to close down her laptop and pack her things away. Some lecturers went far over their time, but thankfully, this one was done the second the clock hit four.

Cara was done, too.

Normalcy, she told herself as she walked out of the lecture hall. *You're trying to get back to some kind of normal here.*

So far, she was succeeding.

Or it seemed so.

She hadn't stayed in bed for hours on end. She went out and did things, grabbed groceries, paid bills, and whatever else needed done. It wasn't like she was a social butterfly, but she made it a point to grab coffee with a couple of friends, and have lunch with her aunt, too. Which was a hell of a lot more than she had been doing before.

Cara hadn't realized how deep her head had been stuck in the sand for all those months. To an extent, she had liked the darkness of being alone, even if the loneliness felt like it might kill her.

She figured, what did it matter?

No one would be able to understand her grief, anyhow.

Cara was right on that end.

No one *did* understand.

But they sympathized.

Maybe it was that the hardest part of her grief was finally waning enough to let her breathe. Maybe she had somehow managed to survive the depression that had sank its dirty claws into her mind for so long. Or maybe forcing herself to do normal things and actually see what was happening around her had been enough to wake her the hell up.

Maybe it was none of those things.

She did know that whatever it was, she was grateful. There was nothing to life, if a person wasn't living it. Lea would have understood that better than anyone else.

"Hey, Cara!"

She had opened the main doors to Hall Three to leave, but turned to face the familiar girl running up to her. Lynn had been one of the few mutual friends that Cara and Lea had shared together, who had come from them attending the university.

"What's up, Lynn?"

The girl smiled widely. "Just wondered if maybe you might want to hang out this weekend? We're all thinking of heading to the new club that opened up in Niagara Falls."

"That club is supposed to be crazy popular right now, isn't it?"

"Yep."

"So, four hours of waiting in line to get inside a club that is so full, you can barely see what's happening five feet in front of you?" Cara asked, slightly amused.

Lynn shrugged. "I guess. You interested?"

"Not this weekend, but thanks."

Cara didn't regret refusing the invite. She didn't have shit going on, she had no plans coming up, and she liked that fine. Lynn didn't seem to mind either, giving her friend a hug before heading back in the direction she came.

Normal, Cara found herself repeating.

Like a damn mantra.

She was coming to learn that sometimes, breaks were good, too. A break from the world, from friends, and from life. It didn't mean she was doing worse or whatever, just that she needed a little time out.

That's what she wanted this weekend.

A little time out.

Of course, *he* would be waiting in front of her apartment building when Cara got off the city bus. Of course, he would be wearing one of those fucking three-piece suits, looking like a goddamn God, as though he had nowhere else better to be in that moment.

And fuck, did he look good.

Cara hated how almost every part of her knew instantly that her attraction to this man was not the least bit containable or innocent.

Gian Guzzi.

Leather driving gloves. Shined, leather shoes, untouched by the dirtiness of the winter in the city. Lazy grin. Confident posture.

Gian.

She didn't have the slightest clue how Gian knew where she lived— she hadn't given him her address that morning weeks ago, and she hadn't even given him her phone number, despite his promise of coffee. She knew that him showing up at the restaurant when she was filling in for a bartender that night a few days back had been nothing more than happenstance, and even then, he *still* hadn't asked for her information.

Almost like he didn't have to.

Like maybe he already knew.

Cara couldn't decide if she liked that, or not.

She stayed back a few paces, as he clearly hadn't seen her get off the bus, and decided to watch him for a moment. He *was* exceptionally beautiful for a man, in a rough, cocky sort of way. When he tugged on the wrists of his leather driving gloves, Cara's cheeks heated with the memory of taking them off, just so he could get his bare hands up her dress in a car.

Nothing innocent about this at all.

Gian both amazed and terrified Cara.

Never had a man had the ability to make Cara so entirely aroused, yet coy at the same time.

She was not shy, yet in a blink, he could make her that way. She was not loud, but he could easily make her scream. She was not controlled by selfish desires, but a *big* part of her still screamed *want, want, want* when it came to Gian Guzzi.

And that was bad all over.

Or was it?

Cara didn't know.

"Are you going to stand there and stare at me all day, or come over and talk to me?" Gian suddenly asked, never once looking away from the opposite direction of where Cara was standing. "Not that I mind your staring, because, well ... *Tu as de beaux yeux, ma chérie.* But I already have a big enough ego to fill this city, no need to go adding to my complex."

That fucking French of his was going to kill her someday.

And she wasn't even sure she understood what he said.

"Did you say I have beautiful eyes?" Cara asked.

Gian's grin turned even sexier as his gaze finally landed on her. "I did—well done, Cara. *Brava.*"

And there went his Italian.

Cara sighed. "You're Catholic, right?"

Sure, he was.

He was French and Italian.

He was a damned Catholic.

"Of course," Gian said, turning to face her more. "Why?"

"Then you're familiar with the Bible and sin. Tell me, is there any place in the good book that explains how much of a sin it has got to be that you can manage to be *that* attractive and charming in three languages?"

Gian laughed loud and hard.

Cara's stomach tightened into a dozen more knots.

Fuck.

Yes, that's what she was.

Fucked.

"There is no such thing in the Bible," Gian assured.

"There should be," Cara mumbled to herself. "It's not fair to all us unsuspecting women walking around, you know."

Gian lifted a shoulder. "There's really only one woman who needs to be worrying about it, at the moment."

"Oh?"

His brown eyes lifted to meet hers unabashed, his grin still firmly in place. "You, Cara. Just you."

She didn't know what game this man was playing, but he was damn good at it.

"What are you doing here, Gian?"

"You owe me a coffee. It also happens to be dinnertime, so I thought you might like food, too."

Cara came a little closer to the back of his Lexus. "And you knew where I lived, how?"

"Constantino is chatty when he drinks," Gian admitted. "I tend to use that to my advantage at times."

"My cousin?"

"Surprised he knows things about you?"

"A little," Cara replied. "We're not really close."

"You don't have to be," Gian said, not elaborating further. "He also mentioned you might have your weekends free, which is why your uncle often calls on you, if he needs an extra hand at the bar like he did the other night."

Cara eyed him curiously. "So, you've been asking about me?"

"*Oui*. Is that a problem?"

"Maybe."

"Funny, *bella*, you don't sound like it's a problem."

Cara barely held back her smile.

Damn him.

"Is your weekend free?" Gian asked quieter.

"My *whole* weekend?" Cara shrugged. "That's a hell of a lot more than coffee or dinner, Gian."

"It is, but shit, go big or go home, Cara. I'm interested in you—*very* interested, love. I'm not about to hide my intentions in that regard. It won't get me what I want, if I do. So if your weekend is free, and you might like a bit more than dinner with me, you should get your pretty ass inside my car as soon as you possibly can, so we can get out of here."

Cara sucked in a sharp breath, stunned and aroused at the same time. With only a few words, he'd provoked her into a reaction, and this time, he hadn't even needed to touch her to do it. He demanded, she reacted.

Damn him, indeed.

"And what would this weekend include?" Cara asked.

Gian waved a hand, smiling. "I've come into some real estate in Ottawa, and I greatly need a break from my life. I'll get to leave this city for a bit—breathe outside of this familiar hell. It's not been a fun couple of weeks. I'd like to see the real estate, *and* enjoy myself while I do it."

Cara wet her lips. "With me."

He nodded, that piercing gaze of his pinning her in place. "With you, Cara."

Well, then ...

"I have to grab a bag," she said.

Gian gestured at her building. "I'll be here when you get out."

"This was not at all what I expected when you said real estate," Cara admitted, taking in the old oak floors and outdated—yet beautiful—pieces of furniture in the two-level penthouse. There was nothing modern about the decoration of the penthouse, and even the light fixtures threw back to yesteryears, when Cara hadn't even been alive. It was beautiful, to be sure, but *old*. "It's like we jumped back in time about fifty years."

Gian hummed under his breath, running his finger along the curved wooden arm of a chaise. Not a speck of dust was anywhere to be seen, yet the place looked like it hadn't been lived in for years. "As far as I know, that was about the time he bought it."

"He?"

"My grandfather."

"Oh," Cara said softly.

"Mr. Guzzi!"

Cara damn near jumped out of her skin at the new voice, though Gian barely moved a muscle except to smile at the newcomer. An older gentleman, and a slightly younger woman, came walking down a spiral staircase. The woman stayed behind the man, her uniform suggesting she was a maid of sorts, while the gentleman's suit said something entirely different.

"We've been looking forward to seeing you, and taking you on a tour," the man said, coming to stop in front of Gian with his hand extended.

Gian shook politely. "Yes, well, the tour won't be needed, Derek, but *merci*."

"But—"

"I think Cara and I can handle the exploring on our own for the weekend." Gian gave her a wink over his shoulder. "Right, *mon ange?*"

"Sure, we can."

She didn't think he had any exploring in mind, to be honest.

"If you're sure," Derek started to say.

"Perfectly sure."

"Penelope comes in to clean and dust Mondays, Wednesdays, and Fridays," Derek explained. "She is done for the day, and all the beds have been stripped and changed."

Something odd took over Gian's features. Cara didn't recognize it.

He cleared his throat, glancing upward at the ceiling. "And which room did he prefer? Or, which one did they use, so I can avoid that?"

"Well, Corrado hasn't been here in more than a decade, Gian. And those items are long gone."

Gian didn't appear to care. "Which one?"

"The only one without a balcony," Derek replied quickly. "Louise didn't like heights."

"Great. I have your phone number if we need anything, so ..."

Derek and the maid seemed to catch on to Gian's unspoken words quickly enough, and made themselves scarce. Cara only heard the quiet click of the front door closing before she turned back to Gian.

He had walked forward, further into the penthouse, toward a row of windows that still had wooden frames, and could be opened from the inside. He crossed his arms, staring out the windows at the old buildings across the way.

"Your grandfather hasn't been here in ten years, but kept a maid on a three-day-a-week schedule?" Cara asked, confused.

"And Derek is on call, too, as he's the building's ... well, like a consigliere, of sorts. This is one of the only suites in this building that hasn't been renovated or updated in some way over the years. They would greatly like me to keep it that way, as it increases the value of the building as a whole, to say the original owner's penthouse is in mint condition from when it was built fifty years ago."

"But you don't want to," Cara assumed.

She hadn't realized it was more than the penthouse that he owned.

"I didn't want this place," Gian muttered heavily. Sighing, he turned to face her again. "Would you mind exploring on your own for a bit? I have a call to make, and I'll order us some food, too."

"Sure," Cara said.

She could tell something else was on his mind.

Gian was good at hiding it, but she saw it.

Whatever it was.

Cara figured it wasn't her place to push. She hadn't come with him for the weekend to pry into his personal life. She had come because, like him, a break from life was just what she needed.

And who the hell said she couldn't have fun while she did it?

"Is this your grandmother?" Cara held out a black and white glamor shot of a beautiful woman, as Gian walked into the bedroom without a balcony.

"No, that isn't Aurora. And my grandmother died two years ago. Heart attack."

Cara's brow furrowed, as she took in the dozen and one other framed photos on the old armoire. Most held the woman, but a few had children, and some, an older gentleman that looked a hell of a lot like Gian, if he were in his forties or fifties.

"Then who is it? Oh, Louise, right?"

Gian stared at Cara, not saying anything.

"What?"

It took her far too long to realize what he *wasn't* saying. A woman named Louise had lived here, and she *was not* his grandmother. A woman who, guessing by the photos and the statements made about the bedroom, had been involved in a romantic relationship with Corrado Guzzi for years.

The photos of the children caught her attention again.

Decades, actually.

"Oh," Cara said quietly, carefully putting the photo back. "Well, then."

Gian shrugged one shoulder, but didn't move further into the room to join her. "Louise died a decade ago, about the time my grandfather stopped coming for his weekend visits. Apparently, he didn't want much to do with the place when she wasn't here, but he also didn't want to sell it."

Cara glanced back at the old photos of the children. "What about their kids?"

"Louise had kids—they weren't my grandfather's."

"Huh."

"You sound ... bothered," Gian said.

Cara's brow furrowed. "Weren't you bothered that he had a whole other life, with another woman, in a different city, that *wasn't* his wife?"

"It was a secret that was not really a secret in our family. I was told—like everyone else in my family—that it was not a topic we were to discuss, for obvious reasons. I didn't feel much about it, I suppose it wasn't my place to. That was, until the deed was handed over to me. Now, I have to consider *too* much."

She understood that.

It couldn't be pleasant.

"Let's get out of this room, then," she suggested.

Gian nodded, and stepped back into the doorway, gesturing for her to follow. "Food is here, by the way."

Cara walked on past, but nearly stopped as she felt his hand find her lower back. That all too familiar shiver crawled over her skin at his touch. "And what comes after the food, Gian?"

She felt his smirk grow as he pressed a quick kiss to her cheek. "*Any* other bedroom but that one, Cara."

Cara crawled onto the foot of the bed, moving up Gian's naked side in nothing but one of his dress shirts. The man woke up at the ass-crack of dawn, and it was disturbing because Cara *liked* to sleep.

She couldn't sleep when Gian wasn't, though.

He wouldn't let her.

Gian had tossed the beige sheets across his lower midsection and groin, but that still left the rest of his body free for Cara to admire. It was quite a sight, especially in the morning with light coming in through the opened windows. For every defined cut of muscle on his body, Cara's attention was caught and spun. He was lean like a runner, yet built enough like a fighter. It was easy to tell over his suits that he was fit, but it was when he was naked that Cara couldn't stop staring.

A *beautiful* man.

Cara laid along Gian's side, though lower than he was, so that her top half ended at his waist. He peered over the book he was reading, those brown eyes of his raking over her form and the shirt she wore.

"Shame you can't go out like that all the time," he said under his breath.

"I could say the same."

"Yes, and then where would all those unsuspecting women be, huh? Falling all over themselves, I imagine. It would be hazardous for me to do that to the world."

"Arrogant ass."

"Complex," he corrected with a grin.

Then, he went back to his book.

His free hand came down to tangle in her hair as he continued reading, his fingers stroking through the strands carefully. He didn't tug or pull, not like he did when he was fucking her, but rather, stroked her hair gently as if to relax her.

And it did.

Before Cara had realized what was happening, her face rested in Gian's palm, and his thumb stroked her cheekbone.

It was intimate.

But not the kind of intimate like the night before, when he fucked her until she couldn't breathe or see properly.

It was sweet.

But not like his pet names, not like his French or Italian nothings in her ear.

Cara was pretty sure this was not how hookups were supposed to go, and she certainly shouldn't be considering feelings for Gian, but he made it difficult not to. This was only supposed to be a weekend away—a break, nothing more. And yet, it felt strangely domestic. Something familiar and comforting, with someone she didn't know all that well.

She decided to get her mind off of that nonsense.

"Are you going to read all morning?" she asked.

"It's good for the brain, Cara."

"So is food. Or coffee. Television. A shower. *Sex.*"

Gian's right eyebrow lifted and his lips curved salaciously. "Those are all good things, too."

"Not good for the brain?"

"Some of them," he said.

Before she could think better of it, Cara snatched his book away and tossed it to the floor. As it landed with a thump on the hardwood, Gian's narrowed gaze turned on her. That one look threatened fun and bad and sinful, all at once. Cara simply smiled back in the face of his unspoken threat.

"Oops," she whispered.

"That was not nice. I was at a good part."

Cara shrugged. "Oh, well."

"That was terribly bratty, too."

"Yes, but—"

Gian lurched toward her before Cara could even get her words out properly. She didn't even have the chance to try and get away from his hands grabbing hard to her waist and pulling her higher up the bed. Her laughter bounced off the walls as his fingers danced over her skin, tickling with killer precision and making her sides ache.

Somehow, though she wasn't quite sure how, Cara managed to get up on her knees, and then stand. Gian followed right behind her, still holding tight and refusing to let her go. She grabbed for a pillow, but he knocked it back down, and she fell with it.

Gian went with her.

That was how Cara found herself pinned under a grinning Gian and how she knew her plan to at least get him out of the bed before noon was *screwed.*

But she was probably going to like it.

"Word to the wise," he murmured an inch away from her lips.

"What's that?"

"Compliance will get you everywhere with me, but brattiness will get you something, too. You like the one, so you'll probably like this as well."

Then, his fingers pressed harder, sliding lower down her sides, and his body followed the same path. Sliding down her body, Gian pushed the dress shirt she wore higher, his lips coming down to kiss against her heated skin every so often. And his tongue ... it lapped at her flesh, taking small tastes of her body before darting back into that wicked fucking mouth of his. Her legs widened for him, and she couldn't even find it in herself to be ashamed that she hadn't pulled on a pair of panties after showering that morning.

"Now, be a good girl," Gian said as he hovered over her pubic bone, "and let me eat in peace, Cara. On your knees, please."

She blinked. "What?"

Gian only tipped his chin up, and that was it. He didn't repeat himself; he didn't like to, she had learned.

Cara's brain finally caught up to the rest of her body and she scrambled to get on all fours like he wanted. She had thought watching him between her thighs would be a nice sight first thing in the morning, but he apparently had other plans.

If there was a torturous, sinful hell, Gian's mouth was it.

It was his tongue lapping against her sex as he spread her ass cheeks wide and grabbed hard enough to leave his fingerprints behind. It was the way he groaned at the first taste of her pussy, so deep and rough that it traveled over her spine before it even reached her ears. It was the curving flicks of his tongue that beat against the underside of her clit over and over again until her legs shook, and she was pushing back into his mouth to *get more*.

And then he was pulling away, those fucking chuckles of his filling her senses with his satisfaction and her growing orgasm that was now lost.

"The taste of you could kill me, Cara. I'd eat you, morning, noon, and night, and I wouldn't even *think* about anything else. It would *kill me*."

She let out a shaky breath, unable to say anything.

She needed a second to think again.

"Do you remember what I told you?" he asked a second before his palm swatted gently against her wet sex. His fingers slid along her clenching opening a second before another soft slap landed against her ass. The sound echoed in the bedroom, making Cara suck in a sharp breath. His fingers—three of them—slid into her pussy, stretching her open and making her back arch from the sudden intrusion.

"About this—your cunt and me, love. What did I say?"

Cara didn't even have to think about it.

Even when she thought they might not see each other again—and certainly not for sex—she still heard those words of his.

"It's yours, when we're together," she mumbled against her arm.

Gian's pleased hum answered her back before he said, "Exactly that,

Cara."

She felt him move on the bed, reaching for something. Cara looked, only to see him pull his cell phone from the bedside table. Gian's eyes turned back on her with a wicked gleam.

"Your pussy is so pink and wet, especially when you want to come. I want you to see what it looks like when you're bratty and greedy, Cara. Let me."

"You'll delete it—"

"Not a chance," he interrupted fast, "but no one else will ever see it."

Just the cadence his tone took on told Cara he was telling the truth. She nodded and his hand slipped over her body with the softest touch again—something she was learning was a sign of his approval, his happiness. He was rough in bed, not that she minded, and the softness only came when he wanted to gift her something back.

Cara heard the phone's camera ding with a familiar shutter-like sound. She looked over her shoulder, only to see Gian's attention was on her body again, and his fingers were pressing deep into her hot sex. Every single nerve ending she had seemed to be attached to her pussy as his fingers slid in and out with a slow assuredness that drove her fucking *mad*.

"I want to come," Cara mumbled.

Her body ached for it.

Her mind screamed for it.

Gian only smirked, his gaze never once leaving his work. She felt his thumb drive upward, spreading her sex open before sliding over her clit with small circles.

"Gian, let me come."

He didn't.

Not right away.

In fact, he pulled away from her again, only long enough to find a condom from a pack he'd tossed aside the night before. Never once did that damn phone of his leave his hand, but Cara found that she didn't give a shit. She wanted *one* thing from him right then.

Just the one.

To come.

He filled her full all over again, his cock much thicker and longer than his three fingers had been a minute before. And yet, there was no hesitation in the way her body took him entirely, and she could *hear* how fucking wet she was as his groin fit tight to the curve of her ass.

"I want to—"

Gian's hand landed where the curve of Cara's ass met her thigh, and it fucking *stung*. But that quick bloom of heat quickly melted into something delicious as he rubbed the same spot. "I'm aware, but you can wait."

"Why?"

63

And why was she so damn whiney?

"Because I like how you sound when you're like this, and you deserve it after what you did to my book." His fingertips danced up her spine before tangling in the hair at the nape of her neck with a firm tug, pulling her head higher. "Just feel me for a bit, Cara. Christ, all I can feel is you."

It was the dip in his tone, the way it roughened and edged, that made Cara shiver. She knew he liked that—enjoyed seeing it—and so she didn't even try to hide it.

His thrusts came deep, but slow, at first. Measured with every flex, and quick on the pull, like he wanted to dive right back in again. Each one brought her higher, right back to the peak of bliss where he'd stop, tease her with his hands and his words, and then start all over again.

And then his thrusts came harder, faster, and even *deeper*. He tossed his phone to the pillows, so he had another hand free. Cara's gaze caught sight of the video playing on the screen of the device, her senses caught between *watching* and feeling. His fingertips dug into her ass, pulling her back with every flex of his hips. The trembling in her legs had spread to every other part of her fucking body, and she couldn't breathe again, not when all she could think about was release, and when she could finally get it.

Gian's hand slid from her hair to her throat, his fingers curving around the delicate line there as he pulled her up from the bed. Her back fitted against his chest as his fingers tightened, and there it was … enough pressure on her throat to make her impending orgasm continue on for what felt like forever.

That little trick of his made her crazy.

"Now you can come," she heard him say, his words a husky murmur in her ear. "And then you can beg me for another and another, Cara."

She would.

He was a drug to her system.

And she did beg for him to tease her and fuck her all over again—*again and again and again.*

Gian had moved the chaise in the sitting room to the old windows that could be opened. Despite the time of year, a warm breeze came in from the windows. Cara found it was a nice place to sit, with her feet propped up in on the windowsill, and her head tucked against Gian's chest.

"So, a therapist, huh?" he asked above her.

She shrugged. "That's the goal. I want to have a main focus, though. Addiction. Recovery. Maybe some child-work."

"Is that because you feel you owe something for your raising, or because it's something you want to personally do?"

"A bit of both."

"As long as you know," he murmured. "When you do something because you feel you owe it, or you have to, you'll never be as satisfied as you want to be."

Gian's fingers roved through her hair as they chatted.

"I know you wanted a break from … everything that happened," Cara started to say.

"I did, yes."

"But you can't only talk about me, Gian. It's not fair."

He laughed, rocking them both on the chaise. "Fair enough. What do you want to know?"

"Well, anything."

"Like what?"

"Your grandfather, maybe. You seemed like you were close, especially if you needed to take a break after burying him. That sounds like someone who needed to get away from their feelings."

Gian cleared his throat. "Interesting way to put it."

"Am I wrong?"

"No. You're very right, actually." He sighed, shifting beneath her a bit. "I don't have time to grieve, in a way, because there's much more happening, now that he's gone. And that feels terribly shitty of me, that my focus can't be on a man who practically raised me for a bit, because responsibility and duty wait on no one."

Cara frowned. "I'm sorry."

"Don't be. Believe it or not, but this *break*, is not entirely a break. I've thought a lot more about my grandfather this weekend than I would have been able to, had I stayed in Toronto. Less bullshit—less noise in my head and from other people."

"I get that."

"Now, your turn," he said.

"For what?"

"A question that isn't entirely safe."

Cara stiffened. "Depends on what it is."

"Too bad—I answered yours." His hand landed on her bare hip under the afghan blanket, holding firm as if to keep her there. "Tell me about your sister. Not the kinds of things you tell other people. How you're feeling. Certainly, not something to placate me. I'll know if you do, *bella donna*. I am not a dumb man."

No, he certainly wasn't.

Cara barely had to think about her response, though. "She was not like me. Lea was the complete opposite of me. And maybe, sometimes, that left me feeling a bit left out when she could so easily fit in and I couldn't, but I always had her, regardless. It took me a bit to realize after she had died that I depended on her for a lot more than being my sister and roommate. I didn't know how to be Cara without Lea."

"Oh?"

"I'm still not sure that I know."

Gian's lips pressed to the top of her head. "I only know you—what you let me know, of course—and I think you do *Cara* very well."

She smiled. "I think you would have liked Lea, though."

"I *like* you, love. And that's the important bit."

"Is it?"

"Sure."

Cara fell silent, lost in the sensations of Gian stroking her skin under the blanket and the comfortable breeze coming in through the window. She hadn't known how much she needed the quiet and a break from life and a city that never stopped moving. Sure, below them, another city was moving like the end was near, but she barely heard a thing.

It was only Gian's speaking again that broke her from the daze.

"We should do this again soon," he said.

"That might make it seem like we're dating, Gian. We hooked up, ran away for the weekend, and now you're planning the next one. I don't get involved with your type of man—I told you that once."

"It's a little late for that, isn't it?"

Cara bit her bottom lip. "Maybe."

"We're doing this again."

It wasn't even a suggestion that time.

"Are we?"

"Oh, yes."

Chapter 6

"Gian."

He almost missed the call of his name by the familiar voice, as he started his ascent of the church steps. It was unusual for his closest enforcer—Chris—to call him by his name, as it was usually "boss" only to the man, but Gian understood why the sudden change.

Edmond clapped Gian on the shoulder as he continued climbing the church steps to a waiting Mass. When the boss was around, Gian could not be "boss" to his own men, as anyone in a higher position than him took precedence.

It hadn't much mattered with his grandfather, but Edmond was not Corrado.

That was obvious to everyone.

"I messaged you this morning," Gian said, turning to face the enforcer standing on the bottom step. "It's not like you to be late, Chris."

The barrel-chested man shrugged his wide shoulders. "Sundays are my off day—that's what you always say, anyway. No business on Sundays. I put the phone away."

"All right, I'll take that."

Only because it was true.

"You needed me for something?" Chris asked.

Gian ignored the passing people—many he recognized—as he reached for the velvet case inside his jacket pocket. Pulling the item out, he rested it on his palm. It was as long as his hand, and about as wide. "I need you to run this across town for me."

"Seriously?"

"Yes. I don't make you run errands very fucking often, so don't start complaining now."

Chris held his hands up, a silent apology. "No worries. Where's it going to?"

Gian didn't answer right away, instead, opening the velvet case to check the item inside for a fifth time since he had picked it up earlier in the

67

week. He'd wanted to give it to Cara himself. He hadn't seen her since the weekend before, but it looked like it was going to be another couple of days before he could drag himself away from the nonsense that had become his life. He figured the gift would be a nice way to tell her to look forward to a visit, and that he hadn't forgotten about her.

In a way …

Inside the case, a black lace, Victorian-styled choker rested on crushed velvet. A small, oval diamond hung from the middle, giving it a bit of regal beauty to go along with the classic. He'd found the item by chance, when he had gone into his jeweller's to pick up one of his Rolexes that needed to be fixed.

There was something about the choker—and the way he thought it might look on a delicate throat—that made him purchase the item without even hesitating.

"A woman, then," Chris assumed as he glanced down at the choker.

Gian quickly snapped the case shut. "A woman."

"You don't usually give gifts to women."

He didn't.

It wasn't appropriate, really.

"She's worth the step out from my usual," Gian replied vaguely. He handed the case over, and rattled off Cara's address. "Redhead, tall, beautiful. You won't miss her, and you might even recognize her. You're not to leave until this is in her hands, and you're not to allow her to refuse it. Understood?"

Chris nodded. "Got it."

"Tell her to text me if she wants someone to argue with about it," Gian added with a chuckle.

He'd plugged his number into Cara's phone the weekend before, and occasionally sent her messages throughout the week, but no actual phone call. He wondered how she would react to the gift, but he would have to settle with the aftermath.

"Go," Gian ordered, pointing in the direction Chris had come.

"Later, boss."

Gian didn't correct Chris's slip that time, but only because the steps had mostly cleared of people. No one was close enough to hear the man's casual use of a title that technically didn't belong to Gian.

Not wanting to be late for Mass, Gian headed inside the church, taking the steps two at a time. He'd missed it last weekend, and two in a row would never be overlooked by his devout Catholic mother.

Not to mention, Gian wanted to be seen.

Especially by the men of *la famiglia*.

With so many younger Capos and foot soldiers upset by the change in power—a change that Edmond had made without their input—Gian wanted to bring some sense of peace. Before any fighting within the ranks could begin, he wanted to stop it. He hoped, though he didn't know how well it would work, that his presence alongside the new boss might keep those men closer to his own age under control of sorts.

Even if Gian didn't entirely trust the new boss.

Gian found his usual seat in the third pew from the front of the church. He rested into the pew beside his younger brother. Domenic—though Dom to his family and friends—passed Gian a curious look.

"What?" he asked.

"You're having Chris run gifts around for you now?"

Gian stiffened a bit in the pew. "Saw that, did you?"

"A few people did. You know, they're talking too, right? You disappeared last weekend, but *someone* knew where you went, and didn't keep it quiet. Add the gift thing to it, and the gossip will fly, Gian. You're not the kind to stir the pot. So, Cara Rossi, is it?"

Fuck nosy people.

And those that couldn't keep their mouths shut.

"Mind your business," Gian told his brother.

Dom rolled his eyes upward. "Not on this, man."

"There's nothing to talk about, so leave it. What I do privately is my own concern, and not for you or anyone else to worry about."

"But you took her away for a weekend."

"So?"

"And you bought her a gift—I saw it, too, it's not a little trinket, Gian," his brother added quieter.

"Again, *so?*" Gian asked, his irritation rising.

"According to Dad, it's one thing for you to hook-up with somebody and go your way. It's quite another for you to be … getting cozy. It makes a statement that you might not want, or the family, if you get what I mean."

"And Dad should mind his own business, too," Gian said.

"Ma—"

"You know, out of everyone, I bet she'll be the least likely to open her mouth and bitch about all of this. And do you know why? Because she knows I haven't been happy on that side of my life in a long fucking time. You know that, too, Dom."

Dom met Gian's gaze, nodding once. "Yeah, I do know."

"Then fuck off about it."

"I don't give a shit how it makes us look, as far as that goes," Dom said, "but I worry about *you*, man. And how it might make a target out of you, given some of the rumblings and the recent changes."

With that statement made, Dom nodded toward the *new* boss, an aisle over and two pews ahead of theirs. As he looked at the boss, Gian wondered how many eyes were watching him and his brother in that moment.

"Might he make a show out of you, to control those who favor you?" Dom asked.

"He's got bigger worries," Gian replied, "like keeping his older sheep happy and compliant. He's not even looking at the younger men right now."

Dom scoffed. "All he's done is piss off a lot of made men."

Yeah, that too.

Still ...

"Don't worry about me, or this, or my business, all right?"

Dom shrugged. "You say that like it's easy, Gian. Grandpapa is dead—nobody's looking out for you like he would have done, so I'm trying to. That's all."

"You're not a made man yet, Dom. There isn't a whole lot of looking out you can do at the moment."

"I do what I can."

That, too, was true.

Gian appreciated it.

But still ... "Stop talking about all of this in church. No business on Sundays, Dom. It's a rule."

"But—"

"You'll never get your button until you learn to listen more than you talk."

Dom finally shut up.

Gian was grateful for that, too.

I got your gift, read the text message.

Gian smiled, typing back, *Oh? Did you like it?*

He knew what her answer would be—yes, Cara liked the choker. It wasn't the choker itself that she probably struggled with, but the idea of accepting a gift from him. After all, it had been a whole *day* since Chris delivered the choker, and Gian got nothing but radio silence in return. He hadn't been particularly surprised about that, either.

When Cara didn't immediately reply, Gian hit dial on his phone's screen, and put it up to his ear as he headed into the restaurant. A business he owned, liked to use as an office of sorts, and had a meeting at later with Constantino and the asshole, Stephan.

They wanted to talk about what had happened with Edmond.

Gian wanted to placate the younger Capos for a bit.

"I was replying," Cara said as soon as she picked up Gian's call.

"You were taking too long. Probably overthinking. As I suspect you've been doing for the last day, *bella*. It's a necklace, one that suits your style, and I wanted to see you wear it, nothing more."

"Gian."

"Hmm?"

"You're being …"

"What, charming, again?" he suggested.

Cara sighed. "I'm agreeable to casual here with you—"

Yes, because apparently casual did not mean dating to Cara Rossi.

Gian didn't give a shit.

"And that means if I want to buy you something, I can and will. You should expect it," Gian interrupted before Cara could say more.

He swore she muttered, "You're fucking impossible."

"Drop the casual bit, and you'll see how impossible I can get," Gian urged with a smirk.

"That doesn't exactly make me want to jump in with both feet, Gian."

"Liar. You know it does."

Cara didn't reply.

Gian didn't need her to.

She'd already told him once …

You make it hard to say no.

"I do like the choker … a lot," Cara finally said, softly.

"Send me a picture with it on, show me."

"You're serious?"

"Would you like to see some of the pictures I already have of you, Cara?"

He didn't even need to see her face to know it was red, like her hair.

Gian laughed darkly, weaving through the restaurant and ignoring the patrons as he headed to his back office. "They're *beautiful*, by the way."

Cara made a noise under her breath. "Pretty sure that was *videos*."

"I took some stills of them. I have an app."

"Oh, my God. I have an app, he says. Like it's not a big fucking deal or something."

"Send me a picture," he demanded again. "Show me how much you like it, sweetheart."

Gian said a quick goodbye, as he had to get some work done before the guys showed up for dinner and the meet. He hated doing it to Cara, as he didn't get to talk to her much as it were, but he didn't have a choice.

To make up for it, as soon as he hung up the phone, he scrolled through the gallery images and videos. He hadn't lied—the video he had took, and the subsequent stills, *were* beautiful. Hot, sexy, and *sin*.

Pure fucking sin.

Porn, at the very least to some.

Art, to him.

He'd gotten a shot of his fingers buried deep into her pussy while she was on her knees, her sex pink and wet, her arousal smeared across his hand. Another of his cock stretching her open, and a quick peek at the handprint he'd left on her thigh. Then, later in the day, he'd pulled the phone out again to catch the way his cum looked, painted down Cara's toned stomach in white, ropey streams.

Gian was terribly careful with his phone. No one touched it but him, and not one single person knew his passcodes to get inside. He wouldn't share the images or videos with a soul, because that wasn't why he'd taken them.

He took them for *him*.

Because it made him hot and it got him off.

Because he liked reliving those moments.

Because his memory didn't do Cara Rossi any sort of justice.

He shot off a couple of the images, and one of the videos he'd shortened to a few seconds. All had been changed to a black and white, and he'd stripped the sound from the short clip, too.

He really liked that app.

Not a minute later, his phone buzzed on the desk as he were going over orders for the restaurant. Gian picked it up, gave the message a look, and laughed hard.

Are those even me?!

Every single one of them, he typed back.

He'd cropped some of the images, zoomed in to keep Cara's body and face from being entirely identifiable. But he wanted her to see what he saw, too.

Beauty.

Sex.

Lust.

The sweetest temptation that had ever crossed his path.

She would certainly be the cause of his eventual unraveling.

Gian didn't think he would mind.

That's porn, Gian, Cara's next message said.

Beautiful porn, he corrected. Then, he sent another right after. *I can do it again, oui?*

Cara's reply had him grinning. *Hell yes.*

He stuffed his phone away, and went back to work.

His mind was definitely not on the orders, though.

"They don't see it like you're *just* doing what you're supposed to do, though, Gian," Constantino argued. "The younger Capos—guys like us— see it like you're standing on Edmond's side of things, here. That you approve of what he did and how he did it."

Gian's jaw clenched, his one and only show of irritation at his best friend's statement. "You, of all people, know I don't approve. But what exactly could I do? I was put in a position where I couldn't do or say anything. He called the vote without telling me that's what it was, and he made the calls on who would be there for it. There's nothing I can do now."

"Not saying anything now certainly isn't helping your fucking case, either."

"Don't forget, it's my grandfather's legacy here, too. And I have to consider—"

"Your last name won't mean shit, with Edmond as the current boss," Constantino cut in fast.

Stephan nodded his agreement. "Everybody—especially the younger guys—knew it was going to be you next in that seat, Gian. It's what Corrado was working towards for years, slowly getting everybody ready for a change. He'd sped it up a bit recently, because obviously, there were some issues between the generational lines, and he probably thought putting you in the seat would help smooth that over."

"Corrado didn't talk about those things with me."

"He didn't *have* to," Constantino pointed out quietly. "It was expected. Edmond took advantage of a situation you weren't ready for and it makes you look weak as shit."

Gian bristled at that comment. "Say that again, *cafone*."

Constantino scowled. "I'm only saying it now for your benefit."

"You weren't ready for it because of Corrado's death," Stephan jumped in again. "Because someone—probably fucking Edmond—put a bullet between his eyes, or ordered it done."

"We don't know that he did it," Gian said quietly.

But he certainly had reason to suspect the new boss.

Every goddamn reason.

"And they were old friends," Gian added. "He's given me reason to think it was him, but that's circumstance, and nothing more. It's not likely that he *did* kill my grandfather."

Gian absolutely planned on finding out, though.

God save Edmond's soul.

"Friendships mean shit in Cosa Nostra," Stephan muttered. "Not when power is right there in front of you, ready for the taking."

Gian passed Constantino a look, not ready to agree to that statement. He'd known Constantino since he was ten years old—unless he had to, unless given no other option, Gian couldn't imagine putting a bullet in his oldest and best friend. They had too much history, too much time watching each other's backs.

Friendship *did* mean something.

At least, to Gian.

"You need to, at the very least, make a statement against what Edmond did to put your own image and respect back in place for the younger Capos," Constantino said. "Don't bite the fucking hand that feeds you, Gian, not with this. Those men would have wanted you, and every time they see you running for the boss, or standing at his side, is another day that they feel like it was you that betrayed them, not him."

Gian considered those words carefully. "And then what if I do, what after that? Then I have a pissed off boss to contend with, and an older generation of men who wouldn't think twice about killing me to get me out of the way. I'm walking a very thin line here."

Constantino shrugged. "So, do it *carefully*."

"Easy for you to say. You're not the one sticking the target on your own back."

"You sure about that, man? Because the way I see it, anyone on your side is not on theirs. And that's a pretty big fucking target, Gian."

Fair enough.

Gian headed out the back entrance of the restaurant, entering into the alley where he had parked his Lexus. After the meeting he'd had with Constantino and Stephan, Gian needed five minutes to himself. He needed to get his thoughts together and figure out whether or not the Capos' warnings had any real merit for him to consider.

Then, his phone buzzed.

Gian pulled the device out of his pocket, ignoring the chill in the air. Cara's name popped up on the screen, but the message surprised him the most. An image file, it seemed. He didn't even hesitate in opening it, his grin growing the very second it loaded.

Tanned skin.

Black thigh-high stockings with lace trim at the top.

Red curls framing delicate shoulders and naked breasts.

And that fucking choker …

She had taken the image in front of a mirror, from her painted-red smile down, but it was perfect. He was instantly hard and no longer giving any shits about his problems.

Took you long enough, he texted back instantly. Then adding, *But so worth the wait.*

He got a wink in response, but that wasn't enough for Gian.

I'm coming over, he messaged, *don't take any of that off.*

Gian didn't even wait for Cara's response before he grabbed the key fob from his pocket, and pointed it at his car thirty feet away. He hit the unlock button, felt his phone buzz, and then the blast came.

Hot.

Loud.

Dead.

Gian was sure he was dead.

Except, dead people couldn't feel pain, and he was in a hell of a lot of pain.

Chapter 7

I'm coming over, don't take any of that off.

Cara stared at Gian's final text message, and then the one she had sent to him right after. *I'm not home right now, at dinner with my aunt.*

The reason it had taken her so long to send him the picture that he wanted—as he was quick to point out when she had finally sent it—was because she was in a rush. Her aunt had called last minute to invite her over for dinner, and as much as she wanted to say no, Cara wasn't very good at doing it.

She'd taken the picture for Gian before she'd thrown on a suitable black dress to match the stockings and heels. Then, she forgot to actually *send* it until the taxi dropped her off at her aunt's home.

Nonetheless, Gian hadn't answered her reply back.

That wasn't like him.

Cara didn't actually spend a lot of time on the phone with him, as far as that went, but when she did, Gian never wasted time on replying. His texts were always an instant response to hers, never leaving her waiting.

It left her with an odd feeling.

Cara shot off another text when her aunt's back was turned, asking Gian what in the hell was up. She stuffed the phone into her clutch before her aunt could see her with it when she turned back around.

Daniele gave Cara another once-over, her gaze lingering on the very short length of the black dress. It fell high on her thighs, enough so that the lace at the top of the thigh-high stockings were visible.

"Were you going out tonight?" her aunt asked.

Cara shrugged. "Nope."

It wasn't a total lie.

She hadn't expected to be leaving a bed, after all.

"You wear outfits like that on regular nights at home?"

"I grabbed the first black dress I saw—it was a bit short. It still worked."

"A bit short," her aunt echoed.

Cara held back the urge to roll her eyes. At twenty-five, she was not about to go explaining her attire, or the reasons for it, to anyone. And certainly not her aunt. "Anyway, what's for supper?"

Maybe if she got the hell out of there as soon as possible, she could salvage some of her night. With Gian, preferably. *If* she could get a hold of him.

"Food," her aunt replied with a wink. "Food you will eat and enjoy."

Well, that was that.

Thirty minutes later, a rigatoni dish soaked in thick, rich sauce was shoved in front of Cara's face. Across the table, her uncle stuffed a cloth napkin into the collar of his shirt as he waited for Daniele to give him a plate, too.

"It's good to see you around more," Claud said.

Cara wasn't quite sure how to respond to that. "It's been a rough few months."

"Yes, but it's better not to wallow. When things can't be changed, you move on. *Capisce?*"

"Yeah, I got it."

She didn't agree.

But that was an argument for another day.

It was only after Daniele had served her husband, and then herself, did she sit down at the other end of the long table. Her aunt said the usual dinner prayer, giving thanks and asking for a blessing from above, before they could even touch the food. It was one of the few things Cara had a hard time with—the blessing, not the actual act of praying. Even through her parents' drunken stupors when she was younger, they never forgot to go to church, make Cara and Lea, and Tommas say their prayers at night, or ask for a blessing when her mother managed to remember to cook food.

Maybe that was it; maybe it was that God had been the thing her parents chose to hold onto, even through their years of addiction, and not the three people they had brought into the world.

Cara really didn't like to think about it.

"All right, let's eat," her uncle demanded.

His booming voice brought Cara from her depressing thoughts. For once, she was grateful for Claud's loud demeanor.

Cara was a quarter of the way through her aunt's pasta dish when the home's landline started ringing. Claud waved at his wife to go pick it up, clearly not wanting to be taken away from his food. Daniele shot him a dirty look as she tossed her napkin to the table and headed for the sound of the ringing phone.

Thirty seconds later, Daniele shouted. "Claud!"

Cara stood from the table at the same time her uncle did. Panic had laced her aunt's yell. She quickly followed behind her uncle, watching as

Daniele passed the phone over with wide eyes and worry setting her lips into a hard frown.

"What is it?" Cara asked her aunt.

Daniele acted as though she hadn't heard the question.

Claud spoke fast—and in Italian—into the phone. As it were, Cara's Italian was a bit too rough around the edges, and she had an even harder time keeping up when someone was speaking quickly.

But she did manage to catch a few words she knew mixed in.

Gian.

Autobomba.

Ospedale.

The name of the hospital was repeated, too.

Claud hung up the phone before Cara had even realized what happened. He waved a hand wildly at his wife. "My keys, get me my damn keys, *donna*."

Cara didn't move as her aunt rushed by her. "Gian is at a hospital?"

"What?" Claud's gaze snapped to Cara, but just as quickly, he dropped the stare and headed for the front of the house. Cara followed right behind. "It's none of your concern, Cara. Enjoy dinner with Daniele; keep her company for tonight."

No.

She refused to relent, her heart beating hard in her chest. "Is that why he didn't message me back earlier? A car bomb, that's what I heard you say."

Claud froze as he tried to put on his jacket. "Why are you even conversing with Gian Guzzi?"

"Because I'm a grown woman and I want to. Why won't you answer my questions?"

"Because I'm not required to," her uncle growled.

Cara straightened like a rod had been shoved up her spine, the familiar sense of being a woman in a man's world creeping into her mind again. This was how it always was for the women in this life—told to turn cheek, shut up, and behave when it counted. She hated that the very most.

"Let me give you a piece of advice, Cara," Claud said, finally slipping his jacket on properly. "You're right, it isn't my place to tell you who you can and can't be running around with, now that your father is dead and your brother has the say over you, but that doesn't mean you shouldn't still *listen* when you are told. My brother—your father—would tell you the same damn thing. Stay the hell away from Gian Guzzi, before you end up in a world of trouble that you don't want and can't handle."

"Aren't *you* a part of that world, too?" Cara shot back.

"You have no idea, do you?" Claud's eyes blazed. "Stay the hell away from the man, Cara."

"I want to go to the hospital."

"No. Not with me, anyhow."

Her uncle didn't even give her a second look before he went in search of his wife *and* his keys. Cara had already called a cab before Claud slammed the front door on his way out.

Fuck him.

She would do what she wanted.

Cara stepped out of the taxi after getting her credit card back from the driver, and stared up at the bright lights of the emergency room of one of Toronto's largest hospitals. She tried to stay away from hospitals—and this one in particular—as it reminded her a lot of Lea. Her twin had wanted to be a general surgeon, and had been a year away from starting her residency, when she died. Another dream cut far too short.

Letting out a slow breath, Cara shook off the unease and headed toward the emergency entrance. Her uncle had about ten minutes on her, so she assumed Claud would already be inside and doing his own thing by the time she figured out exactly where Gian was situated. Maybe he would even be gone by then, and that would be even better for her. Claud would be less likely to make a scene with others around, if he happened upon Cara.

She didn't even make it inside.

"Cara?"

Constantino stepped out of the shadows, a lit cigarette dangling from his fingertips. The cherry-red tip glowed as he came closer. "What are you doing here?"

Why couldn't anything be easy for her?

"Did your dad get here already?" she asked her cousin.

"Five minutes, or so, ago. He left right after. Now, answer me."

Cara tightened the belt on her tweed coat, willing away the cold. "Take a guess."

Constantino cocked a brow. "You probably shouldn't be here."

"Someone already tried to tell me that tonight. Try something new."

"How did you hear about the bomb?"

So it *was* a bomb.

Cara tried not to let that word frighten her too much, but it was *hard*. "I overheard Claud's phone call. Gian was supposed to come over, but I was already heading out. He hadn't answered my message, telling him I was already gone."

Constantino blew out a hard breath. "Don't go around saying that too loud."

"Saying what?"

"Nothing," her cousin muttered. "It's been a long night. Gian's already discharged, anyway. He's not even here, and he's chilling out where he can't be bothered."

Cara stood firm. "I want to see him."

"Yeah—"

"And why isn't he answering his phone?"

"Kinda got smashed on the way down to the pavement, and yeah," Constantino said. "Why don't you head home, and I'll let him know you were here."

Nope.

"I want to see him," she repeated.

Constantino scowled. "Since when did you become so fucking irritating and stubborn? Weren't you supposed to be the quiet twin?"

Cara couldn't quite let those comments roll off her shoulders. "You don't know shit about me. Don't pretend like you do, Constantino."

"Clearly."

"Take me to Gian."

Her cousin shook his head. "Fine. Whatever."

The very moment Cara laid eyes on Gian from across the club's floor, a swift relief coursed through her system. It was a feeling she hadn't quite experienced before, and she didn't know what to do about it. She hadn't realized that from the second she heard *bomb* uttered alongside Gian's name, fear had put her back in robot mode.

She'd gone back to that black space in her mind. Things moved around her, she did what was needed, and went through the motions of life amongst the living, but Cara wasn't *really* there. Not entirely. Not like she should be.

You're catching feelings for someone you shouldn't, her mind taunted. *And for no good fucking reason.*

Cara ignored her inner voice, her attention snagged entirely by the man across the floor. His gaze caught hers, and time stopped as he smiled. Even surrounded by a group full of men, all chatting with drinks in front of them,

Gian looked at her and *smiled*.

A reddish discoloration marred his right cheek, up to his temple, but other than that, Cara couldn't see any visible issues that should be a cause for concern. Then again, she wasn't close enough to tell.

"Wait here," Constantino demanded.

She glared at her cousin's back as he crossed the club floor to the sectioned-off table where Gian was currently seated with the other men. Constantino bent down, said something, and then nodded quickly. That was it, and her cousin took the seat that Gian vacated not a blink in time later.

The club was hot as hell, so Cara pulled off her coat as Gian crossed the space between them, and hung it over her arm. She tried to shake off the lingering anxiety, and seem like everything was fine, but she couldn't quite do it as he came to a stop in front of her.

"You're not who I expected to see showing up here tonight," Gian said.

Cara shifted from one foot to the other. "You didn't answer me back."

"Something happened to my phone."

"Something like a bomb?"

Gian shrugged one shoulder. "I mean, we can do details, but it won't help all that much."

Cara sighed, trying hard not to meet his gaze. If she did, he would surely see all the crazy worry swimming in her mind, and he would know that she actually *cared*. Cara didn't know if she wanted to go down that road with Gian, quite yet.

"Shouldn't you be in the hospital?" she asked quietly.

Gian lifted his arms, and turned slowly as if to let her look him over. "Mild concussion, which means no sleep tonight. I can't hear all that great out of my right ear, but there's no lasting damage. I've got a bruised kidney, but I only need one, anyway."

Cara shook her head in disbelief. "Lucky."

"Some people do say the Guzzi blood is made of nothing but gold, luck, and dirt."

"Who are these people?"

He only grinned.

Cara finally met his gaze then, holding firm. "So, a club is where you decided to come after you get released from the hospital then? Not ... home, or—"

"To you."

His voice turned lower, cool and curious at the same time.

"You don't have to come to me. That's not what I meant or what I said."

"But would you have liked me to?" Gian asked.

Cara reached up to ghost her fingertips along the discoloration on his cheek and temple. "That looks like it hurts."

"Not a lot. Answer my question."

"Why a club?" she asked instead.

"*Dio*, you are difficult when you want to be. Do you know that?"

Cara smiled. "I've been told. Why a club?"

Gian gestured over his shoulder. "Someone thought I needed a drink, I couldn't refuse, given a lot of the shit that's happened over the past few weeks with the family. I've got enough problems, without making a certain group feel like I'm shunning them."

"I don't understand a word you said."

"Yeah, I know, but I like that you're not all that interested in those semantics of my life, anyway."

Cara let out a shaky exhale, and dropped his gaze. "This—tonight—freaked me out a little bit."

"I can tell. You didn't have to come running, though. I was fine, as far as that goes."

"I was gone before I even knew what was happening, so …"

Gian chuckled.

That was all Cara got—one of his husky laughs—before he grabbed her waist, pulled her in close, and kissed her fast. The bruising force of his mouth crashing against hers took her breath away, and all that remaining fear and worry stopped, *just like that*. His hands slid up her sides and cupped under her jaw while his tongue darted into her mouth and gave her a taste of the bourbon he'd been drinking.

Cara felt dazed-like, when Gian finally pulled away.

Breathless.

Stupid.

Spun.

"I knew this would look good," he said.

"Huh?"

His thumbs slid down over her throat, hooking under the delicate lace of the black choker he had sent to her the day before. "This here, it looks perfect, *mon ange.*"

"It does have a certain appeal," she admitted.

"There was a white one—"

"*Gian.*"

"But this one matches those stockings you're wearing, anyway," he said, never missing a beat.

Cara rolled her eyes. "So, hey, if you're good here with … your friends, then I'll head out. I don't need to be here, and you've got my number."

"I am good," he said, "and so are they, so how about—"

"Lea?"

Cara froze in Gian's warm hands like ice water had been poured down her spine. Gian, too, stiffened, his hands tightening to her neck at the quiet call of a name Cara rarely heard spoken anymore. She didn't think it was random, not with the way the man posed the question over Gian's shoulder, or the way Gian's gaze turned cold and hard in an instant.

A beat of time passed, and then another.

Cara's breath felt painful in those moments.

Gian moved to her side, his arm snaking around her waist. Cara faced the well-dressed man, who looked to be around the same age as Gian. Clean-cut, fresh-faced, and good-looking. He certainly wasn't anything to scoff at, and whoever he was, he looked like he *recognized* her.

"Frankie," Gian said, his smile belying the coolness in his voice. "I don't think you've met Cara Rossi, have you?"

The man—Frankie—suddenly appeared as though he had taken a punch to the gut.

"My bad," Frankie said, offering Cara a fleeting smile. "Constantino wanted to know if you were going to head out, Gian."

"*Sì*, I think I am."

Frankie nodded. "All right, have a good—"

"Why did you call me Lea?" Cara asked.

"You're mistaken," Frankie murmured. Then, he gave another nod to Gian. "Later, boss."

He was gone before Cara could question him again, but *Gian* wasn't.

"Come on, let's go," Gian said, turning them both and directing them toward the front of the club. "My place is closer, if that's okay."

"Whatever," Cara replied. "Why did he call me Lea?"

"I don't know."

Gian was lying.

Cara could hear it in his voice.

"*Gian.*"

"Some people in my circles knew Lea from being around, so maybe—"

"No, he sounded like he was in pain when he said it," Cara argued. "That's not a passing friend, Gian."

"Just drop it, *bella*. It's not important."

She didn't think so.

"Why are you lying?"

"I'm not," Gian said.

"I think you—"

Cara suddenly found herself yanked down a hallway behind Gian, and pulled into what looked to be a storage room of some sort. She didn't even have time to ask him what in the hell he was doing, before his lips were on hers again, taking away her words, thoughts, and breath.

"I didn't tell you how much I liked this dress, did I?" Gian asked.

Cara's head fell back against the closed door. "No."

"I do, I like it a lot."

"Who was that guy, Gian?"

"Nobody important."

"Gian."

He either wasn't listening, or he wasn't hearing Cara. As his hands slid up under the short skirt of her dress, and he lowered to his knees, Cara couldn't decide if she really gave a shit in that moment.

"Yes, I really like it. And the length is perfect, because it takes nothing to get it up," Gian muttered.

Hot.

Sinful.

Teasing.

That damn mouth of his was all of those things. And it was the only thing Cara focused on, as Gian dragged her panties down her thighs and his mouth was on her pussy. He had a wicked tongue with more talent than most men had in their entire bodies. He sucked on her clit, his tongue drove fast into the little nub right after, and she couldn't see straight.

"Holy shit," Cara gasped.

Distractions, she thought.

That's what he was doing.

Distracting her.

Fuck.

It was a good distraction.

Sleepy-eyed, Cara leaned in the doorway of the small gym, and tried to get some of the sleep out of her head. Gian didn't seem to notice her presence as his speed on the treadmill picked up from a jog to a thirty-second sprint before it shut off. He didn't even give himself time to breathe before he moved off the machine, and headed to the bar for a set of a dozen chin-ups.

Cara had no idea where this man got his energy.

But shit, it was a beautiful thing to watch.

The power, his body's lines, and the way he focused in on his task … it was all rather beautiful.

Gian dropped to the floor once his chin-ups were finished, and reached for a waiting water bottle and hand towel. Cara let him relax before she cleared her throat to make her presence known to him.

He flashed her one of his signature grins as he came close enough to press a kiss to the top of her head. "Morning."

"How long have you been awake?"

"Most of the night," he answered.

"The concussion, I forgot."

"You didn't need to be staying up with me, anyway. Beauty sleep."

Cara scoffed. "You do *see* me, right? Because nothing about this screams beauty at the moment."

Her hair was wild. Her eyes were sleepy. She had shoved on his forgotten dress shirt instead of her clothes because it was easier. She needed coffee, food, and a shower, and *then* she might be half presentable to the public.

Gian's hand tangled into her messy hair as he brought her closer for a kiss to her cheek. "Shut up and take the compliment, Cara."

Well, then ...

"Fine, but I'm all fucked-out, so don't think you're getting laid for that one this morning."

His laughter came out dark and heady, waking Cara up even more. "Fucked-out, that's a new one."

"I need more time being awake to properly converse like a real human."

"Well, let's get some food in you and then see how you feel," Gian said.

Cara followed behind him as he headed toward his penthouse's kitchen. "Now is probably the best time to ask this, then, huh?"

"Ask what, Cara?"

"Who that guy—Frankie—was last night, and why he called me Lea."

Gian's steps came to a full stop.

Cara damn near ran into his back.

Slowly, he turned to face her, his amusement from earlier gone entirely. "You're not going to drop that, are you?"

"As much as I like you on your knees, eating my pussy like it's the last thing you're ever going to taste, no, that's not going to work today. If that's what you meant to say."

Gian's lips pressed into a thin, unimpressed line. "Cara—"

"I dealt with the distraction last night. Try the truth today, please."

"I don't know a lot about it."

"Tell me what you do know, Gian."

He crossed his arms, and Cara matched his posture in the hallway. She wasn't moving a damn inch until he started talking. Simple as that.

"Sometimes, Frankie runs in the same circles as me, but we're not friends, not like Constantino and I are. But like I said, sometimes we run into one another. As far as I know, from passing mentions or seeing them out, Frankie went out with Lea for a while a year back or so. Those were the few times I actually saw her or came in contact with her."

"Like a few dates, or ...?"

"I think it was more than that," Gian admitted, "but I can't say for sure, and there's certain things men don't ask each other in this business, when women are brought around."

Cara's brow furrowed. "I don't understand. Lea didn't have a boyfriend before she died, and even before that, there was no one she talked about."

Sure, her sister went out and did her own thing. Lea had a social life that didn't include Cara a lot of the time, because she wasn't into that sort of thing. But a man? A boyfriend, for *months*? Cara didn't think so.

"As far as I know, it ended a couple of months before Lea died," Gian said with a shrug. "I only know that because ... well, because I do."

"Because *why*?"

Gian scowled. "Because Frankie got married to the broad that ended up pregnant with his kid; he married her, and it was the right thing to do. That's what a man is expected to do when he knocks a woman up—marry her as soon as possible. I don't know the *personal* details because that shit is private. I know what was presented to me like it was to everyone else."

Cara suddenly felt like someone had sucked all the air out of her chest. "What?"

"Sometimes, it's better to drop things, Cara."

"Did Lea know he was running around with someone else?"

Gian barely blinked. "Maybe it didn't make a difference to her at the time."

It did to Cara.

It was all the same to her.

She thought her twin would have felt the same.

"I think I want to go home," Cara muttered.

Gian didn't even try to convince her to stay.

Cara needed to *think*.

She couldn't do that with Gian around.

Chapter 8

"Johnnie was pulled out of the lake this morning," Constantino said. "All limbs attached, though, so clearly they wanted us to know."

Gian rubbed a hand over his jaw, feeling the stubble he hadn't bothered to shave that morning. "Fuck."

"Edmond is making a point."

"Or the older generation did it," Gian pointed out.

"It's still *for* the boss, Gian."

"Yeah, I know. I'm saying—"

"Johnnie had a verbal disagreement with one of Edmond's favorites the night after your car went boom last week, and all of the sudden, he shows up dead." Constantino scoffed, quickly adding, "Not to mention, he's the second body this week, but he could have been the third in *two* weeks, had the bomb on your car been successful."

Constantino was making all kinds of sense, even though Gian wished it didn't have to be this way. The sudden surge of violence on the streets between the younger and older generation of made men in the Guzzi Cosa Nostra was disconcerting, but not entirely a surprise.

The younger men had taken the bomb on Gian's vehicle as a personal affront, as though it was the boss's one way of removing the last person the men thought might give them a voice. Any verbal or physical action that disagreed with the boss was suddenly met with severe punishment—to make a point, to make the men sit down, and shut the hell up.

"I've been shut out for a week," Gian admitted.

"Completely?"

"No calls from Edmond or his new consigliere. No calls from the older Capos, and any attempts I've made to see them or check in, have been fucked over in some way. He's shutting me out."

Constantino swore under his breath. "This isn't good."

"No."

"What are you planning on doing now, Gian? Reconciliation was fine *before* someone tried to knock you off, but what now?"

Gian didn't have a simple or easy answer for that. "I need to find out who tried to kill me first, and then I'll figure out the rest."

Somehow, he held back from adding.

"Look to Edmond, or one of his minions."

"I'm aware, asshole," Gian said, "but I want a name behind the bomb and a reason first."

Gian still wasn't entirely sure what was going on within his own *famiglia*. Violence, yes. Discontent, sure. Lines had been drawn in the sand, and Gian had attempted not to put himself on either side of it, but managed to get put on one anyway.

"These issues—the problems between the generations—have been ongoing for a decade," Gian said. "Why now, has it suddenly gotten so out of hand?"

"You should already know the answer to that, but the fact that you admit these problems have been ongoing says you have chosen to be blind to the complaints for a long time, Gian."

He let that insult brush off his shoulders.

Sort of.

"It was manageable when Corrado was alive," Gian replied. "That's all I'm saying."

"It was manageable because one side knew that when Corrado was dead, they would finally have what they wanted—a younger boss they respected and had common ground with in *la famiglia*. You, Gian. And they didn't get you. They got another ancient fool in Edmond, who doesn't understand that it's not the forties and fifties anymore, and the rules need to change with the world we live in."

"You're starting to piss me off again; Corrado wasn't—"

"He chose to be blind or placate, too. Don't make that mistake, man."

"He's shutting me out," Gian reminded his friend. "That means he's not going to let me get close enough to put this to an end."

"And the bomb," Constantino said. "Don't forget the bomb."

How could he?

"I have too many things to deal with, all at once. Corrado, Edmond, the men, the fucking bomb. All of it."

"What if it's all the same man behind those things, though?"

"That's too simple," Gian said. "It's too easy. This life isn't easy. Nothing about it ever is."

Constantino didn't bother to argue that point.

"One thing at a time," Gian added, "and whether you want to admit it or not, there are a lot of men who would benefit from putting me in the boss's seat."

"Your point?"

"It's easy to point the finger at Edmond; easier, even, to make me look at him. No one said these men were fucking dumb, Constantino. I'm not going to treat them like they are, it could have been *anyone*."

"I still think Edmond—"

"Yes, because you would also benefit from me, not him, holding the highest position," Gian interrupted. His friend stayed quiet for a long minute. "Do you see my point, now?"

"To an extent," Constantino said quietly.

"Then give me time to think and work this out. I need to talk to people, look them in the face and see if they lie to me. I know these men, I've spent my whole life with these men. It has to be one thing at a time, man. That's how a smart man does it. I won't tear a whole organization apart, in an attempt to rid myself of only a couple of bad seeds. My grandfather *built* this fucking family into what it is, and I won't ruin it."

"Don't take too much time." Constantino laughed, though it came out strained and dry. "You were lucky with the bomb, but that luck won't last forever."

"Yeah, I know. Thanks."

"Just saying."

"I'll call you later," Gian muttered.

He didn't even bother giving a proper goodbye before he hung up the phone.

The elevator door opened, and Gian stepped out to a waiting consigliere for the building. The man smiled, and held out a key fob.

"Your new Mercedes is waiting at the front, Mr. Guzzi."

Gian took the device. "Thank you, Gene."

"Have a good day, sir."

He looked over the key fob for the new Mercedes as he exited the building. The car he'd wanted had to be shipped in from Quebec, leaving him without a vehicle for most of the week. He'd simply used his enforcer as a driver, but he was glad to have his own wheels again. The sleek, black two-door parked in front of the building was running, warming up in the cold March air.

Gian unlocked the car, but he didn't even get the chance to slip inside the driver's seat. Another black car, a four-door Mercedes with dark windows, pulled up beside his on the street. He recognized that damn car, and it took all he had not to ignore it and get inside his Mercedes.

The back window of the car rolled down.

Gian gave the man sitting in the back a look. "Edmond."

"I think you mean 'boss,' Gian," Edmond replied coolly.

"I said what I meant."

Let the fool make of that what he wanted.

Edmond's jaw tightened. "Get in the car. Let's take a drive."

Gian's hand twitched with the urge to reach for the gun at his back, but he knew better. It was broad daylight, in the middle of a very busy street and city, that was filled with cameras for the city *and* the police.

"I'm not sure that's a good idea. I'm not interested in taking a swim in the lake today," Gian said, turning back to his waiting vehicle. "I'm sure you understand."

"Get inside now, or Nathan will paint the side of your new car with your brain matter, Gian."

Well, then.

Gian chose not to question Edmond on whether or not the man's driver *did* have a gun pointed at him in that moment. The windows were tinted too dark for Gian to truly see inside and know for sure.

"Front seat, passenger side," Edmond ordered.

Fuck.

Gian slammed the door of his Mercedes shut, locked the car, and jumped inside Edmond's vehicle as he had been told. Sure enough, the driver and enforcer had a gun out, pointed, and ready to blow. Gian stared down the barrel of the weapon, both irritated and cold inside.

"You know where to drive," Edmond told Nathan. "Take it slow, though, as I'd like to have a chat with my underboss on the way."

"Got it, boss."

Not for a single second, did Nathan drop the weapon as he pulled back onto the road. Gian's gaze didn't move away from the gun, either.

"Unsettling, isn't it?" Edmond asked.

"Be specific. This whole show feels rather fucking unsettling."

"The gun."

"It's not even half as unsettling as a bomb blowing up thirty feet away from you," Gian replied. "Or having your boss shut you out from at least half of your organization. Or getting a sniper shot to the head while you drink your morning coffee and stare out the window. At least with a gun in your face, where you can see it, you know what is waiting for you. It's not trying to sneak up on you when you least expect it."

Edmond chuckled. "Someone's prickly."

"You did ask."

"I did." The older man sighed heavily from the back seat. "Seems we have a problem happening on the streets, don't we?"

"Seems so."

"One would think, given the attention we've received from the officials lately, what with Corrado's murder, amongst other things, that we wouldn't need or want more eyes on our organization," Edmond said.

"I would agree with that."

"Except you don't."

Gian shrugged. "Some things can't be helped. What's happening between the men, the rising discontent, is not *new*. It's an ongoing problem, only now they feel like they can be heard if they shout a little louder, or make a few more problems."

"You see those men through very rose-tinted glasses, Gian."

"I think I take them for their word, and see what they give me," he replied easily. "It's you who doesn't think the younger Capos deserve a voice in this organization. You told them that again and again—you made it even more apparent, when you placed yourself into the boss's seat without allowing them a vote in it."

"Be that as it may—"

"That *is* what it is," Gian interrupted. "There's no other way to look at it, Edmond."

"But there is," the boss replied quietly. "There is, because there is *you*, Gian."

"I beg your pardon?"

"I believe things have gotten out of hand these last couple of weeks, and I place the blame for that squarely on you."

Gian barked out a laugh, and for the first time, glanced away from the gun to stare at Edmond. "*Me?*"

"Yes, you. Had you not given half of my men a reason to believe they could dissent and rebel, then I wouldn't have these problems at the moment. They genuinely assume that by supporting you, they will eventually get what they want. And so, this is what we're going to do about it."

"Do tell."

"You're going to walk yourself back over to my side of things—act as the proper underboss your grandfather trained you to be for the last few years, and shut your mouth about the rest. Because, you see, when the men see *you* getting in line, they'll begin to move back into their proper places as well."

"You honestly believe it's that simple?" Gian asked, amused.

"I believe it's what needs to happen. They're all sheep, they will follow the wolf, as sheep tend to do."

"I wasn't standing on either side of any lines until a *bomb* was set on my car, Edmond." Gian smirked. "And even now, I haven't properly taken a side. I didn't think there was a side to take."

"Then you are stupid and naive. There is always a side, even when there isn't a war to be won."

"A good boss would want harmony in his family, for the sake of business."

"I don't give a shit about harmony, I want compliant *men*."

"I don't think I can help you with that," Gian said honestly. "They have their own mind. The fact you believe they'll follow along with me, simply because I am me, speaks to *your* naivety, Edmond. And considering someone recently tried to blow me up—I haven't put you out of the running for that one quite yet—you can't expect me to jump at the chance to help you, now."

"Well, that's too bad, isn't it?"

The car began to slow, and then pulled off the road altogether. It was only then that Gian realized where they were, and he barely contained his surprise at the apartment building staring back at him.

Cara's apartment building.

"Consider this your final warning, Gian," Edmond said. "Get in line, and help the rest of the men follow along, or I will remove you altogether. It might cause me a bit of trouble after I remove you, a few years' worth of feuding or nonsense, but those dissenters too will learn to shut up, fall in line, or dig their own grave."

Edmond smiled. "I don't mind doing it like that, though I would rather do it the easier way and make it quick. And then, you also get to live and keep your place. It's very simple."

Gian didn't care.

He was still staring at Cara's apartment building.

Why would the boss bring him here?

What point was there to be made with this?

"Do we understand one another, Gian?" Edmond asked.

Gian forced his features to remain cool and calm. "I certainly hear you."

"Consider my words, but I won't give you much time." Edmond waved at the building. "I hear you've been spending a lot of time with a young woman who lives here, so I figured this would be a good place to end our little chat. Have a good day, Gian."

"She's not even home."

It was mid-week.

Cara was at school.

Edmond shrugged. "Walk back, I suppose. The fresh air will do you good, and the time alone will allow you to think. You need both, clearly."

Nathan leaned over, opened the door, and jerked the gun from Gian to the outside.

Fucking great.

Gian waited patiently as the town car's back door was opened by the driver, and Cara was helped from the vehicle. His grin grew at the sight of her wild, red curls and the annoyed expression she sported. His gaze traveled down the maroon dress she wore beneath her opened trench coat; a tight number that stopped a few inches above her knees, made her legs look fucking fantastic, not to mention the heels.

God, the *heels*.

Gian loved heels.

Cara's stare landed on him, and she shook her head. "Do you often send cars to pick people up without any warning and with no indication of what they are going to be doing?"

"Chris told you to wear something nice, didn't he?"

"You're missing the point *and* the question."

"You would be surprised at how many people I call on to do whatever fits my fancy." Gian winked. "But not women, if that's what you meant."

Her iciness bled away a little. "I'll have to take your word for it."

"A man is only as good as his word."

Cara surveyed the restaurant behind him. "Dinner?"

"You're simplifying it, *Tesoro*. It's a date. You and I, *having* a date."

"Why?"

Because he thought she might like it.

Because he didn't want to only *fuck* Cara.

He wanted to know her, too. He wanted to do normal things with her, like taking her to dinner, listening to her talk, and whatever else she wanted to do. He knew very well this woman was worth far more than how well she could take his cock, and he needed her to know it, too.

Gian stepped up to Cara, close enough that he could smell the hauntingly-sweet perfume lingering on her skin. Only a few inches shorter than him, she stared up at him, waiting for what he would do next.

A simple, quick kiss was all he offered before he straightened again with a smile. But it wasn't so quick that he didn't feel the gentle grin of hers form against his kiss before he had pulled away.

"Because it's been a week since I last saw you, and it didn't end well," Gian settled on saying.

Cara looked away. "Well—"

"And you haven't contacted me, either, so don't try to say it's fine. I don't fall for that bullshit."

"I wasn't going to."

Gian was pleased about that. "Dinner, then?"

"I thought it was a date?"

"Dinner is one part of the date, Cara."

Her painted-red lips curved at the edges. "All right, then. Most men actually think to *ask* for a date, though."

"Seems when I ask for things, we end up in a bed, and we don't do much else." Gian chuckled at the sight of Cara's cheeks turning pink at his words. "Not that I mind, but change is always good, too. I tried a different approach this time, let's see how it works out for us."

"Let's be honest here, probably still in a bed."

"At least we'll do something first."

Cara nodded. "Good enough."

Gian's hand found Cara's lower back as they walked into the restaurant. There was no waiting for a table, as he owned the restaurant, and had the private dining area reserved for the evening until his dinner was finished. Once he had Cara seated at the table, the server made his way in with a smile and menus in hand.

"I don't know what I want to order," Cara admitted after the server had offered the specials and what he would recommend. She looked to Gian. "Surprise me?"

"Believe it or not, but if I order for us, it won't be something fancy and pretty."

Cara laughed, gesturing at the silk table cloths and then to the extravagant crystal lighting above their heads. "Even in a place like this?"

"They know what I like," Gian replied with a shrug. "And it's not always spectacular, but something to enjoy. Sometimes, the chef likes to make something that isn't an affair in his kitchen, too."

"I stand by what I said, then."

Surprise her.

Gian only had to nod at the server, and the man was gone from the private dining space. He didn't even need to tell the man what he did or didn't want—the employees knew the owner well enough, and Gian made a point to dine often at this particular restaurant. He *did* like the food, after all.

"How was your week?" Gian asked.

It was a safe topic of conversation. Something he could move into what he really wanted to ask.

Cara made a face. "Busy at school. Quiet all the rest of the time. *Dull.*"

"Why dull?"

Her blue eyes sparkled with mischief. "I get bored when I'm alone."

"You sound surprised at that."

"I never used to mind being alone."

"I'm not very good company for myself, either."

Cara stared beyond Gian, at the artwork behind him. "I find it hard to believe that you spend much time alone."

"Cara."

She didn't look at him.

"*Cara.*"

"Yes?"

Gian reached across the table, and slid his fingers under her chin so that he could *make* her look at him. "If you have something to ask, then do so."

"We're casual, not exclusive. I said that, Gian. I don't *need* to know anything."

"You can still ask, *donna*."

Cara's lips pursed. "That would suggest more than—"

"My God, *ask*."

"I don't *need* to, Gian. That's the point. I was thinking too much this week—overthinking like I do—because of my sister and that guy. She had online journals she used to keep, you know? I went through some because I have her passwords and her laptop. I never did that before. And her phone, too. I still have that. I charged it and read the messages she hadn't deleted."

Gian frowned. "And what did you learn?"

"That it didn't end between them when everyone thought it did. She still saw him occasionally, after he was married. She knew, too, about the other girl before the pregnancy thing came up. Why didn't she ever say anything to me? Why didn't she tell me? I'm her twin."

Cara sighed, her manicured nails rapping against the table cloth as she added, "But then, I know why she didn't say anything, because she knows me, too. She knows I wouldn't have been happy—that I would not have agreed with what she was doing. So, I'm stuck in this headspace of being angry that she left me out of a private thing, and being grateful that she did at the same time. I feel like I didn't know her, or this part of her. It's messed up."

"And this made you overthink because …?"

"Because I don't want to be one of several woman, Gian. I want to be one woman to one man. Except that wasn't what I told you before, so—"

"You are one woman to one man," he interrupted smoothly. "I'm not with anyone else, and I haven't been for a long time. I didn't even do a *casual* thing with women, I did the random thing for an evening and that was it. Things are simpler in my life that way. I have … well, expectations of me, and it's easier when I don't have to bring others into that mess, too."

Cara's fingers stopped their dancing instantly. "Yet, you're bringing me into it."

"Not really. You've made it clear that I am not your type of man because of the business side of my life, Cara. You have no interest in being there. It makes it easy to keep you the hell out of it, when you don't want to be a part of it at all."

"Oh."

"It's an unnecessary fucking complication," Gian said, knowing damn well he sounded crass and harsh. "And I like that we have this way of just enjoying each other, our time together, talking in bed, you thinking you're sneaking up on me in the mornings when I know damn well you are there. Me reading in bed and you wearing my shirts. I *like* those things. They are uncomplicated, easy things for me to do, Cara. You don't ask for more, so I don't offer. But if you did ask, if you did want more, then I would try to give you that, too."

"And you're not doing that with someone else," she said.

"No."

"Or anything else, either."

Gian chuckled lowly. "No, again."

"Okay." Cara gave him one of her brilliant smiles that lit up her pretty, delicate features. "I was also kind of irrationally pissed off at you this week, too."

"For what?"

"Knowing something about my twin that I didn't."

Gian scowled. "That's unfair."

"I told you it was irrational."

True.

"Fair enough," he uttered. "Are you still angry about that? Even irrationally."

Cara laughed a tinkling, musical sound. "Lucky for you, no. I'm not mad, or I wouldn't have come tonight."

"You would have come."

"You don't know that."

Gian's grin deepened. "You came tonight, not even knowing what this was. You came with a tight-as-hell dress on, even though I know my man only told you to dress appropriately for an upscale evening. You came with fuck-me-heels on and your hair loose and wild the way I like. You put the red lipstick on that I like to see stained on my sheets. You would have come, Cara, whether you were pissed off or not."

Her cheeks reddened. "So you're a good fuck—I never denied that, Gian."

"Try again."

She blew out a slow breath. "God, you're insufferable."

"Try again, *mon ange.*"

"I know that means you're calling me your angel. I know how to use the internet, Gian."

"Try again."

"Could you try to be a little less arrogant?" she asked.

"I don't give an inch, because everyone thinks they can take a mile. Try again."

Cara's eyes blazed as she turned them on him. "I came because I like you, and you make it hard to say no, even when you're not asking."

He'd take that.

Fucking right he would.

"Except right now, you're making me want to—"

"Make a trip to the closet private space to get me between your legs?" he asked with a smirk. "Because I only actually need to move my chair closer, Cara, to get that job done with one hand. The tablecloth hides what goes on beneath."

"You are—"

"Are we ready for drinks?"

The sudden appearance of the server made Cara sit straight in her chair while Gian only winked at his companion. "Red wine, and bring it with the food, please."

"Five minutes, Sir."

"Wonderful."

Gian didn't take his gaze off Cara, but he listened to the footsteps of the receding server.

"What did you order us, anyway?" she asked.

"Poutine."

Cara repeated the word, and butchered it the way most Americans and Western Canadians did whenever they said it.

"No, not poo-teen," Gian said with a laugh. "Pou-tin. Or, *pu-tsin* if you're French."

"Isn't that, like, fries and gravy?"

"It's a delicacy, invented by the French. Homemade fries, cheese curds, and a dark gravy, piled into one giant mess on a plate. Everybody has their own way of making it, some add different nonsense to it, which frankly, ruins what it's supposed to be in the end. It's not pretty, but it is delicious."

"And what about *after* the food and wine?"

Gian shrugged one shoulder. "Whatever you want, Cara. I can take you home, and drop you off. I know you probably have classes tomorrow. Or we can go see a movie, maybe a show if you want. It's up to you."

"So, a *real* date, huh?"

"One that ends however and wherever you want it to, *bella*."

She smiled a wicked sight.

Gian knew *exactly* where their date was going to end.

He didn't mind a bit.

Chapter 9

"More," Cara demanded, her voice thick with sleep and content.

Gian chuckled, rocking her body that was tucked tight against his. "You were supposed to be up an hour ago."

"Just read."

"Cara."

"*Gian.*"

He made the sexiest noise under his breath. "You know I can't refuse you when you say my name like that, Cara. That's unfair."

"More reading, less nagging."

"You have terrible morning habits."

"I also have a gorgeous man in my bed and a study group, first thing, that I can afford to miss. Shut up and read, Gian."

In French, actually.

He was reading in French, and Cara *loved* it. She didn't understand a damn word he was saying, for the most part. There was something about his voice that soothed her *and* provoked her at the same time.

With a half-hearted sigh, Gian continued reading. *Les Misérables*, to be exact. She didn't know what to do with this conundrum of a man. He wasn't entirely good, but he wasn't entirely bad, either. He wore shoes and suits that cost more than what most people made in a month, yet ate comfort food and liked cheap beer. He had set a gun on her nightstand the night before, but brought a classic novel in from his car like he needed it just as badly, too. He was educated, high-class, and Toronto elite, but rough, dirty, and full of sin, too.

Cara didn't know what to do with all the pieces of Gian Guzzi.

Not a clue.

The cadence of Gian's tenor changed before his French turned to English as he asked, "You don't even understand what I'm reading, do you?"

Cara shrugged, snuggling in closer to Gian and soft sheets. "Don't have to."

"That's sort of the point of being read to, right?"

"Not right now."

"I don't understand."

"You wouldn't." Cara hummed a happy sort of sound, grinning up at the dark-eyed man staring down at her. "It's your voice. It's an all the time thing, Gian. The way you sound, you probably don't even hear it, but I do."

"And how do I sound?"

She could have said many things.

Sexy.

Lovely.

Comforting.

Arousing.

Deep.

Provoking.

The truth was, Gian's voice—and him, really—was a mix of *all* of those things. Settling on one was not enough. It did not do him justice.

"Dangerous," Cara whispered. "You sound dangerous, Gian."

For a long while, Gian stared at Cara, never blinking or moving a muscle. It was as though he didn't quite know what to make of her statement. "I've never been told that before."

"That's kind of sad."

"Is it?"

"You should know the way you can affect people, Gian. It's more than wearing a suit and a sly smile, with a gun hidden at your back. It's knowing that you only need to speak and people listen. A man with a dangerous voice has far more command than anyone could possibly understand, he needs to know how to use it." Cara rolled over to her back and reached for her phone on the nightstand. She checked the time, and scowled at it. "I do need to get up soon. The study group was okay to miss, but I have a paper I need to hand in for the class after that."

Gian didn't reply, which made Cara look over at him. She found that he was still looking at her, but the intensity she saw in his eyes made her heart stop for a split second.

An appreciation, churned with lust and mixed heavily in his admiration and hunger. As though she was the sweetest, most precious thing to have ever spoken in his presence, and he wanted nothing more than to be right there with her forever. She had seen his many stares before—when he wanted to fuck, his irritation, or his indifference.

This was not the same.

It scared her for a moment.

Something else to add to her rapidly growing pile of confusion.

"I don't know what to do with you," Gian finally said, breaking the silence.

"The same thing you have been doing, I guess."

"It's not enough. It's not nearly enough, *bella*."

She tossed her phone back to the nightstand, and then turned back to Gian, taking her sweet time to crawl on top of his naked body, under the sheets, until she straddled him. One of his hands landed on her waist, his fingers gripping tight to keep her still, while the other slid from her stomach, up between her breasts, and stopped on her throat.

Cara only smiled at the sensation of her heartbeat thrumming under his hand. "I like that, you know. I don't really say it, because I figure I don't have to. But I like that a lot."

Gian's fingers drummed against her throat. "This?"

"Yes. Especially when you squeeze hard enough to take my breath away, like I'm floating for a few seconds, all the control is gone, and it's only a *feeling*. Nothing else. Just the way I feel."

"What else?"

She shifted her weight on top of him, attempting to ignore the length of his erection resting between her legs. It didn't help, really. She only ended up grinding against his cock more, soaking in the silky feeling of his length sliding along her pussy. She used her hands as support against his lower abdominal muscles to keep her steady as she reveled in that simple pleasure.

"Cara," Gian murmured.

That voice of his would kill her someday.

She was sure of it.

Her attention was back on him in an instant, and she remembered what he had asked. "And I like the way you talk when you're fucking me, how you always take and demand, and you rarely ever ask. You don't push, either, but you don't have to. It's raw and it's filthy and I like it that way."

"Why?"

His question seemed simple enough.

Except his voice was laced with huskiness and heat.

"Because there's something about you that's different," Cara admitted quietly. "You use me in bed like a toy, like I'm yours to ruin and fuck however you want to; like your own personal little slut. And then you open my doors, you hold my hand, and you tell me I'm beautiful."

"Of course I do, Cara."

"Yes, *because* you're different. Because there's more to a woman than how she behaves in a bedroom, but most forget not to bring it beyond the bed, too. You don't, and I like that."

She leaned down, close enough that her lips were a breath away from Gian's as she said, "And nobody's ever fucked me quite like you do, Gian."

"That's a damn good thing, then."

That was all Gian said before his lips slammed into Cara's with a bruising, demanding kiss that silenced her mind and made her heart race. His tongue found hers in a familiar dance that came like a comfort, and a battle at the same time. It was only when he pulled away enough to bite into her lower lip that she realized how badly she needed air, but couldn't get in a good breath.

His hips had started moving with the gentle beat of hers, too. Rocking, grinding—putting pressure in the right spot and then taking it away before she could get more.

Cara was sure her juices had soaked his cock already.

She couldn't even find it in herself to be ashamed.

"Why?" Cara managed to ask while his teasing mouth traveled over her throat.

"Why, what?"

"Why is it a good thing that no one has ever fucked me like you?"

His arms encircled her then, one curling around her back and neck so that his hand could grab onto her hair. His other arm went between her legs and up over her ass so his palm laid flat to her lower spine. He held her there, forcing her head back so he could look her in the eyes while her body fucking *shivered*.

"Does it matter?" he asked.

"I answered your questions. Answer mine."

"Because I like that it's only been mine this way," he told her. "The way I fuck you, how you let me have you. Your pussy, your ass, that fucking mouth, and the rest of your body. How you say my name and the sounds you make when you're about to come but you know you need to wait. You're greedy as hell when I'm eating your cunt and then sweet as hell in the morning, demanding that I read to you. When you want to get on your knees like you're about to pray, but all you do is open up that goddamn mouth of yours and suck me dry instead. It's … it's insane, but it's fucking beautiful, Cara. And it's only been mine like that. Someone else might have gotten something else, but I get *this*, and that's addicting. You're addictive."

She took a shaky breath. "And you don't think you're addictive, too?"

His arms tightened to her body and her hair. "As long as it's mine, sweetheart."

She was ruined for anyone else, anyway.

Didn't he already know that?

Well, how could he know, when she was now realizing it, too?

"Who the hell else could make me fucking crazy like you do, Gian?"

He only grinned—sexy, cocky, and pleased.

"You know what I was most pissed off about, the morning after my car got bombed?" he asked.

"What was that?"

"I ruined my damn phone and—"

"Lost your filthy porn."

Gian laughed. "Well, yeah."

"You'll get more."

"Of you? I'd say so."

Cara's gaze snapped to his fast. "Only me."

Gian's grin melted into a smile before he kissed her mouth once more, softer than before. "Who the fuck else?"

Exactly.

"You do have to get up and get ready," he reminded her.

She was more interested in his mouth, hands, and cock.

They were far more interesting.

"In a minute," Cara said absently.

He let her go then, his arms releasing her from that snake-like hold so he could grab her face and kiss her mouth over and over.

Cara rotated her hips on Gian's hard cock once more, determined to get back in her happy place, but he had other things in mind. *Better things.* His hand dove between their bodies, and the next time Cara ground along his length, he filled her full with one hard flex of his hips, driving upwards against her pussy.

She hadn't been expecting the move, if only because he was always so careful to grab a condom first, though she had told him before that she was on the pill. But she liked him this way, too—bare and natural, filling and stretching her full, making her ache with nothing but him.

"Shit," Gian groaned, holding Cara tight to his body so that she couldn't move. "Fuck, I love your pussy."

"Because it's yours."

His nod answered her back, and his eyes closed as she felt his cock jerk inside the tight walls of her sex. She was wet as fuck as her hand snuck between their bodies to feel the base of his bare cock fitted snug to her cunt. Hot, too, she realized.

Cara's fingers slid over her clit with gentle strokes, making her inner muscles tighten and release with each touch.

"Could you come like that?" Gian asked, never opening his eyes. "Just stretched full of my cock and playing with your cunt, could you?"

"Yes, but not as fast as I would like."

"And how would you like it, Cara?"

"You already know."

Gian's eyes opened, making Cara still on top of him entirely. "Yeah, I do."

She hadn't even blinked before one of his hands tangled into her hair and the other found her throat. The second his fingers tightened, choking and pulling at the same time, his hips thrust upward, driving into her again. Cara let him pull her forward, enough to lift her hips and let him pound into her pussy, deep and hard enough to make the rest of the room disappear. It was only the sound of them—his cock slamming into her, her pussy taking him in, all wet and tight, her whines and his whispers—and nothing else.

"Ride me or take it," Gian muttered through his clenched teeth. "Fuck me how you want to, or take my cock the way I know you can, Cara."

"I want both."

She was greedy that way, too. Greedy enough for him to back her ass into his every thrust, but still needy enough to make him pound into her hard enough to make her fucking crazy.

His fingers tightened around her throat, taking away air and making her fly. She knew what was coming. She fucking vibrated for it, anticipated it, wanting his words to make it sweeter, and better.

"Just fucking come and give it to me, then," he demanded. "Show me what's mine, Cara. *Show me.*"

Shit.

She could do that.

All he had to do was *say so.*

Cara stepped out of the shower to find Gian leaning in the doorway. "I know, I'm late."

He held his hands up, grinning in that way of his. "I'm saying nothing about that again. I warned you earlier, you wanted to listen to me read, love."

"Well, it sounded good."

"And then fuck after," he added.

Cara shot him a look. "I didn't hear you refusing."

"Why would I?"

She didn't dignify that with a response, instead drying off with a towel and making quick work of rubbing it through her wet hair. She was going to have to rush to get to school and hand in her paper on time, but she couldn't find it in herself to give a shit.

Gian had jumped in the shower with her long enough to clean himself up before he jumped right back out. Cara was both jealous and irritated to see him standing there with his suit on *and* his hair dry.

It wasn't fair that all he had to do was basically roll over and be ready for the day.

"What do you want, if you're not standing there to remind me that I'm late again?" Cara asked.

She headed past Gian in the doorway, going toward her bedroom for clothes. It was what he said next that stopped Cara in her tracks.

"Your brother called."

Cara turned slowly on her heel. "I'm sorry?"

"Tommas—that's your brother, right?"

"Yes."

"He called when you were in the shower. He wanted me to ask you to call your mother."

Nope.

Cara turned back around and went straight into her room without a word. She dug through her closet, while Gian came to stand in the doorway of the bedroom, watching her in that silent way of his.

"Could you give me a ride to the university?"

"You don't even have to ask," he replied.

"Great. Saves me time."

"I take it you're not going to talk about your brother, huh?"

Cara shrugged. "Tommas is fine. Not my mother, though."

Gian nodded as she passed him in the door. "Fair enough."

"And I'm not calling the bitch, either."

"Ouch," he muttered behind her.

Cara kept walking, picking up her bag and the other things she needed on the way. Her hair would have to dry like it was, but it wouldn't be the first time. "It sounds cold because I mean for it to. I have nothing to say to that woman that will be nice, and everybody knows it. Just because Tommas can muster up an ounce of care for the woman means fuck all to me in the end. I've looked for something, Gian."

"And?"

She turned to look at him, unaffected as she said, "It's not there. Nothing is there. Maybe when Lea was alive, or even shortly after she died, when I was so alone here by myself—maybe then I might have found something. But, now? Now, when I'm almost fully okay and I don't need somebody holding me up, it's gone again. I'm not calling my mother. I have nothing to say to Serena Rossi. She can keep drinking away the shit she did to us kids until she drinks herself into a grave. And even then, I don't care."

Gian's face remained passive and calm throughout her tirade. "I'm sorry, *mon ange*."

"You don't have to apologize. If anything, you're one of the things that woke me the hell up again. I was missing something for a long time after my twin died, and now I don't feel so lost or empty. But you know what does makes me feel that way?"

"What?"

"My mother. Even thinking about her makes me revert back into that shell of a child that played a little quieter than normal, as to not enrage the drunks sleeping upstairs, or waited for her brother to get home so she could eat. That lost, lonely child. So fuck her and fuck Tommas for asking me to care, too."

Gian cleared his throat. "All right. You going to be okay today or—"

Cara opened her apartment door with force. "I'll be fine."

"Really? Because you used more fucks in this conversation than the entire time we've been messing around, Cara."

She locked her apartment up once Gian was out in the hallway with her.

"I'll be fine," she repeated. "I always am."

"Or do you *have* to be?" he asked as she started down the hallway.

Cara tensed, but kept walking. "Does it matter?"

Gian caught up with her quickly enough, his arm curving her waist as he pulled her in tight and kissed the top of her head. It was that simple action—his unspoken concern and care—that slowed Cara's rage.

"It matters to me," he murmured against the top of her head.

Cara sighed. "I'm good."

Gian made a discontented sound under his breath.

"I am," she promised. "Sometimes it spills out, though."

"That's a lot of anger to bottle up, Cara."

They strolled out of the apartment building into cool March air, and Cara breathed it in deep.

"A lot of deserved anger," she pointed out.

Gian nodded as he directed her toward the apartment's parking lot, where he had left his car the evening before. "Sure, except you don't direct it at the person most deserving of it."

"My mother is the type that feeds off attention, negative or otherwise. She uses any time and attention you give her to manipulate you for her emotional games. It's not worth it."

"I'm suddenly feeling like I need to give my mother a visit soon."

Cara frowned. "I didn't mean—"

Gian shrugged as he unlocked his car and then held the passenger door open for Cara to slide inside. Once she was seated, he offered her one of his charming smiles. "You reminded me that despite the fact I am a twenty-nine year old man, I have a mother who still loves me as though I'm her baby. She's always concerned for my happiness, even though she doesn't have to be. I can't even remember her yelling when I was a boy. I have a wonderful mother, and sometimes I don't appreciate her enough. That's all."

Oh.

"I'm sure *she* would like to hear that, too, Gian."

He laughed. "No worries there. I'll be sure to tell her. I think she would like you, Cara."

"Do you?"

"Of course, because I do, *amore*. Maybe you'll be able to meet her soon."

"When?"

Gian winked. "Soon."

Then, he closed the door.

In a blink, he had rounded the car and was inside the vehicle, too. He hummed a sexy sound as the car lit up under his handling, the gears shifting into place as the engine turned over.

"I love this car," he said, "but I do miss the Lexus."

"I can't justify buying a car in a city like Toronto. Everything is a walk away. It would be pointless."

Gian glanced over at her, and then pulled out of the parking spot, heading toward the road. "I travel too much from one side of this city to the other to not have a car."

"Point taken." Cara stared down the road while Gian maneuvered the Mercedes into traffic. Something caught her eye down the way, something familiar. "Is that …?" She trailed off, leaving the sentence hanging as she stared over her shoulder.

Gian followed her gaze, although he was careful not to ram the front of his Mercedes into the back of the car in front of them. "What?"

"There, parked behind that white Toyota."

His teeth clenched.

Cara didn't miss it. "That is my uncle's car."

"Looks like it."

"Why would he be outside my apartment?"

Gian turned back in the seat, his show of irritation all but gone. "Hard to say. Let's get you to classes, Cara."

"But—"

"Hey," he interrupted smoothly, "your birthday is coming up, right? Constantino might have mentioned it, since his is not far off from yours."

Cara's brow furrowed while she tried to decide whether to push him on her uncle's presence outside her place, or call him on his distraction. She settled for answering his question, for now. "Two weeks from Saturday."

"Would a private flight to Quebec be a proper present? We would leave Saturday morning, and be back Sunday evening."

"What's in Quebec, Gian?"

"French. A whole lot of French, *mon ange*. And old buildings, brick roads, shitty drivers, some of the best restaurants, tickets to a ballet, and a fantastic suite booked for a birthday girl."

Cara couldn't help but smile. "A trip to Quebec it is."

Cara nearly tripped over the waiting bags at her apartment door as she rushed to answer the persistent knocking. With only a towel wrapped around her waist, and her wet hair hanging freely around her shoulders, she figured whoever it was could deal with being made to wait, considering it was them who got her out of the shower.

She pulled open the door with a huff, flipping wet curls out of her eyes at the same time. "What?"

A man she recognized—Chris was his name—stood on the other side, waiting with a smile and a large white box with two smaller white boxes on top of them. Pretty, shimmering pink bows had been tied to each box.

Cara's irritation instantly melted away.

"Gian?" she asked.

Chris nodded. "You know it."

This was the second time Gian had sent Chris to her door with a gift—although this looked to be *gifts*. The first had been the black choker she loved so much. The barrel-chested man had politely explained to Cara that should she continue to refuse the gift, he didn't mind escorting Cara to Gian to accept the gift directly, if she was so insistent on not allowing him to do his job. Given that first meeting, Cara knew better than to refuse Chris, when he was only there to do what he had been told.

And it *was* her birthday, after all.

"He could have waited for tonight," Cara mused as she stepped back to let Chris in.

Her birthday had come much faster than she expected, the end of March skipping into her life before she had blinked.

There was no way she could take the boxes and maintain her modesty by holding up her towel. Chris kept his eyes above her chest as he maneuvered through her apartment to set the boxes down on the kitchen table.

"Early gifts, he said," Chris told her. "Something he thought you might like to have for the trip, and the ballet tonight."

"Oh?"

"That's what was told to me. I'll be waiting outside to drive you to the private air strip when you're ready, miss. Do you want me to take the bags at the door down for you?"

Cara gave the guy a smile. "You *can* call me Cara."

Chris shrugged. "I could, but I won't. At least, not yet. The bags?"

"They're only small. I can do—"

"I'll take them, no worries. Finish getting ready."

Chris gave a two-finger wave as his goodbye, and exited the apartment with Cara's small, overnight bags slung over his shoulder. Once the front door was shut, she turned back to the waiting boxes with their pink bows on the table.

"What did you do now, Gian?" Cara wondered out loud.

She thought it was time to find out. She set each of the three boxes side by side, and started with the middle one first, carefully untying the box and pulling off the top. Patent leather, pristine, white pumps rested inside white tissue paper. Pointed toes and six-inch stiletto heels. Vibrant red soles painted the bottom of each shoe.

Cara knew that signature red sole without even having to look inside the heels to check.

Every girl did.

Louboutin.

A small note rested alongside the shoes, and Cara picked it up to read.

Because beautiful legs deserve to be shown off, birthday girl. —Gian

She reached for the largest box, then, wondering what on earth he had stuffed inside that thing, too. It was a good two feet in length and width. She wasted no time getting the bow and top off, only to find more tissue paper this time covering the item inside.

Her hands shook as she removed the tissue paper to pull the white and silver dress out from within the box. White silk, and silver lace and fringe, covered the form-fitting, sleeveless, knee-high dress. There was no flair to the skirt; it was pencil thin, with the same silver lace fringe along the bottom that decorated the sides and bodice. Sparkling beadwork and crystals had been carefully sewn in to the fringe.

A matching clutch also sat inside the box, waiting to be appreciated.

There was no note in this box, but Cara wondered if that was because Gian intended to let the tag on the dress speak for him.

Dolce & Gabbana.

Already, there was a small fortune sitting on her table in a single pair of shoes and a dress. She was reaching for the third, final, and smallest box of the bunch before she even realized it.

Inside, she found a thin, white lace choker. Maybe an inch wide, the delicate lace was soft against her fingertips, and clasped at the back with a small chain with a single, dangling white pearl.

A note rested underneath the choker.

All white, as angels should wear, mon ange. *You're only missing the wings, now. Happy birthday, Cara. —Gian*

Gian had forewarned her during the lead up to her birthday that she would need something appropriate to wear for the ballet in Quebec, but that she wasn't to worry about it. Cara *had* packed something in her overnight bags, which was why she needed two instead of only one, just in case.

Apparently, she wouldn't be needing it after all.

She looked over the items spread across her table, overwhelmed and happy, all at the same time. Gian was smart, though. He had sent the gifts over late, when he likely knew she would be rushing to finish getting ready, and couldn't overthink the gifts or call him on them. It wasn't that she didn't like them—*oh*, she loved them—but she knew what these items cost, too.

She couldn't help but wonder why a man like Gian had no problem with spending this kind of money on a woman like her.

And for her birthday, no less.

These were the kinds of gifts that were meant for the queens of men—women they loved and adored, whom they cherished enough to treat as the royalty in their lives that they truly were.

Was Cara becoming that to Gian?

Maybe that scared her a little.

And Cara didn't have time to think on it.

Which she was sure Gian had known, sending the items over at this time.

Cara backed away from the gifts and headed for the bathroom. She spent the next half hour getting her hair dried into manageable, free curls and putting on a quick bit of makeup to color her eyes and lips. She had managed to clasp the choker on after slipping into the dress and pumps, when a knock beat on her door, and Chris's voice filtered in.

"We do have to leave soon, miss."

"Coming," Cara shouted back.

She grabbed the white tweed coat she had pulled from Lea's closet when she couldn't find something suitable in her own to wear over the white and silver dress. Her sister had owned far too many clothes, and while Cara had slowly started to go through Lea's things to get rid of what she didn't want to keep, she had barely touched the clothes.

Cara pulled the door open to find Chris waiting on the other side.

His gaze fell down over the dress to the shoes and then back up just as fast. He hadn't lingered, and his expression remained neutral. "Gian will be pleased. You look wonderful, miss."

Cara smiled. "Thank you."

"Let's head out."

She followed behind the man, letting him lead her through the apartment hall, down one flight of stairs, and outside to where a black town car sat running in front of the building. It was only a short stroll away. Chris held the back door open for Cara to walk the remainder of the way and get inside, but something caught her eye as she made it to the vehicle.

Another car—bright yellow, which was what caught her attention first—came speeding far too fast down the city road. Black tinted windows made it impossible to see inside.

By the time the car reached them, the driver's window rolled down a few inches.

Cara didn't understand the item that was shoved out the window, not until the color burst from the barrel, and the sound sliced through the air.

Rapid gunfire.

Bullets.

Pain bloomed in Cara's shoulder as she was dragged to the ground. She was frozen, stuck in a strange nightmarish state of reality and memories. She hadn't heard gunfire like that since the day Lea was murdered. It was as though she had been shoved right back into that day all over again in a split second.

She couldn't bring herself out of it, no matter how hard she tried.

Chapter 10

Automatic doors opened in front of Gian, but they weren't spreading fast enough for his brisk pace or patience. His hands slammed against the doors, pushing against the pressure of the mechanical arm to force them open faster.

His heart was in his fucking throat.

His stomach had fallen to his feet.

Time had become unimportant for the moment.

Gian couldn't remember the last time he felt this way—so fucked up in the head, an anxious mess, but still damn cold and calm on the outside.

Corrado used to tell him that *this* was when Gian was most dangerous. That Gian's emotions often ruled him in his choices and behaviors, but it was only when he didn't allow others the gift of seeing his emotions to gauge their transgressions, that it became dangerous. Because he became unstable, and unpredictable.

His grandfather had never said it was bad thing, though.

Another set of doors didn't open fast enough for Gian's satisfaction, and he shoved that set apart, too. A nurse on the other side barely moved out of the way, and she dropped her bags with a squeak. On any other day, Gian would have stopped and helped the woman, but his mind was somewhere else entirely.

A half of a dozen men stood gathered in a semi-circle outside of the hospital room across from the busy nurse station. Gian recognized their faces—friends of his man, younger Capos that had likely heard something happened and come down for support. He appreciated the effort and their concern, but he was neither in the mood to talk, nor interested in playing to the mafia politics.

His car being bombed was one thing.

He always had a fucking target on him.

Cara, though?

Cara was a whole other matter.

"Gian."

"Shit, nice suit, man. Where were you heading, tonight?"

Gian ignored the greetings and questions that were thrown at him as he passed through the group of men. He strolled into the opened hospital room to find Chris cussing a blue streak under his breath as a nurse stitched a three-inch, clean slice on the enforcer's neck.

"Well, if you hadn't moved so much," the nurse muttered under her breath.

"I rolled over in the bed, *cazzo*. Maybe they should have got it closed up better the first damn time."

Gian cleared his throat to gain the attention of both people. When the nurse looked to him, he jerked his head toward the door. "Get out."

The nurse's eyes narrowed. "But—"

"Two minutes, that's all I need. Get out, now."

Thankfully, the woman went without much argument. She did finish the last couple of stitches before she left, though. Once Gian was alone with Chris, he turned and closed the door to keep his next words from being overheard.

"Well, talk," Gian demanded.

Chris resituated himself on the bed to properly face his underboss. "Nothing too bad, a few scrapes from the pavement. A bullet nicked me on the throat. It's fine."

"*Sì*, I can see how fine you are. That's the only reason I came to this room first, instead of Cara's, because I hoped to calm down a bit more before I see her. What the fuck happened?"

"She's fine, too, boss."

Gian grinded his teeth. "That's a matter of opinion at the moment."

"She is. I got her down in time."

"You have one job when she is in your care."

Chris nodded. "And I did that job, Gian. That's why she's getting released tonight and I still have to be monitored until morning before I get my walking papers."

That was true enough.

For the most part, Gian liked Chris because the man was straightforward and took no bullshit, yet he also understood the weight of respect in their world. So, while he would give Gian the truth in a blunt manner that someone else may not, he did it with the respect of a man who knew he was talking to his superior.

Gian's posture softened, but barely. He was still walking on a very thin line of control. He had never been quite so worried, or so pissed off, as he was right then. "What did you see before the shooting started?"

"Very little. I was turned for Cara, I had the door opened for her. I wasn't watching the street—I didn't have any reason to think I should. The bullets started flying, and I was focused on getting her out of the way, that was it. By the time I got back up, my throat was bleeding all over the damn place and the car was gone. She couldn't tell me anything when I asked, it was like she wasn't even on the same planet, all of the sudden. Shock, maybe."

Maybe.

Or maybe it was something else, too.

"So, basically, you've got nothing to help me?"

Chris shrugged, though the action looked painful. "It happened fast. I did my job. There's nothing else to say."

Gian nodded once. "*Merci*."

"You're welcome."

"I'll see you when you're not in a hospital bed," Gian said before he slipped out of the room.

Outside in the hallway, Gian found the group of men had moved farther down from the door and away from the nurse station. Their conversation, however, was still being held at a level that he could plainly hear.

And it did *not* please him.

"So he was what, picking up the Rossi chick when it happened?" one of the Capos asked.

A solider nodded. "Guess so. Maybe that's where Gian's head has been lately—on her, you know."

The men didn't notice that Gian had left the room, nor that he was standing there listening to their conversation a few feet away. He didn't let them in on his presence, either.

"I heard some whispers about that," another Capo said. "He's found himself a distraction, not that I blame him … considering everything."

"Just call her what she is," Constantino said. "Don't dance around it like stupid fucks."

When had Constantino showed up?

He hadn't been there before Gian entered the enforcer's room.

"Is that what you would call her, then?"

Constantino—Gian's oldest and closest friend—nodded. "Sure, I would. What does it matter? It's better that everyone else knows. Those type come second, anyway. Even Gian knows it, too. Why do you think he's running around with her on the low, not shouting it from the rooftops like someone else might? Cara's a fucking catch, don't get me wrong. She's an awesome girl—my cousin, too, so I can say that and know it's true. But to Gian?"

Gian took the few steps that separated him and the group of men, shouldering one aside as he came face to face and toe to toe with Constantino. His friend didn't even look surprised to see him standing there all of the sudden.

"Say it," Gian dared his friend. "Say what you were going to say, *cafone*."

Constantino didn't blink. "We don't have time right now to be running around after your flavor of the month, man, worrying about who might be coming after her next. It's not an important detail, and somebody probably did this shit today to get your attention, since you're too busy to pay attention to what actually needs it right now. She's just a go—"

He didn't even get to finish his statement.

Gian's fist slammed into Constantino's jaw, shutting the man up, making him bleed, and sending him to the floor instantly.

Made men didn't fight. They sure as hell didn't hit other made men. It was a rule. Gian was learning there were some rules that needed to fucking go.

That was one of them.

Gian looked down at Constantino, not bothering to offer his hand to help his friend back up off the floor. "Don't you ever fucking disrespect Cara Rossi again. Not to my face, or behind my back. Don't shout it, and don't even whisper it. If it happens again, Constantino, I will sew your eyes together, burn your fucking ears off, and cut your tongue out. Maybe then, everyone else will understand what see no evil, hear no evil, and speak no evil really means to men like me. Maybe then, they might understand that a woman is worth far more than the title a man puts on her status. Test me, and watch what happens. Speak ill of her again, and I will slaughter you, friend or not."

He didn't bother to wait around and hear what was going to be said next. He had far more important things to do.

Like a woman in the unit upstairs waiting on him.

Cara needed a ride home. Happy fucking birthday to her, he thought miserably. This was not how the weekend was supposed to be. They should have been in Quebec already—hours ago, actually—watching a ballet together.

An apology was not going to make this better.

Of that, Gian was most sure.

Cara said nothing, her gaze lowered to the tiled floor of her bathroom as Gian carefully removed her white tweed coat and set it aside. The front of the beautiful dress that had been one of her birthday gifts was stained a reddish brown—Chris's blood, likely.

She had suffered no open injuries, thankfully.

When Cara did finally speak, her dull tone took Gian off guard. Other than her soft greeting at the hospital when he walked into her room, she had said nothing the entire time it'd taken to get her out, and get her home.

He was not accustomed to this steel-spine, sharp-tongued woman being so … quiet.

"Please don't say you'll buy a new dress to replace this one," Cara said.

Gian shrugged, pulling the zipper down on the garment to expose Cara's back to his hands. He let his palms linger over the warm, soft skin of her shoulders as he pushed the shoulders of the dress down.

"I have a pretty decent drycleaner, actually. He's got a knack for getting blood out as long as it's not too old. A secret trick, or so he says. I think I'll take it to him."

Gian was lying through his teeth.

Blood didn't come out of fabric.

He *would* get a new dress for Cara, he simply wouldn't tell her that was what he had done.

"You don't have to do that," Cara said.

She still wasn't looking at him.

Gian hated that.

"Hey."

Cara let out a soft sigh. "Hmm, what?"

"*Bella mia*, look at me." Gian carefully pulled the dress over Cara's head, and then turned her to face him. Her emotionless expression only hurt him more. "I'm sorry for today, Cara."

"It's not your fault."

Technically, it probably was.

He didn't have to pull the trigger.

"The cops were in questioning me," Cara said, running a hand through her messy curls. "They only got more annoyed when I couldn't give them what they wanted. In case you're worried, I didn't say—"

"I'm not worried about that at all, *mon ange*," he interrupted quickly. "I was worried about you, nothing else."

"Still. I didn't have much to tell either way."

"Chris mentioned you … blanked a bit after the gunfire stopped and whatnot. Like you were frozen on the ground."

Cara shrugged. "It could have been that day in Chicago all over again, because that was all I saw. I could hear Lea asking me to help her, not Chris. My mind is broken that way, I think."

"Or you've got a touch of PTSD. An event like that is difficult to get over, Cara."

"I just …" She trailed off, frowning.

"What, love?"

"I feel like something important happened—or I saw something important—but I can't remember it because all I see is Chicago."

"Whatever it was, it'll come back, if it's important enough. Otherwise, don't stress on it. Certainly not tonight, anyway."

Gian's gaze was drawn to the bruises on the joint of her shoulder, and he had all he could do to quell the rage that suddenly boiled like hot lava inside his gut. With gentle strokes, he let his fingertips ghost over the marks. Chris's attempt to get Cara out of the way as fast as possible had left her with a dislocated shoulder from the force of hitting the ground, and awful bruising around the joint.

"It's not as bad as it looks," Cara said.

"That's a matter of opinion."

It seemed he was saying that a lot tonight.

"You look pissed."

Gian chuckled dryly. "Because it pisses me off that you have any marks. The only marks that should ever be on your body are ones I put there when I fuck you. Nothing more, nothing less."

Cara smiled, but it didn't come off as entirely true. "You don't have to stay tonight. I'm sure you have other—"

"I have nothing to do but sit here with you."

And that was just what he did.

The bathtub practically overflowed with lavender-scented bubbles by the time Gian decided it was filled enough. Steam was already starting to rise in the room as he helped Cara step into the hot, soapy water. He waited for her to get settled in before he pulled a chair from the kitchen into the bathroom, set it beside the tub, and pulled his book out to read.

Out loud, of course.

She liked it.

Cara leaned over and rested her head against his thigh, and Gian sifted his fingers through her silky hair as he read along.

"Other than the whole drive-by thing," Cara started to say.

"Keep going."

"This is mostly an okay birthday."

"I will save the Quebec trip for another time, I promise." Gian bent down to kiss the top of Cara's head. "But it still managed to be okay for you somehow?"

"I didn't realize it until I was in the hospital, but it's my first birthday without Lea. I didn't think about it leading up to today or as I was getting ready this morning. Tommas didn't mention her when he called this morning to wish me a happy birthday. It wasn't on my mind. She was the oldest twin by four and a half minutes."

"You never told me that before."

"Details," Cara said flippantly. "She used to joke and say it was the best four and a half minutes of her life. I'm now six months older than she lived to be."

"Things you don't really consider, huh?"

"I suppose. I was going to say I think she had to be lying about those four and a half minutes, because these past six months have been the worst of my life."

Gian stroked her cheek softly. "You have a good reason for that, though."

"It wouldn't be entirely true." Cara smiled up at him, happier and more honest than before. "The last couple haven't been so bad, really."

Well, then …

He could understand that, too.

"But with the shooting and all," Cara continued, "it brought me back down to reality."

"And what does that mean?" Gian asked.

He wasn't sure he was going to like her answer.

"I don't know right now, Gian."

Yeah, he didn't like that at all.

The cemetery had a quiet, almost peaceful, quality about it. The usual sadness clung in the air, but it wasn't as thick as Gian expected it would be. He stepped out of his car, and looked down the way, noting no vehicles but one that happened to be parked there. Checking his watch, he figured that gave him a bit of time before the men showed up.

Quickly, he strolled through the graveyard, passing by shined headstones and cleaned graves. Fresh flowers—some of the winter kind, but most for spring—rested upon the tops of a great many of the headstones.

All too soon, he came up to the one gravestone he was looking for. His grandfather's. When his grandmother, Aurora, had died, Corrado made sure that the headstone placed on her grave also included his name, birthdate, and a blank spot waiting for his death date to be added. Now, that spot was no longer blank, but rather, carved in identical font and style to the rest of the numbering with his grandfather's date of death.

His father waited on a nearby bench, a paper in his hands.

"Do you come here often?" Frederic asked.

Gian shook his head. "This is the first time, actually."

"How does it feel?"

"Odd."

"Oh?"

Gian bent down to place a handful of fresh flowers along the ledge of his grandparents' stone. "I thought it wouldn't feel like he was here, but it does, in a way."

"Even though he isn't buried yet."

"Like I said, it's odd."

Corrado's body was still waiting to be buried because of the frost in the ground. Another month, and the ground would be soft enough to dig. Gian didn't plan to attend that event, but he figured that he didn't need to.

"Do *you* come here often?" Gian asked his father.

Frederic set his newspaper aside. "Once a week to say hello to Ma. She used to threaten me that if I didn't come to chat with her—even when she was dead—that she would haunt me for it. Turns out, this is like a haunting of sorts, anyway."

"What about for Corrado?"

His father pointed to his temple. "That's all in here. I hear him all the time there, Gian."

Strange ...

"I don't hear him there. Or rarely."

Frederic lifted his brow and said, "Perhaps you're not listening close enough, son."

"Or maybe he thinks he told me enough when he was alive that he shouldn't need to be repeating it now."

"Or that," his father agreed, chuckling. "What did you want me here for today?"

Gian stood straight again, and crossed the path to sit with his father on the bench. "There have been some ongoing problems lately."

"You must think I'm completely out of the loop because I'm not a made man."

"I assume nothing about no one, Dad."

Frederic looked over at his son. "And why is that?"

"Assumptions make for dead men."

His father tapped the side of his head. "See, Corrado is in there, Gian. He simply doesn't manifest to you the same way he does to me."

"And how is that?"

"I often hear him voicing my failures, or his lack of approval. I never gave him what he wanted—except for you—after all."

"But how do I hear him?" Gian asked.

"You hear yourself, son, because you're too much like your grandfather to find the distinction at the moment."

"We weren't entirely the same."

"It's enough," his father said, vaguely. "I know you're having problems with Edmond and his older men. I figured you would, Corrado probably did, too. I think he hoped to make it longer than Edmond, but knew that wasn't going to happen what with the cancer diagnosis. Nonetheless, here you are. I also hear you've found yourself a ... *friend*."

Gian's expression blanked, and he was determined to keep his emotions that way on this topic with his father. "I don't need to hear your opinions on that side of things."

"Yes, well—"

"I also don't *want* to hear it, Dad."

"But what exactly are you going to do with the Rossi girl, Gian?" His father scoffed. "It's not like you can have any kind of acceptable future with her."

"Who says?"

"Cosa Nostra, and you know why."

Gian clenched his jaw. "For a man who didn't want to be a part of *la famiglia*, you're well-versed on things you have no business knowing."

"Thank your grandfather for that."

"You can't thank a dead man, Dad."

"Funny, we're always thanking God for something or other. Didn't he die once, too?"

"Move on," Gian demanded with a disinterested flick of his hand.

"Fine. The problems, you said. I already know."

"Good. Stay low, off the streets, you know, the normal when there's issues popping up. Pass the message along to Ma. I'll tell Dom. I want everyone to be safe over the next little while. That's all."

"That implies you plan to make some moves of your own that might agitate an already volatile situation, Gian."

"I'm not implying it," Gian replied quietly.

He looked across the graveyard to see more cars had begun parking along the road. Most, he recognized. Men—the younger side of the family—that he knew would come when he demanded their presence. Even Constantino's car was clearly visible, though Gian expected his friend to still be a little sour over their scuffle a few evenings ago.

"I'm not implying it," Gian repeated, "because I'm outright saying it now."

"Be careful," his father warned. "Things that often seem clear and straightforward in this business rarely ever are, Gian."

"What matters the most is that someone started a war, and I plan on finishing it."

Chapter 11

Spring was finally in the air, despite already being a couple of weeks into it. Unfortunately, the old adage of April showers bringing May flowers held true for the city, even if the only flowers that would grow were in cement pots between benches on the sidewalks. The wetness didn't seem to want to leave, and it had rained almost every day for a week.

Cara was starting to wonder if she should invest in a poncho and rain boots.

It didn't matter how long she lived in Canada, the weather still took her by surprise every single year. It was as though Mother Nature spent three to four months in a bitter rage Canadians liked to call winter, only to then spend two months in the wet, mucky depression of spring.

Cara tightened the coat around her neck to keep the chill of the wind out, while simultaneously keeping the umbrella high to battle the rain. She weaved in and out of the rushing people on the sidewalk, coming nearer to her destination. A small café just a couple of blocks away from her university that she frequented throughout the week.

All the while, she ignored the shadow of a man following behind her.

A bodyguard, according to Gian. Because she needed one of those now. *Just in case.* The guy never came close enough to speak, and Cara didn't even know his name. He'd never introduced himself, and by the time Cara realized she had a new shadow, she was too irritated over the whole thing and didn't want to discuss it at all.

Cara slipped inside the café, mastering the ability to pull in her closing umbrella through a shutting door at the same time. Somehow, her hair and coat still felt wet, despite having the umbrella up the whole time she had walked the two blocks.

Maybe it was time to look into getting a car, after all.

Cara had the money, as far as that went. She didn't live in luxury, her expenses were very little in the grand scheme of things, and her trust fund was still heavily padded with a decent number. She had her long-deceased paternal grandparents—and her brother—to thank for the trust fund that allowed her several years in a university program without needing to work, though. Instead of dividing up their fortune between their children, they included their few grandchildren as well. Had they only left the trusts in the hands of her parents, Cara had zero doubts that her mother and father would have squandered it away.

The trust funds had then been signed over to Tommas when the twins were still under eighteen years of age, so that he could use it for their education, if they wanted. When Lea died, Cara had been giving a letter from a Rossi family lawyer, notifying her that the details and remaining contents of her sister's trust had been consolidated into hers after expenses were paid.

She had money.

Cara was worried about using too much of it, even for an investment like a vehicle or a more permanent home. She liked money better when she could micromanage it, budget every single red cent, and watch her portfolio continue to stay in a comfortable area for her tastes. Maybe when this final year of university was up, and she had steady income from a job, she might feel okay with spending the money, but not now.

She grew up feeling poor, living like she was in poverty, simply because her parents had not cared to look after the state of their children or their home. She had worn clothes until they were ratty and a size or two too small, shoes that didn't work for a Chicago winter, and sweaters, instead of a proper windbreaker in the fall and spring. Tommas had filled in a lot of those things for his sisters when he could, as he had gotten older, buying them what they needed or paying their school expenses and meals.

But she still remembered what it felt like to be dirt poor, even when she actually wasn't.

Neglect came in too many forms to count.

Cara tried to brush off the lingering sadness from her thoughts as she stepped up to the counter and placed an order for coffee and a bagel. Once she had her order in hand, she took a seat at the far end of the café, tucked into a two-seated table with her back to the wall and facing the windows.

She saw him approach the café before she even took her first drink.

Gian didn't come right in, instead stopping to chat with her new *shadow*. He gave the man a handshake, and only then did he enter the café. It was like all of the nerves in Cara's body suddenly zoned in on the one person around her that affected her the most. She didn't even have to see him to feel him nearby.

It scared her.

It calmed her.

Cara didn't know what to do about those strange feelings, but she knew that she wasn't ready to deal with them. Not yet, anyway.

If anything, she needed time away from the way Gian made her feel.

Time to figure out what in the hell had happened that'd gotten her into this position with a man that she had no business being involved with. Time to breathe, before Gian called her and she stupidly went running for a feeling and a fuck.

Gian smiled as he crossed the café. Unlike her, he didn't stop for something to eat or drink. Like usual whenever he was near her, she seemed to be the only damn thing on his mind or in his priorities. He dropped a quick kiss to the top of her head before taking the only other available seat at the small table.

"How do you walk around without any sort of umbrella?"

Gian shrugged. "You get used to it, really."

"Seven years here. I'm not used to it yet."

"Too wet for you?" he asked.

Cara scowled at the rain pattering against the café's windows. "It's like we go from snow to weeks of rain without any sort of warning or break."

"The warning is the month of April, *mon ange*."

Of course it was.

Canadians.

"Summer is right around the corner," he said, the dimple in his cheek making a rare appearance as his smile widened. "It'll go from wet to hot just as fast, as it always does."

"Sure."

Gian's easy smile melted away fast, and he straightened a bit in the chair. "You don't seem happy. It's not the rain, is it?"

Cara looked out the window again, noting the bodyguard standing under a small ledge to keep from getting rained on. "Thanks for meeting up with me today."

"I've been trying to meet up with you all week, Cara."

"I know. I just … needed a break."

"A break for what?"

Cara blew out a hard breath. "To think."

"All right."

"To breathe," she added.

Gian's lips flattened into a grim line, his face betraying nothing. Cara sometimes hated how easily he hid his emotions when he needed to, as though he didn't want anyone to know his pain or irritation, or even his joy. She was sure it was a learned trait, born out of need because of his position—she knew her brother acted in a similar way—but that didn't mean she understood it. Not entirely, anyway.

"I don't have a lot of time today," Gian said quietly, "and I have to head out for a meet across the city soon. Not that I mean to rush you, but I have to, unfortunately."

Cara nodded. "That's okay. I have another class soon, anyway."

"Did your ... break ... help?"

"Honestly? Not really."

Gian looked away. "I'm not sure what you're trying to help to begin with, Cara."

"This," she said with a wave between them. "A couple of months ago, when we first started whatever the fuck this is, it wasn't supposed to *be* anything, Gian. Fun, quick, dirty, and that was it. That's all I wanted out of it, and here I am, confused again."

"You're confusing me," he said under his breath.

"I didn't want to become integrated in your life—not to the extent that I am. I didn't want to be seen as a target for the people you do business with. I grew up living the sort of life you live, burying people I loved because of their affiliations and business. I was sure that you and I wouldn't ... I don't know."

"It's impossible to live separate lives, Cara," Gian pointed out. "I'm not two different men. I am the same man who carries a gun and acts as an underboss for my *famiglia*, and the man you demanded see no one else but you. The idea that I can constantly keep you from being integrated into all of that is ridiculous, and you should already know that."

"Gian—"

"No, listen to me. That's an idea you rationalized to justify your feelings and why you kept coming back for more. That was your fantasy to keep from worrying too much about what might happen or could happen to someone you give a fuck about."

"I never once hid who I was to you," Gian continued, his voice finally heating with anger. "I never once pretended to be anyone, except exactly who I am. It's like Lea, right? It's the same thing, in a way. You thought you both were good, safe away from your family and their business, but you never were, Cara. You can't run forever, and you're always a part of this thing being born to it. A child *della mafia*. This is who you are, and staying away didn't keep Lea alive. So, what in the hell would make you think pretending that I am someone I'm not would keep reality from catching up to you again?"

Cara felt like he had slapped her.

Actually, a slap might have felt better.

"You didn't need to bring my twin into this, Gian," Cara murmured, her voice thick with pain.

"I only told you the truth."

"You said it to hurt me."

Gian shook his head, sadness coloring up his dark gaze. "You're wrong. I never want to hurt you, Cara."

It didn't matter, she decided. Standing from the table, Cara picked up her bag and umbrella. She left her mostly-unfinished bagel and half-full coffee on the table. Gian didn't stand to see her out like he usually would, instead staying firmly seated with his gaze stuck on the wall behind her.

Coldness radiated from him.

Cara knew that feeling well.

She was damn cold, too.

"I didn't want this, not to be a target again, or hurt because I'm too close to you. I don't want to be shot at when I'm leaving my place or to turn around and see some guy shadowing my every move to keep me safe. I didn't want those things, Gian."

"So what do you want?" he asked.

"I need some more time," Cara replied. "Right now, I need time to—"

"Figure out how you got here with me."

"Yeah."

"Take as much time as you need, Cara." With that said, Gian stood from the table in a smooth motion, never crowding Cara as he turned to leave. "But if you want to save some time trying to figure it out, then give me a shout. I know exactly what got us here, *amore*. Honestly, you know it, too. You're one stubborn fucking woman when it comes right down to it."

"The first non-rainy day in two weeks, and you want to spend it by playing in mud," Cara muttered.

"Not mud, my *flower beds*," her aunt replied with a sweet smile. "I need to get them ready for the seedlings that I'll transplant outside, once I'm sure the frost is going to stay away."

Cara huffed, blowing a stray curl that had fallen in front of her eye out of the way. She resisted the urge to wipe the hair away when it fell right back down again, but that was only because she was wrist-deep in Daniele's flower beds. Or rather, one of several mucky piles of dark soil that was too damp for Cara's liking.

She clearly wasn't a green thumb kind of person.

"Thanks for joining me today," Daniele said.

"No problem." Cara overturned more soil, making sure to pull out any small rocks or dead weeds that had been left over from the year before. "I've been kind of busy lately. Sorry about that, *Zia*."

Daniele shrugged. "Sometimes, that's how life works."

"I suppose."

Cara wasn't going to go into the details of what had been keeping her away and busy, but she figured her aunt probably knew enough to go on without being told. Daniele—considering her husband's affiliations to the Guzzi family—had her own connections to the rumors making the rounds.

However, it wasn't polite conversation to ask about someone almost being shot.

Or who they were fucking.

Daniele was *always* polite.

Always a proper mafia wife.

It was the one thing Cara knew to expect from her aunt.

"So, how have you been?" Daniele asked.

"Busy with school. I thought that since I basically took four months off after Lea died that I would probably be behind, and not graduate on time next year, but I'm on track again now. It took a bit to get there, though."

"Oh?"

"And I got an early spot for a co-op of sorts at a woman's shelter, starting this summer, too. I'll be mentoring the mothers and teen girls, and helping with the outpatient rehab program. Since it's exactly what I want to work in, in a roundabout way, it was a lucky grab."

"That's good," her aunt said absently.

Cara shot a look across the flower bed, only to find Daniele wasn't actually paying her any attention. Her aunt was more focused on dragging the tiny hoe through the soil, overturning it to get the bed ready for planting.

She had been sure her aunt's only reason for asking her over to visit was to pry information out of her, but so far, Daniele hadn't done any of that.

Maybe Cara had been wrong.

Cara went back to helping her aunt clean out the flower beds, before they moved onto the railing pots that were sitting on the back deck. She was half way through filling the hanging pots with a fresh soil and mulch mix when her aunt starting talking again.

"Are you seeing anyone new, Cara?"

Her shoulders grew stiff at the innocuous question.

"Not particularly," Cara answered carefully.

Gian wasn't *new*, after all. And she wasn't exactly seeing him, after their meet at the café the week before. They were a thing, sure, but that meant nothing for now. Or, that's what Cara had been trying to convince herself for a whole fucking week.

"Claud mentioned you were having dinners with a gentleman."

Cara resisted the urge to say her uncle should mind his business. "Did he?"

"Yes, and sleepovers, too."

"Is that what you're calling it, nowadays?" Cara asked, not bothering to hide her sarcasm.

Daniele laughed lightly. "Don't get prickly, I'm only asking to be nice."

"Being nice would be *not* asking, *Zia*. Personal business, okay?"

"I do worry about you, Cara. You weren't your usual self these past few months, and then you seemed to be doing better. I still worry, though, especially if you've gotten yourself caught up in something of a mess."

Cara's brow furrowed as she regarded her aunt. "And what mess would that be?"

Daniele didn't even blink. "Men have a way of causing all sorts of messes that we women are not prepared for. They like to blame the mess on us, of course, but that's only because men fear the fingers pointing back at them when it's all said and done."

"I'm not caught up in any sort of mess, *Zia*."

"For your sake, I sure hope not, Cara."

The news program switched to the oncoming weather for the last few days of April, leading into May, and Cara shut the television off. She let out a hard breath, frustrated at herself that she had once again succumbed to her curiosity and checked the news.

She had been checking the news for three damn weeks now.

Every night, she swore that something new popped up dealing with the Guzzi Cosa Nostra family. Something violent—someone else shot, a body found, a drive-by on a restaurant—and another funeral coming up.

Cara never watched the news, if she could help it. But after her own shooting weeks ago, she had turned the television on while she ate her supper to see what was being said. It was then that she learned just how volatile and violent the streets of Toronto were becoming for made men in the city.

She stayed out of family business for a reason.

She didn't ask questions.

She knew better.

This was exactly why …

Her curiosity once again got the better of her, and Cara watched the news over and over, checking for new stories that might be popping up. She read the Canadian news blogs, because more often than not, reporters hidden behind a screen had more information to offer about crime families and the goings on than what was offered on television programs.

The Guzzi family was in an uproar.

They had been that way for a while.

Gian had never told Cara about it, not properly. She didn't blame him for that, because she had made it clear on more than one occasion that she simply didn't want to know.

The death toll was piling up.

The violence was escalating.

Cara's drive-by shooting had been just *one* event, amongst several attacks. According to sources—though she wasn't sure how trustworthy those could be—the Guzzi family was struggling with an upheaval of power after their long-time boss had died. Gian's grandfather, that was. It appeared as though lines had been drawn between the younger and older generation of men in the family, and it had violently spilled over onto the streets.

It didn't look good.

It sounded all kinds of bad.

Cara worried.

Constantly.

It was every single reason why Cara hadn't wanted to get too involved with Gian in the first damn place. The life he lived was not a right to have in their world. It was nothing more than a privilege that made men and their families fought to keep.

Position. Power. Respect.

That's all the mafia had ever been.

And it scared the hell out of her.

For what felt like the millionth time, Cara forced herself not to grab her cell phone and dial Gian's all-too-familiar number. She had asked for space and time to think, and he had been gracious enough to give it to her without argument. He had not called, not messaged, and he hadn't sent one of his guys to her door with a gift. Even her shadow—the bodyguard that had seemed to come out of thin air—had receded to being simply a faraway annoyance whenever she looked for him. The guy wasn't gone altogether, but she rarely saw him now unless she really searched the crowd hard.

Cara already knew that she was going to fail at staying away from Gian, never mind actually *ending* whatever they were to one another. She was going to fail because she neither wanted to stay away, nor end their fucking mess together.

But she didn't know how to deal with what would also inevitably come with all of that.

The news programs.

The worry.

The violence.

Her fears ...

Cara didn't know how to deal with any of that.

Gian had been right—he couldn't and he didn't pretend to be someone that he wasn't. It was *her* who looked the other way. There was going to come a time when Cara wouldn't be able to turn cheek to the sides of Gian that frightened her, and once she did, there would be no way to look away. There would be no more pretending.

Before Cara fully understood her actions, she had grabbed for her phone and dialed a familiar number, but it wasn't Gian's. She listened to the ringing echo through the speakers as she waited for her brother to pick up the call. She didn't entirely expect Tommas to answer, as more often than not, he called her or she left a message.

But on the fourth ring, he did pick up.

"*Ciao.*"

For a whole ten seconds, Cara didn't respond.

All of the sudden, she didn't know what to say.

She heard the speaker crackle with an annoyed huff before Tommas muttered, "Cara, is that you?"

"Yes," she finally said.

"Something wrong?"

Cara glanced at the blank television screen, and considered how to answer that question. "How do you do it, Tommas?"

Her brother cleared his throat, and then she heard him shuffle around as though he were getting out of bed. "You're going to need to make more sense, if you want a proper answer."

She couldn't help but notice how tired he sounded. Not sleep-tired, but a fuck-this-world kind of tired. It was so unlike her brother. He was laidback, cool, calm, and collected. Always.

Cara had never known Tommas to be anything else.

"Are you sure nothing is wrong?" Tommas asked, when Cara stayed silent.

"Nothing serious."

"All right. Ask me your question again, but make more sense this time."

"How do you care and attach yourself to people who feel like their existence in your life is not guaranteed, but more temporary than you're willing to admit. Like tomorrow, someone gets pissed off or offended and suddenly, you're burying your sister ... or someone else you love."

Tommas sighed. "That's a heavy question for someone who didn't even thank me for wishing her a happy birthday a month ago."

"Thank you for the birthday wishes, Tommy."

He grunted under his breath. "I don't think about it—that's how I deal. And I protect those people as best I can, I do whatever I need to do so that my choices and my actions don't inadvertently hurt them or take them away from me."

"Huh."

"Sometimes I fail, too," Tommas added, a sadness creeping into his tone. "And that kills me, but it's unavoidable."

"Yeah, but ..."

"What, Cara?"

"What about people like me?"

"I do that for you, too. Why do you think you're still in Toronto, huh? Not here, in Chicago, advancing my stupid ass in this fucking family or something?"

"I meant, what about women like me—how do I deal with it? I can't manage it the same way you do, I'm not like you, Tommy."

"That's not an easy answer, Cara."

"Try me. Give me something."

"Why are you even asking this shit?"

"I need to know how to *deal*," she said sharply, offering little else.

"I only know what I see around me," Tommas replied quietly. "Or rather, the women around me. My cousin's wife, or the women in my family. My friends' wives, or *famiglia* daughters that bury their parents with dry faces and shaking hands. They're *strength*, Cara. They are the picture and embodiment of strength all around me. They handle their shit far better than any of us men ever could. They cook dinner, wipe children's faces, do what they have to do, and they smile when faced with their fears. I don't know how they do it, because I am too busy trying to keep allowing them the chance to cook their dinners, love their messy-faced children, and have no fears, all the while. Do you understand?"

"But you're part of the reason they're in that sort of life, Tommas."

"And all we made men do is make the best of what we know, Cara. Nothing more, nothing less."

She took the time to absorb her brother's words.

Tommas always gave it to her straight, after all.

He didn't pretty shit up.

"Oh, there's something else you need to know," Tommas said tiredly.

"What's that?"

"Serena's body was found this morning by the maid. Suicide, apparently."

Cara wished she was surprised to learn the news of her mother's death. She wasn't.

Something else that was ... inevitable.

"I'm sorry," Cara said softly.

"Are you?"

"For you, Tommy. I'm sorry for you. You've dealt with her your whole life, longer than I ever put up with her. You would only do that—and keep doing it—because somewhere inside, you hold affection for her."

"Not anymore," Tommas murmured. "I can let you know when the funeral is going to be."

"I would rather you didn't."

"That's what I figured."

"Please bury her beside Dad, not on the other side of Lea."

Tommas mumbled his agreement quickly.

"Cara?"

"Yes?" she asked.

"I don't know what's going on, or what made you pick up the phone to ask me all of this tonight, but there's really only one thing that matters in this life of ours, anyway."

"And what's that, Tommas?"

"Do what makes you happy. Be where, or with whom, or do whatever you need to do to be happy. Take that risk—it's worth it. Because this life is fleeting, and tomorrow might be the last time you smile, so it's better to spend today happy."

Chapter 12

"Sit, sit!" Gian clapped his hands twice, helping to quiet the men milling around the long dinner table. He waved at the waiting seats, and the men began to fill them. "Dinner is served."

As he said those words, two women, and one man, strolled into the dining room, each holding platters carrying all sorts of foods. Once the food was set down on the table, the help left and then returned with pitchers of drinks.

After they were gone for good, Gian waited to see if any man at the table would reach for food or a drink before he approved it. None did.

Instead, they looked to him, waiting.

As all good made men did for their boss.

It had taken Gian a couple of weeks to really get used to the fact that a great portion of the Guzzi made men saw him as exactly that—their boss.

He thought it appropriate to hold their first unofficial dinner where the last man they respected and followed as a boss had his, too. At Corrado's home, at his dining room table.

Maybe he had done this for a bit of nostalgia, too.

Gian took his own seat, said a quick prayer as had become a custom when sitting down to eat dinner with family, and then he waved again. "*Tutti mangiare.*"

His order for everyone to eat was no faster out of his mouth before the men began to reach for the hot dishes. He wasn't particularly hungry—a shitty by-product of his stress, likely—so he sat back in a chair that had once belonged to his grandfather, and enjoyed the sight of the Capos and enforcers filling their plates.

Conversations filtered around the table between men, some discussing the events and attacks that had escalated rather violently over the past couple of weeks. Gian allowed them those discussions, and only joined in if he was directly asked a question. He found that he learned a lot more, and the men *talked* a lot more, when they had a boss who cared to hear what they had to say.

All but one man at the table was made.

Gian turned to his left, where his brother Dom was stuffing his face with pasta. "Hungry, *fratellino*?"

Dom bristled. "Only little compared to you in age, Gian."

He laughed. "Relax. You're lucky to even be here."

"Yeah, I know."

Being unmade, Dom shouldn't be allowed to share the same experiences with made men until he had earned his seat at the table and his spot within the family. But ... Gian remembered times when his grandfather had allowed *him* to sit at the table, and to have a voice. He figured that had been Corrado's way of making his intention clear about giving his grandson his in to the family.

Gian was only doing the same for Dom.

In a way ...

"So, do you think—"

Dom's question was interrupted by a ringing phone. Gian recognized the familiar sound instantly, but because he wasn't sure why his grandfather's house line would be ringing, he looked over the table of men to see if it was one of their phones. None reached for their phones. Corrado's mansion had been kept running ever since his death, as the Guzzi family had often used it, and no one was quite ready to put it up on the market officially. Even the cook, maid, and the man who ran errands and greeted guests stayed in the house, with pay.

But they never mentioned the home getting calls.

Eventually, the ringing stopped.

The maid stepped into the dining room, pressing her palm over a cordless phone to keep her voice from being heard on the line. "Mr. Guzzi, there's a call for you."

All eyes turned on Gian. He stood from the table, leaving the men behind with a demand for them to keep eating, and that all was fine. Although to be perfectly honest, he wasn't sure what in the hell was going on.

Just outside the dining room, he took the phone from the maid and put it to his ear. His usual Italian and French greeting slipped out before he could think better of it. "*Ciao, bonjour.*"

"Gian, how are you this evening?"

Gian stiffened in place. "Edmond. Why in the fuck are you calling me at Corrado's home? And better yet, *how* did you know I was here?"

"I know a lot of things."

"Oh? Try me with one."

"Fifteen men sitting around your grandfather's table. Would you like their names? Sixteen, actually, if you include your unmade brother."

"Spying, now?"

"Hardly." Edmond scoffed. "You simply never think to look at any of those young gentleman like you should. They're not all trustworthy, Gian. Each of them has an ultimate goal in mind where this organization is concerned. Sure, it's true enough that some of them tie those goals to you being their boss, but some … some, probably do not."

"You're wasting my time."

As Gian spoke, he had moved through the left wing of the mansion, heading toward the front of the estate. He checked out the windows, to make sure none of the men stationed outside had taken a hit, and that there was no funny business going on. He didn't trust Edmond as far as he could throw the fat bastard.

"It's been a rough couple of weeks, hasn't it?" Edmond asked out of the blue.

Gian let the curtains close, and headed back the way he came toward the dining room. "Depends on who you think it's been rough for. On my end, I think it's been mostly okay. *You* were the one who started this nonsense, remember. I only recently joined in with a few attacks of my own. I can't help it if my attacks are more direct and successful than yours are."

"You assume everything, Gian. Don't you know what they say about assuming?"

"I know you're trying to play some kind of game with me, and my food is getting cold. I'm not in the mood."

"Too bad, it's time to listen. My attacks were pointed, and only done to either calm a situation, or make a point. They didn't have to be direct to be successful. That's what you fail to realize, Gian."

"Are you done?" he asked Edmond.

"Not even close. I know exactly why you're doing this."

"Do tell."

"You think I killed your grandfather," Edmond said simply.

Gian's jaw clenched. "Partly, but it's not the only reason."

"Yes, yes. The younger men, they want a boss they picked, they want to act like spoiled children who have their hands held when they're scared to do what they're told. We've been over this."

"Your bias is showing again, Edmond."

"So be it, they're a dime a dozen. They can be replaced."

"You're wrong again," Gian shot back. "Made men are not commodities to be replaced. Not in this Cosa Nostra."

Edmond laughed. "You have a lot to learn."

"It takes time, or so I was told."

"Be careful not to run out of it before you even get the chance to properly get started." Then, Edmond said quieter, "But you do think I killed Corrado."

"It no longer matters."

"It does, or this would not be happening."

"Wrong again," Gian murmured. "Corrado is only a small part of this. Cosa Nostra is not about the one man on top, but all the men who wait on his direction. It's not *me* who has forgotten that, Edmond. Good luck, but we both already know how this will end. I could ask you to make it easy on me, but we both know you won't."

Gian hung up the phone without a goodbye, handed it to the waiting maid, and joined his men at the dinner table once again.

None of them asked him what was wrong.

Nothing was wrong.

He had this shit under control.

Gian popped the top off his beer, took a long swig, and glared at the game playing on his flat screen television. "I don't know why you bother to watch this, man. The Leafs haven't done well in decades, and this isn't going to be their year."

Constantino bristled. "Be a proper Canadian, would you? Don't diss the Leafs like that."

"He's more of a Montreal fan," Dom remarked from the Lazy Boy chair. "Depends on who is winning at the time."

"That's a fucking shame," Stephan put in. "Pick a team and stick with it."

Gian had news for them. "Since you three are watching the game on my huge ass television, sitting on my comfy furniture, drinking *my* beer, and you're not at your own places, you can shut the fuck up now or get the hell out."

"Jesus, you're an asshole tonight," Constantino said absently, his attention snagged by the Leafs' player cutting down the middle of the ice. "Why are you so miserable lately?"

Gian took another swig of his beer, refusing to even entertain that goddamn question. His mood had been less than pleasant and for quite a while, it had only been getting worse. He had managed to hide it, for the most part, when he needed to. Lately, especially the last few days, his bad attitude had been showing itself more often, bleeding onto others that happened to be around him.

Like easy fucking targets.

Gian knew better; he was smarter than allowing his emotions to rule him or control how he went about his days and business.

Lately, he couldn't help it.

"It's nothing," Gian muttered, setting his beer down to the coffee table.

He took a seat beside Constantino, and decided to watch the game and get the night over with. It had been a while since he'd actually done something with friends—even if Stephan had showed up with Constantino earlier—so he might as well make the most of it.

Gian had forgiven Constantino for his slip at the hospital, and what he'd said about Cara, but it was a one-time only thing. His forgiveness had come easy once his friend apologized, but that was only because Constantino had been his friend for so damn long that he found it hard to stay pissed at the guy.

"But don't be surprised when the Leafs lose again, like they always do," Gian said. "They are the most boring hockey team to watch—nothing changes, from season to season."

Stephan shot Gian a look. "You should get laid. Maybe that would pull out whatever stick got shoved up your ass."

Constantino chuckled under his breath. "Hey, there's an idea."

Dom wisely chose to stay quiet, but that could have been because he had shoved a half of a slice of pizza in his mouth.

Lucky for him.

"Fuck off, both of you," Gian warned, never taking his gaze off the television.

"So that *is* it?" Constantino asked.

"What?"

"You need to get laid, Gian."

For fuck's sake …

"I need you to mind your business," Gian said, his irritation rising.

Take the fucking hint.

"Yeah, that's what it is," Stephan said with a nod. "Cara—the Rossi chick he was running around with—hasn't been seen in a while."

"My cousin," Constantino said, "I don't need a reminder, Stephan. I know who the fuck she is."

Gian's teeth was starting to grind so hard that his molars were aching.

"What I'm saying is, Gian here, wasn't running around with anybody else, so if she's keeping a low profile *without him*, then he isn't getting pussy from anywhere." Stephan laughed under his breath at the glare Gian passed his way. "Yeah, that's exactly what it is. No pussy makes for an irritated mess of a man, doesn't it, Gian?"

"I'm two seconds away from throwing all of you assholes out of my penthouse," Gian replied.

"Hey, I'm just eating pizza," Dom mumbled around a bite in his mouth.

Gian ignored his younger brother.

"Stay the hell out of my business," he told them all. "And that is the last fucking time I am going to say it."

Because mostly, he hated how right the guys were.

He hated how easily they had picked up on his mood and the reason why.

He missed Cara like crazy.

Space, he reminded himself. *You're giving her space.*

And also driving himself insane at the same time.

Gian had hoped Cara would get her shit figured out and all would be fine between them. He hadn't expected … this. Weeks and weeks of waiting, of wondering, and of being entirely fucking alone.

He almost hated how much control that woman had over him.

Except he couldn't hate that at all.

"If you're lonely or something," Constantino said, "then why don't you go home, Gian?"

Gian raised his brow. "I *am* home. And Cara wanted space. Although, that's not your fucking business, either."

Constantino shook his head. "I didn't mean here, man."

All right.

Fuck this whole night.

Gian didn't even bother to kick the guys out.

He left.

Gian whipped his car into the parking lot belonging to Cara's apartment building. He checked his phone again, and then triple-checked it *just to be sure.*

Would you pick me up? My place.

That was all Cara's text message had said. Gian had barely gotten his confirmative reply typed out before he had pulled an illegal U-turn on a downtown street and headed his lover's way. He'd only meant to clear his head when he'd left his place earlier, but this was perfectly fine, too.

Gian checked his phone once more, ready to send a message to Cara that he was there, but he didn't need to. Cara appeared outside the passenger side window, Gian unlocked the door, and she slid inside without a word.

He pulled out of the parking lot while Cara was still buckling up her seatbelt.

"Where to?" Gian asked.

Cara stared out the side window, never looking at him. "I don't know. Somewhere … quiet?"

"We can do quiet, *bella mia*." Thankful for the lack of traffic, Gian headed toward the bay. It was a bit of a drive, but it would be quiet and private. "Do you want to grab some food or something?"

"Sure."

"Anything specific?"

Cara shrugged. "Anything unhealthy and greasy."

Gian chuckled. "Junk food, then."

"What else?"

It took an hour to grab food, and drive all the way to the bay. Gian pulled the car along the metal fence that kept vehicles from going too far ahead. He had only put the car into park before Cara leaned across the seats, grabbed his jaw in her hands, and pulled him in for a kiss. It was not a sweet, hello kind of kiss. It couldn't be one of those, when her tongue invaded his mouth and she tried to get closer. It was more of an *I want* kind of kiss.

Gian was more than willing to give where Cara was concerned.

"So we're doing this first, then?" he asked against her mouth while pulling his leather jacket off at the same time.

"Yes."

So sure.

No hesitation.

"Whatever you want, Cara."

Gian hooked an arm around Cara's trim waist, and yanked her into the backseat of the Mercedes. He used the space between the front seats to get back there, but it sure as fuck wasn't an easy fit, and Cara fell hard into his lap with a breathless laugh.

He moved so his back was to the door, bringing her along with him. Burying his hands into her hair, he held tight so he could get more of her pretty mouth against his while he had the damn chance. But that only made him want more of her to taste—her cheeks, jaw, and neck. All the spots that he hadn't been able to kiss and bite and taste for *weeks*.

He had time to make up for.

Cara, apparently, had different plans. Her hot mouth started traveling down over his throat, her tongue lapping at his pulse point for a moment before moving on again. Gian decided all he could do was let her do her thing as she lowered even further.

"Jeans, a T-shirt, and a leather jacket," Cara said, working the button and zipper on Gian's jeans. He lifted off the seat enough to let her pull the jeans and his boxer-briefs down, and pull his shoes off. "I think this is the first time I've seen you without a suit."

"You've seen me without one."

"Being naked doesn't count, Gian."

"You've seen me in workout clothes."

"Which is basically a pair of shorts," she pointed out.

"I wasn't planning on leaving the penthouse today," he said in explanation.

Cara pulled his T-shirt up, and for the first time, Gian let go of the hold he had on her hair to allow her to slip the clothing off. "This is a good look, too. Relaxed. I liked the leather jacket."

If she liked it …

"You can take it," he said before pressing another hard kiss to her mouth. "Now, stop talking and start sucking my cock like you were working on doing two minutes ago."

Cara's eyes narrowed playfully. "How do you know that's what I was going to do?"

"Well, if it wasn't, it's sure as fuck what you're going to do now."

She winked and started lowering down his body again. "Lucky for you, that was the plan."

Of course it was.

Cara liked to say that it was him who had a gift with his mouth and tongue, but he didn't think she was aware of her little *talent*. The second her lips encased his cock, and she took him deep into her throat without slowing once, Gian was in fucking heaven. She always knew how to suck him, hard on the swallow, and looser on the way up. Her tongue swirled at the head of his shaft, while her teeth teased along the pulsing vein that matched the beats of his heart.

And *fuck*, she didn't give him a break. She didn't slow.

She sucked and sucked, while her fingers dug into his thighs. She didn't stop when his fingers weaved into her hair so that he could hold her down on his cock, and her throat flexed in the best way around his shaft when his hips bucked upward, wanting more still.

"Shit, shit, shit," he mumbled in a hard groan. "Suck my fucking cock, *Tesoro*. Just like that."

He called Cara a lot of things in bed.

His slut.

An angel.

Sexy. Beautiful. Filthy.

But *treasure*—that one probably fit her best.

Especially when she was sucking him off.

Only something precious and treasured could make him feel as crazy and high as she did when she was fucking him or sucking him dry.

Sex—for Gian—had become something of a nuisance in his life, to deal with when he got the chance. It slowly became a secondary need that took a back seat to his daily responsibilities and the duties that always had to come first.

Not with Cara.

With Cara, sex became a form of his affection. It was yet another way to communicate. It let him *feel*. He was always relaxed—never bothered or worried about outside issues—whether he was on his knees between her legs, or she was above him looking down. He focused in on her, nothing else, and it wasn't such a fucking nuisance to be taken care of.

It was an urge that was constant. Unrelenting.

She was always on the back of his mind now, in one way or another. When he wasn't with her, he was working out a way to be with her. In her effort to have space from him, all she had managed to do was make Gian even more fucking obsessed with her than he had been before. He controlled the urges well enough, but it was like constantly balancing on a very thin string, ready to break. He didn't want her running scared from him again, he wanted her *with* him.

The sound that tore from his throat was almost inhuman, his words jumbling together as the pressure and heat in his spine suddenly grew to the point of no return. He managed to get something out, a mix of "fuck, I'm going to come" and "shit, don't stop." He wasn't really sure what he said, he couldn't hear it. His ears were ringing as his load emptied into Cara's waiting mouth. She kept his cock tight to her lips and deep in her throat as his cum shot out with enough force to make him dizzy.

Like the good girl she was to him, she swallowed every last fucking bit of it down, too. Then she cleaned his cock with her tongue, and kissed her way back up his body until she was sitting sweetly in his lap, straddling him. The pleased curve of her lips told him that she *liked* sucking him off, if only because it gave her some control between them.

She didn't know it, but she had all the control now.

Gian pulled Cara in for a bruising kiss, her lips warm and swollen against his. Despite having just emptied his fucking balls, his cock was still painfully hard, because he wasn't done. It wasn't that simple when it came to Cara.

"Thank you for wearing a dress tonight," he said.

Cara lifted a single brow high. "Why?"

"It makes this easier, and faster."

He'd needed to get undressed entirely, she only needed her skirt lifted up and her panties pushed aside. Then, he could *finally* get back to the heaven and home that came with fucking Cara Rossi.

Gian lifted Cara's skirt and turned her in his lap so that her back pressed to his chest. His hand flew between her thighs to feel what belonged to him there. He buried his face into her sweet-smelling curls as he yanked her panties aside, and brought her down on his length without giving her time to prepare for it. He didn't want to wait, he was so fucking tired of waiting after *weeks* of it.

But *shit* … it was worth it. Every hot, slick, tight inch of her sucked him in and held him in place like she wasn't going to let him go. Seated deep in her cunt, Gian could breathe again for the moment.

"Oh, fuck," Cara breathed as she squirmed on his cock in the best way.

"Christ, you're wet. How hot do you get sucking me off?"

"It's not normal."

Her words were a mumble. A hot, airless mumble.

"It is," he said with a chuckle, his fingers tangling into her hair. "Now, you got what you fucking wanted—you made me come. Give me what I want, Cara. Give me what's mine, *mon ange*."

Her pussy. Her orgasms. Her sounds. All of that belonged to him when they were like this.

Every bit of it.

"Just give me a sec—"

Gian tugged firmly on her hair, quieting whatever she was going to say. "Fuck me, Cara. *Now*."

She didn't need to be told again, lifting enough to ride him while he pulled on her hair and kept a hand between her thighs at the same time. He liked the feeling of his cock and her cunt against his fingertips. He could feel everything, from the way she stretched open every time she lowered on to his cock, to the rhythmic pulse of his heart beating in his shaft. All her juices slicked them up, and he wanted to see her clean his fingers off when they were done.

Gian's fingers pressed tighter to her cunt, not quite grabbing it as she fucked him, but firm enough for her to feel it. She grinded her clit into his palm at the same time. "All mine, Cara."

"Yours."

Of course, it was.

He hadn't realized how unhurriedly such a thing could build inside him—such a vindictive, needy, greedy, beautiful thing like love. He'd never been in love before, and when he finally understood that he had been slowly falling in love with Cara, he'd been too stupid and too selfish to stop it. He liked the way it felt, after all, even when it hurt.

So yes, all of her belonged to him.

And he wanted her to know it.

Cara dug through the bag of fast food, pulling out a cheeseburger and fries, and setting her bare feet up on the dashboard. After cleaning up, she'd opted to kick her flats off on the floor of the car.

"Busy couple of weeks?" Gian asked.

She handed him over the bag. "Nothing unusual. Mostly boring."

"That could be considered a good thing."

"It could."

"But?" he pressed.

Cara smiled a bit. "But I missed you, too, so that kind of sucked."

Gian didn't even bother to hide his grin. "Eat, love."

She did, pulling out fries to chew on. Once they were gone, she said, "My mom killed herself, or that's what my brother said."

"Oh."

That felt stupid to say.

Gian didn't know what would be appropriate. An apology felt wrong, considering Cara's feelings regarding her mother. She didn't look entirely sad about it, but she didn't appear to be happy, either.

"Are you going back for the funeral?" he asked.

Cara shook her head.

"Why not?"

"Her death is enough closure for me," Cara admitted under her breath. "I don't need to watch her be buried, too."

"You could have called me."

Gian heard the slight bitterness in his tone, though he wished he could have hidden it better. He didn't want to be angry with Cara for asking that he give her space and time alone. It also wasn't that easy. The longer it had stretched on between them with no word from her, the harder it had become for him to deal with it.

"There was nothing to say," Cara said dryly. "Not about Serena Rossi, anyhow."

"You could have called for—"

Cara glanced over at him, her knowing eyes quieting him instantly. "I wanted to call. Every day. Multiple times a day. Every chance I got. Whenever I looked at my phone. It didn't get easier not to pick it up, but neither did watching the news, seeing shootings and hearing all the problems piling up all over the city. I had choices to make, Gian."

"Like what?"

"Like if I wanted to keep doing this with you. Whether or not I was okay with what that might mean."

He cleared his throat. "And?"

Cara unwrapped her burger. "I'm here, aren't I? I called, didn't I?"

She was.

And she had.

"The only thing that would make this food better is beer," Cara said.

"I could have brought some or picked up a six-pack." Gian set his burger and fries up in his lap. "We couldn't have come out here, though."

Cara shrugged one shoulder. "We'll grab some on the way back to my place."

"Is that the plan?"

"Yep. That's the plan."

"So, we're going to act like everything is good and you didn't run off scared?" he asked.

"We will if you stop bringing it up."

"We *are* going to talk about it, *mon ange*. And other things, too."

She sighed, rolling her pretty blue eyes upward at the same time. "Fine, but we're eating first. Maybe fucking again, too."

"I do love the way you think, Cara."

Her smile was sinful. "I know you do."

"And you."

Cara glanced over at him, her eyes knowing and the silence stretching on. *Now or never*, he thought to himself. If he could feel it, he should be able to verbalize it. How else was she going to know the craziness he constantly felt whenever she was near?

"I love you," he added, quieter.

"I thought we were eating first before all of that."

They would.

Gian nodded at her food. "Eat, but it changes nothing. I said what I said."

She wasn't running this time.

Chapter 13

"What do you want, red or white?" Gian asked, holding up two bottles of wine for Cara to choose between.

"I thought we were grabbing beer?"

"We are, but you like wine more. Which one?"

Cara eyed the two bottles and said, "Which one do you think I'd prefer?"

"The red for tonight. White for a meal."

"Lucky guess."

"Or I pay attention," Gian replied just as fast, slipping the bottle of white wine back on the shelf. "Red wine is good for rich dishes, too, you know."

Cara crossed her arms as she rounded the corner of the aisle, plucking the red wine from Gian's outstretched grasp. "How can you say you love someone when the only thing you've ever done with them is fuck?"

Gian cleared his throat, glancing at a customer in the next aisle who looked their way. A simple glare from him sent the patron heading in another direction, fast. Then, his gaze was back on hers, the intensity pinning her in place.

"You know that's not true," Gian muttered.

"What—that all we do is fuck? It's *very* true."

"Wrong. We do a hell of a lot more than that. I can't help that all of the things we do happen to get mixed up in the fact we like to fuck a lot, Cara."

"Well—"

"So I'll never read to you in bed again, or in the bath, or anywhere else. We won't stay in bed, talking and talking and fucking *talking*, about everything and anything that comes to your mind. I'll act like you don't enjoy being quiet, and that you smile even when you're sleeping. You don't need to tell me shit about your mother and father, or your brother, and never mind even thinking about saying something when it comes to your dead sister. I'll pretend like I don't know shit about what you like, the things you do, or who you want to be when you graduate in a year. And—"

"I get it," Cara interjected softly. "I shouldn't have said that."

"Be more specific."

"I'm being difficult, Gian."

"Clearly," he responded dryly.

"Say it to me again."

"Say what?"

"What you told me in the car earlier."

"That I love you?"

"Yes, that," Cara said.

Gian didn't hesitate. "I love you, Cara."

His inflection didn't change a bit. Neither did his expression. He said those three little words so easily, as though it should be obvious to her, him, and the world that he felt for her in that way. He felt so deeply, so intensely, that he could tell her he loved her privately in a Mercedes, where no one could hear or in a liquor store, where a cashier waited for them to pay and customers milled around.

He said it.

He said it like he meant it.

He said words Cara didn't understand.

Oh, she got the love bit—that she understood well. Too well, probably. She understood that he *did* love her, because she felt that way, too. She felt alone when he wasn't there, she heard his voice in her dreams, and she felt him all around her when he was gone. She missed him constantly, she worried where he was when he wasn't with her, and her best moments had been spent in comfortable silence and sweet whispers with this man.

Of course, she loved him.

It was all the *hows* that made her pause.

It was the *how did this happen* that stopped her from saying it back.

"Why are you staring at me like that?" Gian asked.

"Why don't you ask me to say it back?"

"I don't need you to."

Cara glanced away from the honesty in his gaze. "But you *want* me to."

"That's not what you asked. You asked *why*. I don't need to hear you say something that I already know, Cara. And do you know how I know?"

"I'm listening."

"I know you love me because I can count on one hand the times you've asked me for something, or needed something from me, or wanted *just* me until tonight. I can count on one hand, but I'd only need one finger to do it. Just tonight—that's the only time you've ever taken something from me that you wanted. You called, you wanted me with you, and that says more than anything else you ever say possibly could."

"And why is that?"

She didn't mean to be so goddamn defensive, but it was hard. Her walls were her go-to defense for anything that seemed like it might reach too far inside her emotions or cut her too deeply, when it was all said and done.

Gian was definitely one of those things for Cara.

On both accounts.

"Because you don't need me," Gian said, his tone lowering an octave with the frankness his words took on. "Not in the grand scheme of your life, you really don't. It might fuck you up for a while to send me on my way, but you would come out fine in the end. That's what women like you do, right? You get hurt, brush yourself off, and get on with it—with life. Everybody fails you in one way or another, that's what you've been taught."

"Gian—"

"It's true. Even if they don't mean to, or it's a by-product of someone else's actions, they hurt you. Your parents, your siblings, or friends. And so you prep for the next person you let in to hurt you, too, and when they do, you get to fall, dust it off, and keep going with a few more bruises on your soul."

She almost hated how he saw those things.

She wanted to hate that she had never needed to tell him those things.

"But what's more amazing," Gian continued, "is that you let me in. And that, in some crazy way, you still lower your walls enough to let someone climb over for a time. So here we are, you waiting for me to fuck up, even if I do love you, and even if you do love me, because it always happens, regardless. And you'll be fine when it does—if it does—because that's who you are, Cara Rossi. And we don't get to be anything but exactly who we are."

Cara's exhale felt painful as it rushed out, but with that pain came a sense of relief. "Saves me the trouble of explaining all of that to you."

Gian shrugged. "I never asked for an explanation."

"No, you didn't," she agreed quietly. "Don't you think it's a little sad that you love someone who is just waiting for the other shoe to drop?"

"I think it's sad that the woman I love feels like she has to wait on that at all."

Well, then …

"What about all the shit I don't like?" Cara asked. "The business you do, the things that life has taken from me, and how it hurts me? What if that bitterness I feel and the distrust that's settled deep inside of me never goes away? Doesn't that—in a way—reflect on us? Doesn't that make us doomed?"

"There are a million things that could doom us, Cara," Gian said, stepping forward to stroke her cheek and push a stray curl behind her ear.

She smiled at his touch, feeling that familiar shiver race down her spine at his contact. "You know what else could doom us? That instead of taking that risk with me—jumping off the cliff that scares you—you want to debate how and why I love you inside of a liquor store at ten at night. Because that's what you'll keep doing, about everything, on all the little details about us, instead of just *being*."

Cara frowned. "You don't know that."

"I know you worry about details all the time. Right now, you're worried about the details of us, of something like *love*. That should be the easiest, most honest thing you can feel. And your very nature is to question it, Cara, and to question me."

"I don't *want* to."

"But you do. And you know what, that's okay, too. As long as you *be with me*, I don't care about the rest. I don't care about those details and the nonsense. I don't hear the noise of everyone else telling me what I should or shouldn't be doing with you. I don't give a single fuck about any of that, because I love you. Nothing else matters. The rest will figure itself out on its own. I believe that entirely."

"Why would anyone tell you not to be with me, Gian?"

That time, he was the one to look away.

Cara didn't miss it.

"Like I said, it doesn't matter."

She wondered if it *should*, though.

"Say it, again," Cara demanded.

Gian—once more—didn't hesitate. "I love you, Cara."

It became easier to hear each time he said it.

It became easier to believe.

It became easier to understand.

"I want you to say it back," he told her, "but I don't need you to say it because I want you to. I don't need you to say something that scares you enough to send you running away from me for three weeks, only to call me when you can't take it anymore. I don't need you to justify what I already know, *amore*."

"But?"

"But I do need you to be with me, Cara. That's all."

An older gentleman slipped down the aisle, making Cara move closer to Gian to avoid being bumped into by the guy's shoulder. She didn't mind.

She liked it there.

"I do, though," she said.

"Hmm?"

"Love you, Gian."

His smile grew and he kissed her quickly before pulling her into his side. Heading toward the cash with a six-pack under his arm, and a bottle of wine in her hand, Cara felt … settled. For the first time in weeks, she was okay.

"Now do we go back to pretending like we're good and the last few weeks didn't happen?" Cara asked.

"There's no need to pretend. We're perfect, *mon ange*. We always were."

"In a crazy way, maybe."

"In *our* way," Gian murmured before he kissed the top of her head.

So, maybe loving this man wasn't such a bad thing after all.

Maybe.

"Now, we're going to go to your place, put one of those ugly fucking rom-com things on you like, get drunk, and then fuck tomorrow morning away," he told her as he sat the liquor down on the counter.

The cashier's eyes widened, and her cheeks pinked as she reached for the wine first to ring it through. "Usually, I'm supposed to greet customers, but I'm not sure what to say right now, so excuse me for saying nothing."

Gian flashed the girl a smile. "Just tell me what I owe."

"Thirty-five, twenty-two," the girl said faintly.

Cara couldn't even bother to feel embarrassed as she shook her head. "You are awful, Gian."

"Yes, and you love it."

They did exactly as he said they would—shitty movie, liquor, and all. But even when the morning came, and Cara was sure she was going to die from the way Gian's tongue fucked her senseless, she still wanted to hear him say it.

Again and again.

Over and over.

"Say it again," Cara demanded in a whisper.

Gian's chuckles rocked against her inner thigh, and then higher as his lips kissed a path from her pubic bone to below her right breast. "Again?"

"Again."

"*Ti amo. Je t'aime.* I love you. I can say it in three languages, *donna*, what more do you want?"

Cara wasn't sure what she wanted, really.

Not entirely.

More mornings like this, definitely.

Soft sheets. Sunlight on her face. Gian in her bed.

Was that how love was supposed to go? Cara didn't know.

If it was, she had already been doing *this* with Gian for months.

So why did it feel different now?

Why was it *better*?

"Again?" he asked, hovering over her on the bed.

Cara smiled, pushing up on her elbows to kiss his mouth that tasted like her. "I love you."

Gian smirked. "Again?"

"Always."

Chapter 14

Gian found it was a strange feeling to have so many eyes watching him, waiting on him to speak. Like his words and his direction, was the only thing that mattered. Of course, he'd always been in some sort of position of power, regarding the mafia as an underboss. He always had some sort of control. His direction had always been followed when he had given it.

This didn't feel entirely the same.

This was different, because his word had become law to these men. To them, there was no one above him, no one for them to look at to ensure the direction he was giving, the demands he was making, were the right ones. It was only his word, and his wants, that now mattered.

Before, Gian had not felt the heavy weight of that kind of responsibility on his shoulders where the men of his Cosa Nostra were concerned. He shared that weight between himself, his grandfather, and Edmond. He'd never fully understood how important it was to say the right thing, to make the right choice, the first time.

Maybe he had been spoiled in that way.

"As we expected, Edmond is not backing down," Gian said. "But no one is surprised about that, right?"

None of the men answered, not that he expected them to.

It was their time to listen.

It was his time to talk.

"There's only one thing to do now—push harder, put more pressure on him, on his men, on his territory—where ever the hell we need to, in order to get what we want. None of us should want a street war. As it is, we have too many bodies piling up. We have too much official attention. The police won't leave us alone. The bigger problem is, neither will Edmond. He's not going to back down, and we won't either."

Gian stopped his spiel long enough to take a drink from the server that approached his table. Two fingers of whiskey burned all the way down his throat as he drank it in one fast gulp. He probably should've sipped the drink, as it deserved, but he wasn't in the mood. What he wanted, were quiet streets, compliant men, and Edmond in a grave.

Gian didn't think he was asking for much.

However, if their lives were that simple, then everything would be a hell of a lot cleaner. And as the old saying went, nothing worth having would come easy.

It was his own fault for not being better prepared for this.

Gian only blamed himself for that.

He had spent too much time after Corrado's death, stuck in his own problems, wandering around lost in his own world. Instead of handling the issue that was Edmond from the very beginning, Gian had let it fester. And now what had been a small wound, was a gaping, infected hole, eating away at his *la famiglia*.

"You could always hire someone to finish Edmond, if that's what—"

Gian's gaze cut to the Capo in the corner booth, and the action quieted the man instantly. "Like he did for my grandfather?"

Or, Gian still assumed that had been done by Edmond. He had no reason to believe otherwise, and the fool didn't offer one.

"Well ..."

"Say it. That's what you mean."

The Capo gave a single nod. "Fine, *sì*, that's what I mean, boss. Consider what we might gain by ending it quicker."

"In a coward's way," Gian said slowly. "A way that makes *us* the coward."

"No—"

"*Yes.*"

"He wouldn't be the first to die by the hands of a hired gun," the Capo muttered under his breath.

"You're right, he certainly wouldn't be."

The Capo also had a good point. Killing Edmond by way of a hired man, someone he didn't know and was not expecting, would end everything. Strangely, Gian did not feel okay with making that call, regardless of the positives that could come out of the situation. He felt—in a way—that it would make him no better than Edmond, killing his rival and not giving the man even a chance to properly defend himself.

Had Corrado been given the chance to see his death coming, might it have ended differently? Would his grandfather have made the choice the Capo was suggesting?

Gian didn't have the answers for those questions.

And he wasn't Corrado Guzzi.

He was only himself.

"But the answer is no," Gian said firmly, "so drop it."

The Capo's confirmative reply was enough for Gian to move on, satisfied his point was made.

"This will all be over soon enough," he assured. "Just keep doing what you've been doing. Clearly, someone wanted a war, and now they've got one. Maybe once they realize that they've gotten what they wanted, it won't be as nice, after all."

Despite wanting to get the hell out of the meeting with the men, and get on with his day, Gian ordered lunch and readied himself for more conversation. As an underboss, he had simply needed to check in on the Capos and their dealings to make sure everything was on the up and up. His responsibilities kept him on the move, going from one man to the next, without stopping for very long. As a boss, he was learning it was not quite the same.

He had to talk.

A lot.

He had to listen, too.

It almost made him miss the years before he was a made man, when all he had to do was slam his fist into someone's face to get what he wanted.

Life was not that easy, now.

Frankly, it was better he had learned to tamper his temper. Bosses— good ones—didn't need to use violence as a first resort to get business done. That simply wasn't how Cosa Nostra men behaved. Gian had been lucky enough to get all of the roughness out of his system *before* he earned his button, and it made the transition of becoming a made man easier.

To an extent ...

His phone buzzed in his pocket as the men droned on around him. He almost didn't pick up the call, as all the people who would usually be calling him at that time of day were sitting around the restaurant, waiting on their meals. Cara, the only one who might call him, should have been at university.

When the buzzing persisted, Gian pulled the cell out and checked the screen. The sexy image of Cara shooting him the peace sign and winking lit up the phone. Gian answered the call instantly. He put the phone to his ear as he stood from the table, turning his back to the men and walking away so his conversation couldn't be overheard.

"*Ciao, bonjour.*"

"I saw it again."

Gian tensed. "Saw what, *mon ange?*"

"The car. The *car*, Gian. I saw it again!"

He didn't have a damn clue what she was talking about, but the frantic pitch her tone took on was enough to make him turn back and head for his table again. He grabbed the jacket hanging off the back of the chair, waved Constantino off when the man stood with questioning eyes, and headed for the front of the restaurant.

"Okay, you saw a car, Cara. What car?"

She made a desperate noise that cut him deep, her panic searing through the phone like she was standing right in front of him. She was across the city, but damn it, Gian swore he could feel her fucking fear radiating all the way to him.

He was already out of the restaurant and moving toward his car and waiting enforcer by the time she gained enough of a breath to answer him.

"The *car*! With Chris—that day, Gian. All the noise and the gunfire. The fucking car!"

"Are you sure?"

Gian only asked because Cara insisted she remembered nothing about her drive-by attack, except the pain she felt when she hit the ground. She didn't have distinct memories of what happened leading up to it, and discussing it was an emotionally taxing event.

"Yes," Cara hissed. "I saw it and *I knew*."

Now they were getting somewhere.

"Where are you right now?" he asked.

"At the café I like. I wanted a snack before my next class."

"Can you stay there?"

"I'm not leaving!"

Her screech almost made his ear bleed.

"I'm twenty minutes away, Cara. Get something to drink, I'll be there by the time you're done."

"Okay."

Fuck.

He wished she didn't sound so frightened and panicked. He knew she had a lot of baggage regarding the drive-by simply because it reminded her of Lea, and of that event. Her memories of her attack were clouded with the ones she had of Lea's, and even trying to talk about it put Cara in a bad place. That—and only that—was the reason why Gian didn't push.

Gian scrubbed a hand down his face. "It's fine. It'll all be fine, *bella*."

"Hurry," she mumbled.

"Already on my way. Try to relax."

Easier said than done, he knew.

Gian said goodbye, and slipped his phone into his pocket as he took the keys to his car from the enforcer. He did not leave his car unattended after the bomb incident. "Follow me in your own car."

Chris nodded. "Got it, boss."

Gian broke at least a dozen traffic laws, but he cut the twenty-minute drive in half. He couldn't find a place to park, so he simply yanked his car over to the side of the road right in front of the café windows, ignoring the horns honking behind him.

Cara flew out of the café damn near to the second Gian cut the engine, and jumped into the vehicle without even looking over her shoulder once. He pulled the car back onto the road, much to the chagrin of the other drivers he had cut off, and hit the gas hard.

"I thought it was going to happen again," Cara whispered in the passenger seat.

"It's not going to happen again. Tell me what you saw."

"The car."

"Yeah, I got that. I need a bit more info to go on, though."

Cara let out a hard breath and ran her fingers through her hair. "I don't even know how I forgot that was the car—it's so fucking *yellow*."

Immediately, Gian hit the brakes and pulled the car into the nearest parking lot. "Say that again."

"What?"

"The color of the car."

"Yellow?"

Gian nodded. "You're sure that's what it was."

Cara blinked. "It was yellow. I see cars all the damn time, but not one like *that*."

"All right."

Gian cut the engine and got out of his vehicle, rounding the side to open Cara's door. She simply stared up at him, unsure of what she was supposed to do. Chris had pulled up behind them, his car still running and waiting.

"Come on, get out," Gian said, holding his hand for Cara to take.

"Why?"

"I have some business to handle, now."

"Do you know who owns the car?"

"I know who owns a *yellow* car," Gian replied unfazed. It was an odd color to have, especially in their business, when the intention was *not* to draw attention. "And that's not for you to worry about."

Chris had finally exited his own vehicle as Gian managed to convince Cara to get out of his car. He nodded to the man, and urged his lover toward the enforcer with a smile that was entirely forced.

Because inside?

Yeah, there he was *pissed*.

"Chris will take you to my penthouse for the evening," Gian said. "I will be home later."

Cara glanced over her shoulder at him. "Will you?"

"Of course."

After he hurt somebody.

Louis Portella.

Gian repeated the name as he tugged his driving gloves at the wrists, making sure they were snug against his skin. He watched the twenty-three-year-old solider, Edmond's grandson, stroll out of a strip joint with a grin on his face and not a fucking care in the world.

He figured he ought to let the guy have his happy moment. Shortly, there would be absolutely nothing for the guy to be happy about.

Quickly, Gian stepped out of his car, keeping the engine running. He hit the button on the fob to unlatch the trunk as he pulled his tie free from around his neck at the same time. Crossing the small parking lot without missing a beat, Gian came up behind Louis before the guy even knew what was happening.

Gian had already checked the place out while Louis was inside, enjoying the entertainment. The only camera was located directly in front of the business. None were set off to the side, where the cars were parked. He chose to strike now, because the lot was empty, and he didn't know where Louis was heading next.

Time was always of the essence.

Gian used his tie to wrap around Louis's neck, pulled it tight, and forced the man to the ground. Effectively cutting off the man's airways and his ability to shout for help, Gian pulled the fool back across the lot toward his waiting trunk.

A single, hard kick to Louis's face stopped the man's fighting. Dead weight was a bit harder to pull along, but Gian didn't mind. It was easier to stuff an unconscious man into the trunk of a car, rather than a conscious, fighting one.

Blood trickled out of Louis's nose and mouth, staining the gray interior of the trunk. Gian made a disgusted noise at the sight, knowing he'd have to send his car in to have the interior ripped out and changed, before he slammed the trunk closed.

A half hour later, Gian used the barrel of his gun to poke Louis in the forehead to wake the man up. It took a whole minute for the guy to gain enough bearings to realize he was sitting in a junk yard, inside a beat-up Toyota. Louis yelled for a good two minutes, and Gian let him, knowing no one was coming to help.

It benefitted Gian greatly to know people who knew people.

Like a man who owned a junk yard.

"Didn't your grandfather ever tell you it was a stupid idea to buy a yellow Camaro?" Gian asked.

Louis blinked. "W-what?"

"Your car. The color. It's fucking ostentatious. You can't miss it driving by. It might as well be screaming at you to look at it."

"My c-car."

Gian poked the guy in the forehead with the barrel of the gun again, harder the second time. "That's what I said, dipshit. Pay attention."

Louis tried to move away from Gian, but he didn't get more than a couple of inches in the shitty, worn-down driver's seat. After all, Gian had tied the bastard's hands to the steering wheel, and his legs to the gas and brake pedals.

"What the hell?" Louis asked, yanking on the restraints.

"It's easier when you can't run," Gian explained. "Now, about your car."

"Fuck you."

"Stupid boy."

Gian cocked back the hammer on his gun, aimed, and pulled the trigger. A single shot plugged into Louis's knee, blood splattering over the car and out the door. Gian didn't bother to move when the blood flew, simply stayed like he was and let it stain his suit. It would have to go after tonight, anyway.

Louis's shouts of pain made Gian smile a bit.

"You can keep yelling, but the owner has stepped out for a while to grab some late night snacks," Gian lied.

The truth was, the owner of the junk and crushing yard was waiting in his office for when Gian drove out of the lot. The man would then pick up his payment, left in the usual spot, and junk the Toyota by crushing it with a hundred other vehicles that night without so much as looking inside.

"Now answer me," Gian continued. "Didn't Edmond tell you that color was a bad choice for a car?"

Louis nodded.

"Of course, he did. I remember him bitching about it shortly before Corrado died." Gian chuckled. "Pretty sure he threatened to *junk* it, when you weren't home one weekend."

Louis cleared his throat, water in his gaze.

For the most part, the man hid his pain well.

"When did Edmond order you to do the drive-by on Cara and my enforcer?"

"He didn't—"

"Don't try lying," Gian interrupted swiftly. "It was pure fucking luck that nobody saw your yellow piece of shit that day, and nothing more. The problem is, somebody *did* see it. She only happened to remember it today.

Lying makes this last longer, man. See how that works?"

"He told me to use another car," Louis said hoarsely. "I couldn't get my hands on one."

"Stupid."

The man nodded, his silent agreement.

"Why Cara?" Gian asked.

"She was a means to an end."

"The end being what, exactly?"

"He wanted to get you to fall in line," Louis said. "You weren't following the fucking rules, okay? He said taking something away from you might put you back in your place."

Edmond had a lot to learn about Gian, but he saved that lesson for another day.

"Tell me about the bomb, and Corrado," Gian urged.

Louis's brow furrowed. "What?"

"The bomb on my car. The murder of my grandfather. This isn't fucking rocket science."

"I didn't do those things."

"I didn't say *you* did them. I want you to tell me what you know about them."

"Nothing," Louis said quickly. "I know nothing."

"I fucking told you not to lie." Gian sighed, already readying and aiming his gun for Louis's other kneecap. "You had to make this hard—"

"I'm not lying! I swear, I swear I'm not fucking lying!"

Gian barely held back from plugging the asshole with another bullet. "Why in the hell should I believe you?"

"I'm going to die, anyway," Louis mumbled, his gaze never leaving the gun in Gian's hand. "What good does lying do for me now?"

He had a point.

"So you know nothing about those two events," Gian said, wanting to clarify.

"Because my grandfather didn't do them," Louis replied.

"You don't know that for sure."

"I know Edmond said he would have had Corrado shot from behind, so at least the funeral could have been an open casket."

Gian clenched his teeth so hard at that admission that his molars ached. "Did he now?"

"He didn't need to kill Corrado. He was already *dying*."

"How the fuck do you know that?"

"I didn't know—my grandfather did. Edmond told me *after*. Why kill a man that's already got one foot in the grave, huh?"

Gian didn't have the answer for that one.

And he was done with this conversation, now.

Standing, Gian brushed off his pants. Louis looked up at him in enough time to see Gian's gun pointed directly at his head.

Always look at a man when you take his life.

Corrado's words echoed in Gian's mind.

He deserves that respect.

Gian pulled the trigger, and didn't look away.

Chapter 15

Cara woke with a start, jerking upward on the couch at the sound of a door slamming shut somewhere in the penthouse. She scrubbed her eyes with the back of one hand as she went in search of the cause of the noise. Soon, she had narrowed it down to a bathroom, as the sound of water ran heavily behind the door. She assumed it was Gian, because he should have been back by now, and Chris had not followed her into the penthouse when he'd delivered her there earlier.

"Gian?" she called, rapping her knuckles to the white wood.

"Sorry, *ma chérie*. I didn't mean to wake you. Head into bed, I'll be there in a minute."

She knocked again, instead. "It's like one in the morning, Gian."

"Yes, I'm aware."

"Open the door."

A heavy sigh followed the request, but she heard the latch on the door unlock. Cara opened the door herself, stepping in to find Gian stripped down to his boxer-briefs as he scrubbed a bar of soap up and down his arms with forceful strokes. Bloodstained clothes rested at his feet, forgotten beside a waiting trash bag.

Gian picked up a cigarette from the counter, and took a drag, exhaling thick, white smoke to the ceiling. That was a new thing.

"Since when do you smoke?" Cara asked.

"Not very fucking often, that's when."

Gian continued his work like Cara wasn't even in the room, dragging the bar of soap against his fingernails until he seemed pleased that it had done its job. On the counter beside his burning cigarette, a Berretta sat dismantled, as though it too were waiting to be cleaned.

He was almost mindless in his task, barely paying her any attention. Scrub, wash, dry. Scrub, wash, dry. He scrubbed parts of his body that Cara was sure had nothing on them. Occasionally, he'd glance into the mirror for a moment, or lift up his burning cigarette for another drag, but then he was right back at his task once more.

Cara had a million and one questions to ask. The part of her that hated these sights, and knew good and well what they meant, wanted to demand answers so she could confirm what she already understood.

The bigger part of her that loved Gian, didn't say a thing. It was a choice she had to make. So she made it. Cara found it surprising, how easy it was to make that choice.

"Do you need something?" Cara asked.

"Not at the moment, sweetheart."

"Okay."

Cara turned to leave the bathroom, deciding it was best for them both if she left him alone to do his business. She didn't need to be there to see it, and she didn't think he needed her there, watching him like a bug under a microscope. Plus, the longer she stayed there, the more curious she became and was liable to start asking questions she knew better than to ask.

Neither of them needed that.

"Wait," Gian said quickly, "there is something."

Cara spun around to face him slowly. Gian had rinsed all the soap off his arms again, and was now patting them dry with a towel that he dropped onto the pile of bloody clothes once he finished with it.

"What is it?" Cara asked.

"Remember when I promised you that we would do that trip to Quebec again sometime?"

"Yes."

"I was thinking I could extend it a couple days, if you don't mind taking a couple of days off school. You head out tomorrow, and come back Sunday evening."

Cara's gaze narrowed, as she was not a stupid woman, and she had *not* missed how he posed his words carefully. "*Me.*"

Gian stood firm, his gaze never wavering from hers. "*Only* you, Cara."

"No."

"Chris would be happy to accompany—"

"Gian, that was supposed to be a trip for *us*, not just me. And *no*, I am not taking someone else—especially not another man—on it with me!"

"Technically, it was a trip for your birthday. So *oui*, it was only for you. I was going to tag along."

"You're playing word games to distract me from what you're not saying."

Gian's expression hardened as he replied, "Fine, then I'll say what I mean. It would be best if you got out of the city for the remainder of the week and weekend. It will give me one less thing to worry about, as I do some digging into some people and business that I should have done a long time ago."

"I'm not going anywhere, Gian."

"Cara, now—"

"The answer is no."

"Fuck, you are stubborn when you want to be," Gian grunted under his breath. He turned back to the sink, going back to his task as though that would get him back on track, and Cara's refusals didn't matter. She had news for him. "Don't force my hand here, *bella.*"

She stuck her hands to her hips, determined to make him hear her. "You can't order me around from place to place."

"Can't, *mon ange? Can't?*"

"That's what I said."

"That's the wrong word, Cara. I can *do* whatever the hell I please, so long as you are safe and comfortable while I do it. Nobody said you had to be happy about it, though."

"Then what's the right word, your fucking highness?"

Gian's brow dipped in his irritation, his dark gaze flashing over to her in warning. "Won't, Cara. I *won't* do something you ask me not to. See the difference?"

"I see you being an asshole."

Before Cara had even blinked, Gian pushed away from the counter and came for her. His hand caught her around the back of her neck, he pulled her close, and his mouth came crashing down on hers in a fast kiss that seared her from the inside out. It took her fucking breath away, all the languid strokes of his tongue against hers, and the way his fingers tightened to hold her still. He didn't let her move away, even when he stopped kissing her.

"Stop being difficult," he murmured against her lips.

Cara let out a shaky exhale. "I'm not going anywhere that you're not going, Gian."

"I love you, Cara, but you're killing me."

"You don't really want me to go anywhere, either."

"I want you *safe.*"

"With you," she said, kissing him quickly, "I'm sure I will be."

"Chris," Cara greeted as the man held open the restaurant door for her. "Thank you."

"Very welcome. Have a good dinner, miss."

He still wouldn't call her by her name, no matter how many times she insisted. She figured she could break him of the habit, eventually.

Gian was waiting for Cara beyond the entrance of the restaurant, his sharp, black suit making her gaze travel over his fit form to appreciate the sight of him standing there like he was. With his hands clasped at his back, and his stare focused on something inside the restaurant, he seemed almost relaxed.

Cara knew that he couldn't possibly be as calm as he appeared on the outside. Gian's mind always ran a million miles a minute, and with the problems he had been having lately, she was sure that only made it worse.

Yet, there he stood. Like a fucking rock in a hurricane. Refusing to move or be moved. Unflinchingly calm in the eye of a storm. Always strong.

Cara wondered if this man knew his strength, or the power he wielded because of it. She was positive that if *anything* made Gian a formidable threat to the men in his business, it was this right here.

"Something caught your eye?" Cara dared to ask as she approached.

Gian's head turned, his lips tugging into a sexy grin as his gaze landed on her sapphire-blue, body-con dress. He didn't hide his wandering gaze, making Cara smile and her cheeks heat up. "Something certainly has now, my beautiful girl. How was your day?"

"Long, but I got through it."

"Chris wasn't too pushy when he showed up to bring you to dinner, was he?"

"Chris is always pushy," Cara joked, "but I blame that on his very impatient boss."

Gian winked, his arm curving around her side as his hand laid flat to her lower back, above the swell of her ass. "He's paid very well to put up with me, trust in that."

"I'm sure. Have you ordered?"

"We have, yes."

Cara's brow furrowed. "We?"

As far as she had been told, this was supposed to be a dinner for only her and Gian, no one else. She certainly hadn't expected guests to be included, too.

Gian bent down to kiss her forehead, his fingers pressing lightly to her back to urge her to walk forward. "Seems I wasn't the only one who made reservations here, tonight. They suggested we merge the tables, and I didn't want to be rude."

"Like you give a shit about being rude."

He chuckled. "For some people, I do."

"Well, who is it?"

"Constantino and Stephan, actually."

Cara didn't bother to hide her discontent.

Gian only laughed harder. "We'll be gone before you know it, and I know you were told to pack a bag to stay with me tonight at the penthouse, so stop moping."

"I'm not *moping*."

"What would you call that frown, then?"

Cara eyed him from the side as she said, "A displeased smile."

"Nice try. Don't mope, love. It's not a good look on you."

"I wanted you to myself *all* night. I'm not asking for a lot."

Gian pulled her impossibly closer. "I'll make up for it, but if you insist on that moping of yours, I'll be forced to take whatever action necessary to put an end to it."

"Including having dinner alone?"

"I told you, it would be rude."

"Then, how—"

"I do own this place, and there's a lovely private office in the back. Private in the way that no one can see inside, but they can certainly *hear* a lot."

Cara's body heated instantly. "Stop that."

"I've given you fair warning. Stop the moping. Fix your face, beautiful."

She shot him a playful glare before plastering on a smile that made Gian nod in approval. She had done it just in time, too, as they rounded a half-partition wall to come to a stop at what would be their table.

Constantino and Stephan—a man she hadn't seen since that night months ago, at the club with Bambi—sat chatting together, seemingly unaware that Cara and Gian had arrived. They only took notice when Gian pulled out Cara's chair, and then pushed her in closer to the table.

"Evening, cousin," Constantino greeted.

"Constantino," Cara replied.

Stephan only nodded at Cara before going back to his conversation with Constantino, like she wasn't even at the table. Cara didn't mind, really.

Gian's fingers stoked Cara's thigh under the table after he too had taken his seat, though his hand never wandered higher. No, he simply continued his light, teasing touches, reminding her of his earlier threat to make her smile, if needed.

The *bastard*.

God, she loved this man.

"The food should be here soon, if you want to wash up or anything," Gian told her.

Cara nodded, thinking she should do just that. Chris hadn't given her much time to do anything except throw on something appropriate after she'd arrived home from classes. "I'll be quick."

"Bathrooms are toward the back, *bella*."

A quick kiss later, that was all but ignored by the other men at the table, and Cara headed for the bathrooms. She made fast work of washing up her hands, and did a check of her little bit of makeup in the mirror, finding her lipstick, eyeliner, and mascara had held up remarkably well throughout the day. She fluffed her curls with her fingers, resetting some of the waves, and headed back out to the table.

She nearly rammed into a familiar man as she rounded the hallway corner leading back out onto the restaurant's main floor. For a brief second, as she apologized out of habit for not paying attention, she hoped he wouldn't recognize her.

She knew that was a foolish wish.

Of course, Frankie would recognize her face. Her features were a perfect match to her dead twin's. And from what information she had gathered from Gian and Lea's online, private journals, the two had been involved for quite a while. It still made her a bit uncomfortable, given the circumstances of their relationship, but Cara was now sadder about it, more than anything else.

She wished Lea had told her.

"Cara," Frankie said, taking a wide step back.

"Frankie."

He shifted from foot to foot, shooting a glance over his shoulder before looking back to her. Nervousness wrote heavily all over his actions.

Cara cleared her throat, waving toward the semi-private area. "I should get back to my table."

"Sure, but first, uh … could I apologize?"

"For what?"

Frankie shrugged one shoulder. "A while back—at the club when you showed up. I probably came across as rude, and that wasn't my intention. You shocked me, and your face, it really took me off-guard. I'd seen you from afar before, with Lea, but never up close like that. When she said identical, she meant that quite literally, I guess."

He offered her a tentative smile that Cara returned. "It's okay."

"It's not, Cara. I am sorry."

She nodded quickly. "Thank you."

"How are you?" he asked, posing the question with a careful tone. "Don't feel like you have to tell me, if you don't want to. You certainly don't owe me anything, but in a way, I feel like I might know you. She talked about you often, even though we tried to be casual and keep the personal shit out of it all."

"She's doing well," came a deep voice from behind Frankie.

Cara's gaze flew to Gian, who had clearly come looking for her, and she smiled a bit wider. "I am. I'm doing a lot better now."

Frankie murmured something fast in Italian to Gian, who shrugged in response, as though he hadn't a care in the world.

"All is fine," he assured Frankie. "As long as she says so."

"It is," Cara said. "Thank you again, Frankie."

Gian side-stepped the man as Frankie headed down the hall toward the men's bathroom. "I need to make a call, Cara. Can you find your way back to the table without running into someone else?"

She laughed at his teasing. "I'm sure I can."

"All right, get going. The food is waiting."

He dropped a kiss to her forehead before he headed down the hallway, bypassing the bathrooms altogether and exiting through a back door into what looked like an alleyway.

Cara wasn't all that interested in sharing a table with her cousin and Stephan while Gian was gone, but she sat back down with a smile and surveyed the pasta and salad dish that had been set out for her.

"What the hell took so long?" Constantino asked.

"And where's Gian?" Stephan added.

"I had a conversation with someone," Cara replied, "and Gian is making a phone call."

"Who?"

Cara glanced at her cousin. "Pardon?"

"Who were you talking to?"

Jesus.

Why were people so nosy?

"I ran into Frankie coming out of the back," she said, offering little else. Constantino should know enough to know who Frankie was—or had been—to Lea.

Constantino made a noise that sounded unpleasant under his breath.

Stephan shot his friend a look. "Relax, man."

"These *donnas* make it fucking hard," Constantino muttered. "First the one, now the other. It's a damn shame, like they don't even care how they look or how they're making the rest of us look."

"I beg your pardon?" Cara asked sharply.

Constantino paid her no mind, still going on to Stephan in his way. "You know what I mean, Stephan. You're not quiet about what you do running around with that girl of yours, but at least Lea had the fucking decency to keep out of sight when she was with Frankie, for the most part. This isn't any different, no matter what anybody says."

"*Constantino*," Cara snapped.

Her cousin's gaze cut to hers. "What?"

She wasn't entirely sure what Constantino was going on about, but she certainly didn't fucking like it. She definitely wasn't going to sit back and let him compare her relationship with Gian to the one Lea had been involved with, where Frankie was concerned. She didn't see how the two *could* possibly compare. It was like apples and oranges.

"If you have something to say to me, then say it," she told her cousin. "But keep in mind, your opinion of me, my business, and what or *who* I choose to do are none of your fucking concern."

Constantino rolled his eyes. "That's exactly the fucking problem. You don't care that everyone else is looking at what you're doing, and seeing it for exactly what it is, Cara. Playing a man's whore, nothing else. It's shameful."

Cara felt like he had slapped her. "Why am I playing any man's whore? Because I'm not like every other *principessa della mafia*, getting married the first chance I can, and making sure every little fucking thing I do is approved by a man in my family? Is that why? You know what, don't bother answering."

She stood from the table, already done and wanting to get the hell out of there. She could take a fucking cab home, for all she cared. She wouldn't, however, be sitting there for another second longer.

"Go fuck yourself," she told Constantino before leaving.

Chapter 16

The first thing Gian noticed when he returned to the table was that Cara was absent. Right off the bat, that put him on edge. Constantino ate his food with heavy forkfuls, as though he didn't have a problem, while Stephan picked at his plate and chatted away on his cell phone.

"Where's Cara?" Gian asked.

He didn't even bother to sit down.

Constantino shrugged. "She left."

"Say that again."

It didn't even come out as a question.

His friend let out a heavy sigh, dropping his fork to his plate with a loud clatter. "I said, she left, Gian."

Gian reached for the cell phone in his suit jacket, but hesitated before pulling it out. "And why the hell would she leave, exactly?"

Constantino made a dismissive noise under his breath, going back to his meal. "She didn't like what she was told, I suppose."

What. The. Fuck.

Gian sincerely hoped this was not another incident like he'd had with Constantino at the hospital, but it was looking worse and worse by the second. "I'm going to give you ten seconds to explain what in the fuck that means before I drag your ass out of this restaurant and beat you fucking senseless."

Made men didn't fight.

It was a rule.

Gian no longer cared for that particular rule.

Especially not when Cara was involved.

Stephan cleared his throat, dragging Gian's attention to him for the moment. The man quickly said goodbye to whoever he was speaking to on his cell phone, hung it up, and put it in his pocket. Standing from the table, Stephan dropped his napkin down and pulled money from his wallet, letting it fall by his glass of water.

"And where are you going?" Gian asked.

Stephan jerked his head in Constantino's direction. "As much as I like this stupid fuck, sometimes he goes too far."

"Hey—"

"You do," Stephan interrupted Constantino. "There are things you need to *not* talk about, or give your opinion, and a guy's girl is one of them."

"Is that where you stand on the line for this?" Constantino asked.

Stephan nodded sharply. "You're damn right it is. Call me when you get yourself straightened out, Constantino. And make sure you *apologize*. Even if it is Gian."

Gian let that barely-hidden insult brush off his shoulders, but only because he had one fucking idiot to deal with for the moment, and he wasn't in the mood to handle two. Besides, Stephan never made an effort to hide his dislike of Gian, in the grand scheme of things. Constantino, on the other hand, had been doing some pretty underhanded shit that left Gian fucking unsettled.

Like whatever *this* was.

"*My* apologies," Stephan said as he passed Gian by to leave.

Gian let him go, never budging an inch, even when Constantino went back to eating his food again. That only irritated the shit out of Gian more.

"Sit, eat," Constantino demanded. "We'll talk this out. I fucked up, big deal. It happens."

Gian didn't sit. "How did you fuck up, though?"

"She mentioned running into Frankie." Constantino waved a hand as if to dismiss what he was about to say next. "I might have mentioned that it doesn't look good on our family to have her running around with you, doing what she's doing, like she is. Just like it didn't look good when Lea was involved with Frankie a while back."

Gian bristled all over. "And you think this is even remotely the same?"

Constantino, stone-faced and dry-toned, said, "It's exactly the same."

"You're wrong."

"No, I'm not, *and* I'm within my rights to say so, if I want to. She's a woman of *my* family, regardless of where her brother is. So, who gives a shit if her father is dead, and her brother is too busy finishing out a war in Chicago to look after his sister's business? I'll speak for them—what you've done with my cousin is a fucking *shame*, Gian."

"You're way out of line," Gian murmured, forcing himself to keep his tone level.

"You know I'm not. Fact is, Cara is now good for what you've used her for, and very little fucking else, man. That's the sad part. Nobody else will ever look at her and think, shit, wife material or anything of the sort. You've ruined that, and I don't even think she *knows*."

"Constantino, I warned you once, didn't I? I warned you—friends or not—I would fucking hurt you, if you spoke badly about Cara again."

Constantino dropped his fork again, standing from the table and moving to stand toe-to-toe with Gian. Neither man moved a muscle, neither looking away from the other. It took every ounce of willpower Gian had left in his body to keep his hands down at his sides, clenched into tight fists he was ready to throw.

"What's worse, Gian, is when you are boss at the end of all this, when it's all said and done, she won't matter. Not for more than what you've already used her for, and maybe even for less. She won't be *allowed* to matter. No whore—"

Gian was pretty fucking sure he broke a knuckle on impact of punching Constantino in his ignorant, disrespectful fucking face. He barely felt the pain, and since he felt like one punch wasn't good enough, he landed another two, back-to-back, sending his friend sprawling to the floor of the restaurant.

Constantino wasn't knocked out, but he was pretty damn close. Gian figured that had been enough to make his point—he didn't need to do more, not when the guy was now bleeding and groaning on his back like an idiot.

Gian checked his knuckle.

Not broken.

Dislocated.

He gritted his teeth, and reset the knuckle as he heard a server approach from behind. With a single wave, the server retreated. One of the many benefits of owning the place, he supposed.

Bending down, Gian turned Constantino's head to make the man look at him. "I warned you, man. I won't be doing it again. We're done. You mean less than shit to me at this point. And unless you pull your head out of your fucking ass and work out a damn good apology for this one, you're going to remain that way. It doesn't matter to me, one way or the other."

Constantino laughed hoarsely. "Just tell her the truth, Gian. See what *she* says."

"There's nothing to tell."

Gian knocked on Cara's apartment door, ignoring the pain that bloomed in his swollen, bruised knuckle. She hadn't answered his calls as he'd left the restaurant, or the ones that he'd made on the drive over. A quick check with Chris, who had been designated to follow Cara for safety reasons again, had confirmed that she was at home.

Chris didn't have more information to offer, though.

"Cara, open the door," Gian said quietly. "I know you're here, *mon ange.*"

Silence answered him back. He understood why. It still hurt like hell. He'd take ten dislocated knuckles over her rejection. Funny, how love worked that way.

Gian knocked again. *"Cara."*

"Did you know that in Italian, *cara* means dear?"

Her quiet question filled him with a sense of relief. She hadn't opened the door, but it was a start. Gian would take it.

"Of course, I know," Gian said. *"Mia bella cara, amore."*

He heard the lock unlatch on the door a second before Cara slowly pulled it open. She stood on the other side, the apartment's darkness shadowing her in the hallway light. She had lost the dress from earlier, and the heels, too. Clean-faced, any makeup had been removed, and she'd tossed her wild hair up into a messy bun. An over-sized T-shirt fell at her mid-thigh, and she looked ready for bed.

"I'm sorry I left without at least waiting for you," she said, crossing her arms under her breasts and staring off to the side. "I got angry and I only wanted to leave. So I did."

"It's fine."

Or, it was now.

Gian understood *why*. He had simply reacted in a different way than Cara had, perhaps a less than proper way, considering his status. Even Cara had walked away when she was offended, Gian had definitely not.

"I'm sorry for whatever it was that Constantino said to you," Gian said. "He has no business putting his opinions in where they're neither wanted, nor warranted. And trust that he absolutely knows that, now."

Cara nodded. "Sure."

"You don't sound sure, sweetheart."

She looked up at him, sadness coloring her blue eyes. "Did he have a point, though?"

"No, absolutely not."

"Really? Because if he feels the need to say that running around with you looks bad on me, and if my uncle felt the need to warn me away from you, then why not think something *is* wrong with it? And what is it that's so wrong? I don't understand. I'm not doing anything wrong, am I?"

"No," Gian rushed to say. "There's nothing wrong with this—with *us*. There never has been. Some people have their opinions because they're stuck in a different time, with different rules. Women should do as they're told, as they're expected to do, and not what they want to do. I'm not of that mindset, Cara."

She frowned.

Her sadness hurt him as badly as her silence.

"And who the fuck cares about those people, anyway?" Gian asked. "I sure as hell don't. I only concern myself with what you think and feel, not them. They get no say in this or us. None at all."

"Then why did I let what someone else thought bother me so fucking much?"

"Because you're allowed to have feelings, Cara. You're allowed to demand respect from other human beings. No one has any right to make you feel less than them, especially when they don't know who you are in your heart. They don't know you. Not like I do."

"You really do know the right things to say."

"I say the truth, love."

Gian stepped forward, opening his arms to test the waters. Cara gave him one of her small, sweet smiles before letting him wrap her in his embrace. Slowly, he walked her backward enough that he could kick the door closed behind him. Tangling his hand into her soft curls, he tilted her head back far enough to steal a kiss from her pretty mouth.

"Anyone who even thinks to breathe a bad word about you in my direction deserves every fucking thing they get," Gian told her, his calm voice belying his inner rage that had finally simmered a bit. "You're mine, Cara. I love you. Nothing else matters."

It was shocking to him in that moment how savage and brutal his love could be. That, without care or consideration, he would willingly and happily hurt someone he thought of as a friend simply because they had hurt *her*. The possessiveness that nearly always filled him whenever Cara was too far away was suddenly settled when she was in his arms, and his restlessness finally drifted away when he could touch her again.

This wasn't wrong.

He wasn't going to let her, or anyone else, say otherwise.

"Fuck," Gian snarled, pulling his mouth away from Cara's as she laughed. "I'm going to kill whoever that is."

"No, you won't."

The persistent knocking on her apartment door had effectively cockblocked him in the worst way. He had *just* gotten her out of bed, and ready to sit down and eat something—a feat in itself, where Cara and mornings were concerned. He thought a nice fuck on the kitchen table would be a reward for his good deed before breakfast, but apparently, that wasn't going to be the case.

Cara pushed Gian away, and jumped off the table, pulling the oversized shirt down her thighs a bit more. "It's probably Chris."

Gian's gaze narrowed. "You don't know that."

"No one else visits me. And I know he's trailing me again. You're not as smooth as you think, Gian."

"Never mind, you." He swatted her ass with a firm pat, sending her flying into the living room with a giggle. "Cover up with something. You're indecent."

"You pulled me out of bed this way!"

"Yes, *for me*. Not for the neighbors."

Cara stuck her tongue out at him, but still pulled an afghan blanket over her lower half as Gian headed for the door. A quick check through the peephole confirmed Cara's theory. Chris waited behind the door, his gaze trained on something down the hall.

Gian pulled it open with a scowl. "Do you not know how to use a fucking phone, or what?"

Chris barely blinked in the face of Gian's rage. "Did I interrupt your morning—"

"Finish that statement."

The enforcer grinned instead.

The fucker.

"What do you want?" Gian demanded.

Chris held up the item in his hands; a brown box, taped across the top, though the tape had been sliced through and it looked as though it had been opened. "This was delivered to me this morning by a friend, of sorts."

Gian eyed the box. "What friend?"

"One of Edmond's enforcers that knew I was more likely to question him first, before shooting. I suspect that's why the old fucker sent him over."

Well, then.

Gian took the box, looking over the cut tape again. "Why did you open it, if you were told it was meant for me?"

"One bomb is quite enough for you, don't you think?" Chris asked quietly. "I didn't go through the contents, only cut and opened to make sure nothing was waiting to go boom."

Gian wasn't the least bit surprised that Chris had chosen to take the risk of opening the box himself before handing it over to his boss. It was that length of loyalty that made Gian appreciate the man even more.

"Thank you," Gian said.

Chris nodded once. "And I am sorry about, you know, interrupting. If

I did."

Gian scowled again. "Yeah, you did."

"Sorry, boss."

"Don't worry about it."

With a quick goodbye, Gian closed the door on his man, and headed back for the table. Cara seemed distracted by whatever was on the television, and Gian used that time to his advantage. He pulled open the top of the brown box—no bigger than a shoebox—and emptied out the contents. A small memory card rested on top of a tablet, and photographs fell across the table.

A small, hand-written note fell out last.

A gift, it read. *This has gone on long enough, Gian. Here is what you've been looking for, and it's time to end the rest. —Edmond*

Gian's gaze scoured the photos first.

Constantino.

A man Gian didn't recognize.

He distinguished quickly enough from the images that a trade of sorts was happening—money exchanged hands in the darkness of an alley, and that was it. A few other pictures, taken in the daylight, showed Constantino having multiple meetups with several younger Capos, and even a few of the older ones.

That might not have been such a bad thing, but it unsettled Gian. It bothered him because Constantino had no reason—no business—to be running between Capo to Capo, not when he had his own territory and crew to manage. The dates on the photographs showed Gian that all of those meets had happened *before* Corrado's murder.

Gian glanced over at the couch, seeing Cara was still lost in the television. He plugged the memory card into the side of the tablet and turned it on. He put the volume on low as he scrolled through the images and the one video that loaded from the card. More photos of Constantino showed up, although these showcased him visiting *Edmond*.

Gian tensed all over as he pressed play on the one video the card held.

A video of Claud Rossi lit up the screen, taken off to the side, slightly grainy, but still distinctive enough for Gian to discern who was in the room with Constantino's father. Edmond, and Matthew, the new *boss's* consigliere.

"He's gotten himself mixed up in some kind of shit this time," Claud said.

"Do tell," Edmond urged.

"I think Constantino's found himself over his head. Maybe he overheard me talking to my wife that the boss seemed unwell, or something. He jumped off my radar a lot more often than he usually does, and I took notice."

"Me, too," Edmond said. "Or rather, he was close to Gian. I needed to keep an eye on everyone close to him for a while."

"I didn't want to speculate."

"But you *did*."

"I can't have my son hiding things from me in this business, not in this life of ours," Claud muttered heavily. "It makes for dangerous things. I followed him, sometimes, and noticed he was trailing Gian some days, others he was off on his own. I started looking around, asking some questions to the men in the crew. A few pointed me in the direction of the kind of business Constantino had been asking about."

"What kind of business?"

"A hired man."

Gian's chest tightened painfully at what he was hearing. He didn't want to believe it, but certain things—his old friend's behaviors over the last few months—had left him with a bitter taste in his mouth.

"That's not all, though," Edmond said. "After Corrado, I was having a lot of the men watched, because everybody knew that kill came from the inside. I wanted to know *who*. I owed it to Corrado because, like him, I didn't see it coming until it was too late."

Claud shifted on his chair. "And what did you find, boss?"

"He had the bomb planted on Gian's car. I got photos of the meets and the payment exchanging hands. It speaks for itself."

"Gian is his friend."

"Gian is his way to the top," Edmond corrected with a shrug. "Gian was not making the moves that perhaps Constantino felt he should be after Corrado's murder, and so, I believe he thought to simply *push* Gian in the direction he wanted."

"As in, he didn't mean to kill him, only knock him down for a bit."

"So he would get up swinging." Edmond chuckled. "Frankly, no one knows Gian better than Constantino, if you think about it. Maybe he knew exactly how to push to get what he wanted."

Edmond had a good point, as much as Gian hated to admit it. Constantino had, on more than one occasion, made comments about Gian's habits. Like *always* using his car starter to start his vehicle in the winter, even though it was hard on the engines to do so in the freezing cold weather.

"And if he had fucked up?" Edmond considered out loud. "Well, then I suppose Constantino probably thought of Gian as fodder. He would still get what he wanted, in a way. A war between the younger and older generations that would open up seats all the way across the board."

"What do I do now?" Claud asked. "He's my son."

"He's a made man," Edmond replied just as fast. "And because of that, you'll let him answer as one, no matter who demands their retribution.

That's how made men have always done this—it's how we always will."

Gian shut off the tablet.

He had never agreed more with something Edmond said.

He never would again.

Chapter 17

"Something smells fantastic," Gian said as he came up behind Cara at the stove.

She leaned into his touch, grinning when his kiss landed softly on the pulse point of her throat. His hand rubbed her back as he peered over her shoulder.

"What are you making?"

"A steak and potato mess," Cara replied, "fit for a king."

"I don't think you've ever cooked for me."

"You always order in."

"Not always, but it is faster."

Cara rolled her eyes. "*You've* never cooked for me."

"I'll rectify that soon."

"Can you even cook, or will you grab a bunch of takeout and set it up on dishes to make it look good?"

Gian swept her hair further behind her ear and nipped playfully on the lobe. "How little you think of me, pretty girl."

Cara tried damn hard to hide her shiver, and failed miserably. "So you *can* cook?"

"I have a French mother who had an Italian mother and a *very* Italian grandmother from my father's side. Yes, I can cook. I learned with bruised knuckles from my grandmama's favorite wooden spoon. My mother, on the other hand, preferred the French dishes, and I found those easier to make, really."

"Why was that?"

"Different teaching methods," Gian said with a chuckle. "Of course, the only reason they thought to teach my brother and I to cook was because my sister absolutely refused to do anything in the kitchen, and they needed to pass something on."

"Ah. Well, then you owe me something Italian *and* French."

"I will see what I can do."

"I'll hold you to it," Cara said sweetly.

She went back to attending her steaks, slathering them in a special homemade sauce that very few people had the recipe to. She preferred to cook her steaks in the oven, rather than on a frying pan. The meat always came out a bit more tender.

Gian moved around her in his penthouse, grabbing items out of the fridge and setting them up on the counter for Cara when she asked. He also pulled out a beer, popping the top off and taking a hearty swig from the amber-colored bottle. Just the way he stared at her, told Cara something was on his mind.

What, exactly, she didn't know.

She could just *see* it.

Their ruined date a few nights earlier had mostly been brushed under the rug. Cara hadn't seen her cousin since, and she didn't plan to seek the asshole out. Gian, on the other hand, kept Cara closer than ever since that evening and the morning after. In fact, he'd packed a bag for her to bring to his penthouse, and he hadn't let her leave since, only for school.

Cara didn't mind, really.

She liked being there with him.

"Everything okay?" Cara asked.

Gian shrugged. "It could be better, but I'll get there."

"Do tell."

"It's not for you to worry about, *bella*. Just nonsense making noise in my head, like it sometimes does. It'll all go away soon."

"If you're sure …"

"Positive." Gian took another drink from his beer as Cara slipped the casserole dish, filled with the marinated steaks, into the oven. "I do have a question for you, though."

"Oh?"

"What do you want in the future?"

Cara straightened quickly as she closed the oven, and leaned against the warm metal to regard Gian as she spoke. "For what?"

"Us, I guess."

"I want you," Cara said simply.

"That's a broad statement, though. I meant … the details, Cara. Of life, you know. The little things. What do you want with me in all of that?"

"What's brought this on?"

Gian smirked in that way of his. "I told you once that if you asked me for something more, I would try my very best to give it to you. I've done that so far, but now I wonder what you want beyond what we have, that's all."

"I want *you*," she repeated firmer.

"Yeah, but—"

"Everything, Gian. I want everything with you."

"Everything," he echoed.

"I mean, yeah. As it comes, you know."

"With me."

"Who the hell else?"

Gian gave her one of his usual smiles, leaned forward, and pressed a kiss to her forehead. "All right, then. That's all I needed to hear."

"And nothing's wrong?"

"No, I needed to hear that. From you."

It was one of the strangest interactions of Cara's life, certainly the oddest she'd ever had with Gian, but who was she to question the things that roamed around in his mind? Sometimes, he was so quiet, she wondered what his mind must be like.

"I have some shit to do, so give me a shout when the food is ready, okay?"

Cara nodded. "Sure."

Something was definitely wrong, she decided as Gian walked away.

She still didn't call him on it.

"Gian?" Cara rapped her knuckles on the opened office door and peered in to find Gian still had his head bent down as he looked over something on his laptop. "Supper is ready."

"Can it wait for a minute?"

"It's set out on the table, but it'll be warm for a bit."

"Good. Come here for a second."

Cara stepped into the office, taking a seat on the couch closest to the window. "What's up?"

"I bought you a ticket. It's for tomorrow afternoon. To Chicago's O'Hare."

She wasn't sure she heard him right.

"I beg your pardon?"

Gian looked over at her, his expression blank as he redelivered the news. "You're going to have to leave for a while. I need you to go, for your own safety, as things are not good here on my end of things. Chicago is the best place to send you, considering everything."

"No."

"Cara—"

She stood fast from the couch. "Absolutely *not*, Gian."

"It doesn't matter how much you argue with me about this, and I know you're going to try, *mon ange*, but it's already been done. The ticket is bought. You'll be in a first-class seat tomorrow afternoon, on your way to Chicago."

"Like hell."

"I already talked to your brother as well. He knows when to expect you. He'll be there to pick you up."

Cara didn't care, and she was no longer listening. "I'm not going *anywhere*."

Gian sighed. "Is that how you want to do this then?"

"I want to stay with you, Gian!"

"If I didn't have to send you away, if I could choose any other option but this one, I would do that, Cara. I can't. This is the only option that completely takes you out of the equation. That way, I can focus on the things I need to for a short while. The faster I get you into a safe zone, the quicker I can get you back *with* me. Don't you understand that?"

"I said—"

Gian held up a single hand, quieting Cara instantly. "It is for your best interests."

"Fuck you."

He barely reacted to her stinging insult. Even *she* was surprised at the venom that her tone held.

"Are you angry that I'm sending you away, or because of *where* I'm sending you, Cara?" he asked.

She refused to give him an answer. Instead, she headed out of the office, going back the way she had come from the kitchen. Gian's footsteps echoed behind hers, albeit slower than her anger induced speed.

"Don't run away from me," Gian called out from behind her.

"Go to hell, Gian."

"Stop swearing at me, Cara."

"Not likely."

She held back from calling him an asshole, but barely.

"Is this what you're going to do, then?" Gian asked, as Cara strolled into the kitchen. "Fucking run because I did something you don't like?"

"I'm not—"

"You *always* run when shit goes south, Cara."

Fuck him again.

She made her way to the plate she had made for herself, and sat down at the table to eat. Gian stood at the other end, in front of his own plate, with his arms crossed as he stared her down.

"What are you doing?" he asked.

"Not running, clearly. I made food. I want to fucking eat it, if you don't mind."

Gian's jaw clenched. "And then what? Because Chicago is non-negotiable, Cara."

She ignored him, grabbing a steak knife to cut into the slab of meat on her plate.

"You're going to be on that flight tomorrow," he said when she stayed quiet.

"Will you shut the fuck up and eat?"

Gian yanked the chair out from the table with more force than was necessary. The two of them ate like that, both irritated and angry with the other, silent and stewing in their frustrations. Cara barely looked at Gian, and she could *feel* his damn eyes burning into her.

She hated that he had been right. She understood shit was bad in Toronto right now for him and the Guzzi family as a whole. He had been going non-stop for days, on the phone, out of the penthouse, and then back at odd hours. She overheard some of his phone calls, though she knew better than to eavesdrop.

Shit was going down.

Or it was about to be going that way *fast*.

Gian was trying to prepare as best he could for it.

Cara was likely one of those things, but he was *so fucking right*. It was not that he was sending her away, but where he was sending her away to. It was Chicago, and all the hell and pain that was about to accompany her on a long trip down a memory lane she didn't want to walk through.

Certainly not alone, anyhow.

And fuck him for knowing it would hurt her, and doing it anyway.

Fuck him for that.

It was only after they had finished the food, after she had cleared the table, that the yelling really got started between them. She had never fought with Gian, certainly not with raised voices and something to actually shout about. Not for something she was truly angry with him over.

This was not the same.

It was the first time Cara yelled in a long fucking time.

She raged.

She was *pissed*.

Gian let her.

She had the distinct feeling he did that because regardless of how much she screamed, fought, swore at him, and said no, she was still going.

And it was going to hurt.

A lot.

Chapter 18

Gian closed his laptop the second he heard familiar mumblings coming from down the hall. Cara sounded less annoyed than she had the night before. He took a phone call as he listened to the soft patter of feet down the hall, followed by the click of a closing door. The bathroom, likely.

By the time he was done with his call, Cara stood in the office doorway. She hadn't bothered to put any clothes on; she still wore that frilly, delicate lace that she'd gone to bed in. And that was only the panties, not the bra. She had simply tossed his dress shirt on—unbuttoned—which did very fucking little to cover her breasts.

Never mind what it did for his cock.

Bathed in morning light from the wide office windows. Sleepy-eyed. Mussed hair. Peeks of her soft, smooth skin, from the valley of her tits all the way down to the lace of her panties, demanded his attention. Her lips had turned a faded, stained red from the lipstick she had been wearing the night before.

Gian was sure his maid was sick and tired of trying to clean red lipstick stains out of his white sheets.

Fuck.

He wished he cared.

Cara leaned in the doorway. "Morning."

"You seem more pleasant today," Gian said.

"I was pleasant last night."

"After you yelled at me and then ignored me for hours."

Gian had never imagined a time would come in his life when he found himself controlled by the ways of a woman. At least, he hadn't expected that control to come *because* he loved her.

Cara had no idea of her control over him.

She probably thought Gian pulled the strings.

How wrong she was ...

"I know you're not happy about Chicago, Cara."

"It ... seems like a bit much," Cara said. "Like an overreaction, maybe.

I could go anywhere, but that's where you think I should go."

"Your brother is there. You have family to look after you until I think it's safe to ask you back. It won't be for long. It's only a precaution, *bella*. Sending you to a safe house is one thing, but sending you out of the country is even better."

"Safe." She scoffed. "You do realize that the last time I was in Chicago, I buried Lea."

"Yes, but—"

"Because someone *killed* her."

Gian nodded, knowing this was one of Cara's hot-button issues. "I'm aware, but shit is different down there now. Calmer, even. Your brother recently took over as the new boss. It might do you some good to settle a few things while you're down there. And by settle, I mean stuff in your heart—the things that keep causing you pain. Your father died, you didn't go to his funeral. Your mother killed herself not too long ago and you didn't go back for that, either. And even if not for them, then for Lea. You miss her all the time. You say it enough, like you left her behind."

Cara glanced away at that statement. "I hate Chicago."

"You hate how it makes you feel, *mon ange*. That isn't the same thing. Time to face that head-on, and bury it for good."

"Easy for you to say." She blew a stray curl out of her face. "I'm not going to put up more fight about Chicago."

"No?"

"I tried that yesterday."

Gian smirked. "And it didn't work."

"Seems not."

"It won't be for long, like I said." Gian checked his watch. "And you have three hours before you have to be at the airport."

"Breakfast, then? I can cook or we can order in."

Gian took the sight of Cara in again, drinking in her show of skin, the curves of her hips, and her delicate lines. Every inch of her was a giant tease to him. A wonderland to explore, and to use to satisfy the darkest urges beating through his mind and body. Those damn urges only increased whenever she was nearby.

"They won't serve what I'm interested in," he said with a grin.

"Oh, my God. You are insatiable."

Gian shrugged.

This wasn't news.

"Insatiable would imply that I don't give you a break. In case you forgot, you slept alone in my bed last night. *Unfucked*, Cara."

Her cheeks pinked. "Yes, well—"

"By *my* choice, too," Gian interjected quickly.

"I'm surprised you didn't jump at the chance for angry sex,

considering the way you go on in bed all the time."

He cocked a brow. "Angry sex is unhealthy. Like anything that's unhealthy, it's usually too enjoyable for its own good. Before you know it, you're causing fights, just to fuck and get that feeling back. Not interested, *bella mia*. We have enough to argue about, without adding nonsense like that in, too. Sorry."

Cara's blue eyes twinkled with her surprise. "That was not a response I expected."

"I'm full of surprises."

Gian crooked a finger at Cara as he leaned back in his large office chair. She didn't question his motives. She walked right over to his side with one of her sly smiles, anticipation burning brightly in her gaze.

Once she was close enough for him to reach out and grab her, Gian did just that. Cara sprawled into his lap, cradled in his arms. Her legs hung over the arm of the chair. The button-down shirt of his that she was wearing had spread open more, exposing the swell of her breasts.

Gian couldn't help but run the tips of his fingers over the peaks of her already-taut nipples. Then, he gave them a pinch, making Cara gasp and arch her back higher, closer to his hands again for more.

Cara gave him a stern stare that only make him chuckle. "How do you live with yourself?"

"Like you," he said, "I've learned to love it."

"You're terribly—"

"Cocky. I know."

"You could at least let me say it."

"You're not saying anything that I don't already know."

"Smartass."

"Yours, though," Gian murmured through a grin.

She preened in that happy, pleased way of hers.

"You always say the right things."

"I do, don't I?" he asked.

"And then you ruin it just as fast," she said with a shake of her head.

"Let me make up for it."

Cara peered up at him through her thick lashes. "And how do you plan to do that?"

"Orgasms. Morning orgasms."

"Well, then."

"They make up for everything, Cara."

"Yours certainly do," she agreed.

"And you wonder why I have a fucking complex, *amore*."

Cara shrugged. "More orgasms, less talking."

"But you like it when I talk and fuck you."

"Yes, but at the same time, Gian."

Fair enough.

"Get those fucking legs open, so I can get to what's mine, Cara," he demanded low.

With a sweet little sigh, she did as he wanted, widening her legs over the arm of the chair. His gaze roamed over the shape of her hips, to the line of the panties keeping her pussy covered with a scrap of lace.

"I love it when you make it easy on me."

Cara's grin turned sinful. "Sometimes, you like to take it, too."

He agreed, but his attention was elsewhere now.

He had a goal.

Get Cara off.

Do it again.

And then fuck her until his brain wasn't such a mess.

Good plan, Gian told himself.

Hopefully, it would be enough to sedate him until he got his stubborn, sexy girl back, but he doubted it. Cara was an obsession for Gian. From the way she talked, to the way she walked. All her smiles, and when she grew quiet. How she felt under his hands and beneath his control. Her desires and fears.

Their *what ifs.*

All of it.

Every single bit.

Gian was so fucking obsessed.

"Will you be my good girl this morning?" He traced the shape of her lips with his fingertips. Cara kissed the digits before sucking the tips into her teasing mouth. "Can you be patient, or will you turn greedy again?"

Cara released his fingers from between her lips to say, "I thought you liked your greedy slut, Gian?"

He grabbed a handful of hair at the back of her head and pulled her up for a bruising kiss. He enjoyed when she melted into the demands of his kiss, but he liked it even better when she fought for control.

Even if she always lost.

Gian pulled away, letting Cara fall back into his lap. "You know I do, but I like it when you listen and behave, too."

"I can listen—I *will.*"

"And?"

"And I'll be your good girl, Gian."

"That's all I ask."

Cara licked her lips, squirming under the feel of his hand slipping beneath her panties. Gian's fingers skimmed over the small, trimmed patch of soft hair to get to the heaven between Cara's legs. Her thighs opened wider as he found her hot little clit—something else that was damn greedy, when it came to her body. He wanted her cunt wet, tight, and needy when he filled it with his cock, so he worked her clit until she shuddered and moaned her way through her first release.

All the while, she stayed as still as possible on his lap, never demanding more, and simply taking what he offered. He'd stroked her hair while he teased her clit, and watched the blues of her eyes deepen in color when the bliss raged.

Cara let out a slow stream of air as she calmed in his lap. "I'd demand you give me another, but ..."

"But?"

"Good girls don't demand anything, do they?"

Gian smirked. "No, they say please and thank you, and patiently wait for more."

"This is a lot of work, Gian."

"I always reward you."

"*Thank you.*"

"Good. Now ..." As he'd spoken, he'd been running his fingers with firm strokes over the entrance of her cunt, feeling the heat and juices of her arousal smearing to his digits. "I want you to take off my tie."

Cara radiated curiosity and anticipation as she reached for his throat with careful hands. She loosened and then pulled his tie free. Gian worked her pussy with two fingers, pumping deep and curling into her G-spot with every thrust. He could feel the shake in her legs, hear the way her breath caught, and he knew then that her second orgasm was coming on fast. Cara continued her task until the tie was limp in her hands.

Pleased that she had focused on his demand instead of getting off first, he sped up the rhythm of his fingers until she was crying out with another orgasm.

Cara's back lifted in a beautiful arch. "Oh, my God, Gian." His tie had gotten twisted in her clenching hands. "You know I love you, don't you?"

He chuckled. "Yes, but tell me again."

"I love you, Gian."

Gian pulled Cara into a proper sitting position on his lap. He gave her a kiss—softer and slower than before. "Of course, you love me like this."

"And when you're not like this, too," she promised.

He wondered how long that would last, though.

"Your tie," Cara said softly, offering the item between them like a gift.

"Thank you." The silk slid into his hand, and he shot Cara one of his wicked grins. "Don't panic too much when I take away your sight and make you feel for a bit."

Cara tapped his cheek gently with a shaky hand. "I never panic with you."

Gian took that as her permission.

She barely moved an inch as he blindfolded her with the tie, although her hands gripped tighter around his forearms. He unwound her fingers from his body, and placed them in her lap.

"Be good," he said in her ear.

Gian took a moment to admire Cara like she was—blindfolded, sitting pretty in his lap, and so trusting.

"Hold still," he warned, when Cara squirmed.

He could see her questions getting ready to fall from her lips, but he didn't give her the chance to ask them. Quickly, he lifted them both from the chair, and sat Cara on the edge of his desk. He moved whatever items out of the way that he didn't want knocked over or broken because of what was coming next.

"Tell me how you feel," Gian said as he pulled his own shirt off and dropped his slacks.

"Hot," Cara answered instantly.

"What else?"

He pulled the length of his cock from the confines of his boxer-briefs, and fisted his shaft with firm strokes from the base to the tip. His heartbeat pulsed against his palm.

"Greedy," Cara admitted with a pretty pout.

Gian kissed her lips for that admission. "Good, that's how I wanted you, *mon ange*. My greedy, good girl." He placed her palms to his chest. "Hands on me—it's time to feel for a while. Don't hold back, Cara. I want your cunt squeezing my dick until I can't breathe, and your screams need to be loud enough that I will hear them tomorrow. Understand?"

She nodded, her wild red curls bobbing along with the motion.

"*Perfetto.*"

And he didn't just mean her compliance.

"You might hear the camera on my phone," he said, wanting her to know so that she could refuse. She never did.

"Please fuck me, now."

"Definitely greedy."

"*Very.*"

He dragged his hands over her curves, taking in each soft breath, shiver, and goosebumps that came after his touch. Her responsiveness was his drug. The way she let him love her, use her, *fuck* her, was addicting. She barely moved an inch—only lifted a little—as he dragged her panties down and let them fall to the floor.

"Just feel," he reminded her as he slid the head of his cock through her sex. Her arousal soaked the tip when he flexed forward enough to open her up and let her know that he was a moment away from filling her full. "Don't you fucking move, now."

Cara bit her bottom lip hard. "But—"

"*Cara.*"

She quieted instantly.

Gian left only the head of his cock seated inside the tight heat of Cara's cunt, feeling her sex contracting around him over and over. He reached for his phone. He caught the video of his dick sliding all the way in, the way her thighs widened and her body let him stretch her full. He got the sight of his cock pulling back out, soaked with her cum, and how his shaft throbbed in time with his heartbeat. He lifted the phone enough to catch his thumb sliding over Cara's plump lips and then his hand curving around her throat.

"*Please*," she whispered.

That was all he could take before he tossed the fucking phone to the side, his control gone again. He palmed Cara's ass roughly as he slammed his cock back into her cunt again. There was nothing quite like the contractions of her pussy, flexing around his length, while her fingernails scored hot lines across his chest, and her sweet sounds echoed in his office. He couldn't seem to fuck her fast enough—or hard enough—to satisfy the need beating in his chest. He never could, because as soon as he was done, he knew he would only want more.

Cara's heels dug into his lower back as he pushed her down on the desk, slammed his mouth against hers, and fucked them into a mindless oblivion. Her cunt was so tight that she felt like a hot glove made just for him.

It was only after she had come again, that he pulled his tie from her eyes, and let the pressure building in his spine take over. Her body looked best, spent and sweaty on his desk, his cum spattered up her stomach, and his cock pulsing against her inner thigh.

Then again, she always looked damn good.

It was only hours later, when Gian walked Cara to the waiting car outside of his penthouse, that he finally allowed himself to think of something other than her. He thought about the coming days.

"Message me when you land, Cara."

She kissed his cheek with a smile. "Yes, Gian."

"I'm serious."

"I will."

"I will fly down to Chicago to spank your ass, if you don't."

She grinned. "Don't tempt me now."

Always testing him.

Gian gave Cara a quick kiss and helped her into the waiting car. "It's going to be a busy week, so if I don't pick up your calls, try not to worry. It's just business."

"Got it. I love you."

"*Ti amo*, Cara."

Closing the car door was the last thing Gian wanted to do, but he did it. He watched the vehicle pull out onto the street. It was only when he couldn't see the car anymore, that he turned and headed back for his building.

At the front door, Chris waited. The enforcer said nothing as he followed Gian inside. Once they were in the elevator, Chris turned to him, his expression blank.

"Are you ready for what comes next, boss?"

Gian readjusted his tie. "For duty, always. For the rest … we'll see."

The rest would have to come first.

And then duty would be waiting, too.

Gian answered the buzzing phone, and continued stirring his stir-fry. *"Ciao, bonjour."*

"Constantino is on his way up, boss."

"Thank you, Chris."

"Call me if you need me, or when it's done."

Gian agreed, hung up, and went back to cooking his food. Usually, he was too busy to cook, but when he found the time, it was a relaxing process. God knew that he needed to be relaxed today.

Gian lowered the heat on the stove, covered the food, and headed for the elevator entrance of the penthouse when he heard the familiar ding signaling a visitor was headed up. He tossed a dishcloth over his shoulder, using the ends to wipe his hands off as he went to greet Constantino.

His most trusted friend.

Or … that's what Gian had once believed. He now knew that to Constantino—no matter the man's intentions—those words meant nothing. All it had taken was a box, a few careful conversations, and a series of sad realizations, for Gian to understand those words also meant nothing to him as well.

Affection would never cloud his judgement again.

Not after today.

He was not willing to play the blind fool to any man, even if it was to his benefit.

Constantino was half way down the entrance hallway when Gian met up with him. The man wore a big smile, and clapped Gian on the shoulder in greeting as he jokingly looked him over.

It had taken Gian making a phone call to Constantino that included

187

him saying *he* had overreacted, apologizing for hitting his friend, and promising it was all water under the bridge, to get the man at the penthouse. *But* that was all it'd taken, because like Gian in the past, Constantino was predictable where his best friend was concerned, and he didn't want to fight or be on bad terms with Gian.

Gian had only needed to mention Edmond as well, and Constantino was hooked, line and sinker.

It was stupid of him to be, yes.

That was what blind affection did to a man.

"Jeans, shirt, no shoes, *and* a dish towel. Are you playing homemaker today, or what, man?"

Gian laughed, and headed back toward the kitchen while Constantino followed behind. "Taking a break today, that's all."

Constantino sniffed the air. "And cooking, apparently."

"Someone needs to feed me."

"So hire someone."

"It clears my head." Gian gestured at the many chairs around the table. "Take a seat and we'll chat."

Constantino took a seat that faced the kitchen, allowing Gian the chance to watch the man as he finished his stir-fry. He would never turn his back on this man again.

The sad thing was, he hadn't even needed to turn his back the first time. Constantino had simply stabbed Gian in the chest when he wasn't looking. And when Gian did finally notice and asked what happened? Constantino pointed the finger at someone else.

Like any good coward would do.

"Where's the girl?" Constantino asked.

"She has a name. You know it." Gian opened the pan and stirred the contents up. "Cara—use her name."

"Are you still pissed about what I said at the restaurant? I apologized for that, and I only spoke the truth. Like *you* should be doing, man."

He had apologized when Gian called. Although, it had taken some careful prompting on Gian's part to make it seem as though he felt he overreacted that night.

"It's the point of the matter, Constantino."

"Fine. *Cara.* Where is Cara? The other night when you called, you didn't want me coming over because she was here."

Gian checked the clock. "She's probably watching that show she likes. It would be on at this time in Chicago."

Constantino perked. "Chicago?"

"Flew in yesterday."

"She did that herself?"

Gian chose not to answer. He certainly wasn't about to say that *he* had sent Cara away, and raise Constantino's suspicions. He wanted the man thinking that nothing was wrong, like water under the bridge.

Much like the idiot had fooled him.

"That's where she is, anyway," Gian said, pulling the pan from the stove. "I don't know when she'll be back."

That wasn't entirely a lie, either.

Gian didn't know when he would send for Cara. After he had finished business, the smoke had cleared, and it was safe. A week, maybe two. He couldn't let his need to have Cara close cloud his judgement about what was best.

"Better she go," Constantino said.

Gian pulled plates from the cupboard. "Pardon?"

"Cara. It's better she left. She fucks with the way you do things—how you see shit—but you don't seem to notice."

Gian refused to let Constantino push on that nerve. "Maybe she does."

"You know she does."

"Hungry?"

"I could eat," Constantino said.

Gian prepped two plates of food, keeping an eye on the other man at the same time. Constantino seemed entirely unbothered and calm, sitting there, as though he didn't have a thing to worry about.

"I suppose you don't, huh?" Gian asked as he delivered the plate of food.

Gian then took a seat directly across from his old friend.

"Don't what, man?"

"Worry," Gian clarified.

Constantino shrugged, shoving a bite of food into his mouth. "It's a waste of time to worry."

"That, or you feel … privileged. Safe in your spot because of me."

Constantino's brow furrowed. "Is something wrong?"

Gian shook his head. "Should there be?"

"Not that I know of."

"Then, no."

"All right." Constantino went back to his food as though nothing was wrong. Just as Gian expected he would.

"Have you ever heard of blind affection?"

"When a person lets their personal feelings get in the way of what should be obvious?" Constantino asked.

"Exactly that."

"I could see why some people might struggle with it."

"Me, too," Gian agreed.

"So, you said when you called that you're finally ready to finish this out with the boss, then?"

"And more." Gian smirked. "Never call Edmond the boss in my presence again."

Constantino offered an apologetic smile. "My bad."

The man didn't seem to notice that Gian had yet to touch his own plate of food.

"But, that was what you said," Constantino pressed.

"And more," Gian echoed. "Do you want a beer?"

"Sure."

Gian left the table, and grabbed two beers from the fridge. He sat one down at his spot before moving around the table to hand Constantino's bottle over, but he didn't move to return to his seat again.

"I'm not the only one between us that suffers from blind affection," Gian said quietly. "Because if you didn't suffer from it, too, you would have known better than to ever trust me after you betrayed me. All lies come out eventually."

Constantino's head snapped up, his wide—understanding—eyes flying to Gian. It was already too late. Gian hadn't removed the dishtowel from his shoulder until then, and he'd quickly twisted it into a rope of sorts. He had the rope wrapped around his friend's throat before Constantino could even attempt to fight back.

Gian pulled the makeshift rope tight, his emotions bleeding away as a blissful numbness took its place. Constantino fought back against the hold, clawing at Gian's arms and hands, trying to topple over his chair, and even kicking at the table. The plates and bottles jumped with every hit and kick. Gian still held strong.

"I'm not sure if you killed my grandfather for yourself, or because you knew what would happen after his death. I don't know if you meant to put yourself in a higher position because of me, but you clearly intended to use me for something."

Constantino's struggle continued, but Gian paid it no mind. His fighting would end forever soon enough.

"I put it together after Edmond sent me a box with info about the bomb set on my car and who put it there—you. You were stupid enough to try to play *his* side, too, just in case you needed to. I saw the pictures of you heading to Edmond's place, going in and out on all days of the week, when you were trying to get *me* to act against him. That was your mistake. He's a snake, too, like you. And if he thought *I* might get rid of a problem with you, then he was willing to take the risk of telling me."

Gian sighed. "And I thought, *why*. Why would you do that to me, and what else would you do? What else had you done? You knew—despite how fucking ignorant you've been lately—that I would never look to you, Constantino, because you were my friend. And I trusted you. You took advantage of an already-volatile situation, and pushed us all over the edge, because you knew that no matter what, *I* would keep my friend on top."

He pulled the rope tighter still, feeling the man's fight finally begin to leave. "You taught me a lesson that Corrado never did. A lesson he *couldn't* teach me. You have to be ready to kill absolutely anyone that stands at your side, because no one can be trusted."

Gian still didn't feel anything when Constantino's body finally fell limp. He undid the rope, let the corpse fall forward, and then he covered the man's head with the unraveled dish towel.

"Fuck you for being the one to teach me that lesson."

He returned to his seat, popped open his beer, and ate his food.

Life went on.

It always did.

"Last chance to back out," Chris said as Gian handed his gun over.

Outside the restaurant, the street was quiet. As though it—and the shops lining the streets—knew what was about to happen, and that it was better to be out of sight, safely hidden away.

"Why would I back out?" Gian asked.

The enforcer made a show of taking Gian's jacket off, showing to whoever was watching inside the restaurant that he had no hidden weapons to bring to the meeting.

Chris handed Gian's jacket back. "I didn't think you would, I simply said the option is there."

"Would you?"

"No."

"Why?"

"Legacy," Chris said frankly. "The respect of it all."

"Some might think that this is the ultimate *dis*respect," Gian pointed out.

"Those people will never and could never make the choice you are making today."

And that, at the end of it all, was exactly why Gian was doing what he was doing.

"Some men are made for this," Chris added, "and some aren't. Which one are you?"

"I'm tired of my ability being questioned."

"Then good luck, boss. I will be waiting out here when it's over."

Gian gave the man a nod. "Don't miss, Chris."

"I never do."

Gian waited as the enforcer crossed the street, and jumped into his vehicle. Then, he turned and entered the restaurant. This was the most dangerous part, he knew. Simply entering the place with no backup, no protection. It was a hostile environment, and he could easily become a target.

Inside, Gian was surprised to find the place mostly devoid of people. No patrons sat at tables, and no employees served the few men sitting at tables.

"Gian." Edmond stood from his seat at a center table, facing the windows. *Lucky.* "I'm pleased to see you show up today."

Gian crossed the space, ignoring the looks of the men waiting to see what he would do. Only a couple were men that Edmond had asked to come along, others were ones Gian told to be there because of the boss's request. Apparently, Edmond thought having a few men witness their meeting would be better than a larger group.

Let word travel, Edmond had said.

Standing toe to toe with the man, Gian finally spoke. "I took care of the problem on my end, the one you let me know about."

Edmond nodded, seeming pleased. "And come to your senses at the same time about the rest of this fighting and nonsense, I assume?"

No, not really.

He *had* decided enough was enough, though.

"Grudges tend to kill a lot of people in this business," Gian said with a shrug of his shoulders. "I need to learn to let bygones be bygones."

"Good, good."

Then, Edmond held out his hand, the one with a ring that was all too familiar to Gian. It had belonged to his grandfather for years, and while Corrado should have been buried with it, someone had removed it from his home before it could be collected for the funeral home. Constantino might have been the one to pull the trigger where Corrado's death was concerned, but Edmond had not been an honorable man in his intentions after the fact.

Gian could never, and would never, forget that.

He would not forget a shooting intended to *keep him in line* that nearly killed Cara, either.

Things like those were unforgiveable.

The *bygones.*

"Well?" Edmond asked, still holding his hand out for Gian to take. "Are we going to settle this like proper made men and move on as your grandfather would have wanted us to do, Gian?"

The man intended for Gian to bend down, and kiss his ring. Had it been his grandfather, Gian would have done it without question. Because it was Edmond, the significance made him hesitate.

Still, he bent down, grabbing Edmond's hand and bringing it close to his mouth. Gian didn't kiss the ring, though, he simply held it there for a moment.

"You have no idea what Corrado would have wanted," Gian murmured low enough for only Edmond to hear. "But I certainly do."

Gian dropped Edmond's hand, without having kissed the ring, as glass shattered. He straightened to his full height, getting the brief chance to stare Edmond in the eyes for only a second before the man's body began to sway.

A perfect sniper shot had hit Edmond square between his eyes. Blood trickled down from the wound. Death already stared back from his eyes.

This was appropriate, considering ...

Gian let the body fall as one of the men inside the restaurant shouted, a panicked realization starting to take over about what had just happened. He paid the men no mind as he bent down and removed his grandfather's ring from Edmond's slack, lifeless hand, only to slide it down his own finger.

Standing once more, Gian turned to face the men with a smile. Shocked faces stared back at him, unmoving and frozen in time.

Chris was one hell of a shot.

Word would *certainly* be traveling now.

"I'll answer to Don or Boss, only, and anything else will cost you a body part of your choice," Gian said quietly. "Now, I need someone to move this body."

Chapter 19

Cara missed her bed—or better yet, Gian's—the moment she opened her eyes and looked around. The unfamiliar bedroom staring back at her wasn't necessarily off-putting. The big bed, earthy tones, and soft bedding were comforting enough, as far as that went. But it wasn't home.

Her body knew it instantly.

She'd already been back in Chicago for a week, and no matter how many times she woke up in the guest bedroom of the Trentini mansion, it was still startling. It only reinforced her desire to go back to Toronto; the need to be home in familiar spaces thrummed deep.

It was only Gian's demand that she stay away until he called her back—when it would be safe again—that kept her from booking a ticket.

Well, that, and her brother.

Tommas was not letting her go, either. Each time Cara brought up her desire to return home sooner than she was allowed to, her brother was quick to shut that idea down. Things were happening, he would say. She was better, and safer, right where she was for now.

Cara knew better than to argue with difficult, stubborn men. Or rather, she knew which battles to pick.

This was not one.

Cara rolled over in the king-sized bed, ignoring how empty it felt to sleep in such a large space with no one else to help fill it up or keep her company. She had been alone for so long, happy to find occasional fun with a man, but perfectly fine to send him packing before morning even arrived. She couldn't quite say the same, now.

It was only a *week*. The loneliness growing in her heart should not have been taking up so much fucking space, like a weed getting out of control.

Love made things difficult.

Complicated, even.

Cara thought it was kind of lovely, too.

She missed Gian.

Terribly.

Cara found her charging phone on the nightstand, and brought it closer, squinting through tired eyes to see if she had missed any calls or messages throughout the night. There was nothing, and that only hurt a little more. She *had* talked to Gian a few times over the week, but it was never long enough. Their conversations never had enough substance. She couldn't see his face to tell if he was simply hiding something to make her less worried, or if there really was nothing she should be concerned about.

She knew the truth.

Gian wouldn't have sent her away if he didn't absolutely have to. Of course, something was wrong. Of course, he kept their conversations short and the depth of them at a shallow level, in order to ward off Cara's anxiety.

She didn't quite know how to tell him that it really wasn't working. She was still lonely and worried. She still wanted to go home, regardless of what was waiting there—good or bad.

Still, she stayed put.

Cara rubbed a hand over her face, wavering on whether or not to call Gian's phone. It was early to be calling—seven her time, which meant it was eight in Toronto. Gian ran on his own time, though, which happened to be like a well-oiled machine. Up before six, breakfast and a workout, and then out the door before nine, if he could help it. He ran on the same schedule like it was his default. It didn't matter if Cara was with him or not, his internal alarms rarely changed.

She scrolled through her contacts, found Gian's, and hit the green phone button beside his name. The call rang and rang, four times, then five and six. On the seventh, his answering recording picked up, and she ended the call before it even beeped.

Something wasn't right.

He *should* have picked up.

Cara tried to push the worries aside, knowing it could be a million other things, too. Like a late night which had him sleeping in, though that had never been a thing before. Or an early meeting with whomever, which caused him to silence his phone. The second option was more likely, so that was what Cara chose to accept.

For now.

Even knowing that Gian would see the missed call and realize Cara had called him, it wasn't quite enough for her. Maybe the man *did* have her a little fucked up in the head and heart. A bit too crazy about him, and them, even after she had told herself not to go that far with someone like Gian Guzzi. He was everything she wasn't supposed to like—not his business, his arrogant, overly confident attitude, or his life. None of it was supposed to attract Cara like the dumb moth to the pretty flame, and yet, he had.

He was the first damn thing on her mind in the morning.

The last thing to cross it at night.

She kind of wanted him to know that.

He does like his pictures …

Cara grinned at her inner voice, got the camera set up on the phone, and held it out far enough to get a shot of her in the sheets, with the morning light coming in through the window behind her. The stark, white light contrasted against her body, but not quite enough to hide the fact that she had been sleeping in very little, just black boy shorts. Her hair was a curly mess, framing her face wildly, with no makeup to be seen.

It actually wasn't too bad.

It was usually Gian taking the pictures, teasing her while he did so, but constantly going back through the images whenever he got the chance. She had gotten more than one text from him with an image or short video clip of her that were nothing short of *porn*. She knew when he was doing it during their encounters, as he always told her, and she never minded enough to tell him not to.

A shot of her on her knees, with his cock in her mouth. A three second video clip of his cock filling her pussy full. Each one—new or old— was like a snapshot of memories for Cara that suddenly came back in a rushing wave. She was positive that was exactly Gian's point in randomly sending the pictures or videos for her to see.

It turned her on like nothing else. It was filthy, like his mouth and everything else about him. He managed to make her body hot in a crowded room, and he could be across the fucking *city* while he was doing it.

No one knew a thing.

She did.

That was enough.

Cara sent off the image in a text before she could think better of it. And then, not wanting to sit and stare at her phone until she finally got a response, she forced herself out of bed and toward the attached bathroom.

Gian would answer.

Eventually.

Cara's phone finally buzzed with an incoming text as she neared the dining room of the Trentini mansion. She nearly checked what the text said—likely a message from Gian, as no one else bothered to text her anymore—but stopped at the hushed, yet sharp, voices coming from within the dining room. Her brother, and his fiancée.

"Have you even *asked* her?" Abriella demanded.

A loud sigh followed right after. "No."

"Why the hell—"

"Because *why*, Ella," Tommas replied harshly, not even posing it as a question. "Why is it any of my goddamn business what she does, or with whom, for that matter? Why does that matter; why should it matter? It doesn't. It never should have mattered to anybody but you and me, when it was us and our business, and it doesn't matter with her and ... whoever the fuck she chooses to run around with. She's twenty-five, a grown ass woman. Look me in the face right now and tell me to put constraints on her, *only* because it might look bad on the rest of us. Is that what you want me to do, to be, like the rest of them?"

Cara knew right then and there that they were talking about her, and likely Gian, but she didn't have the first clue as to why. She decided to stay where she was, and see what else she could learn before she made her presence known to the couple.

"I-I ..." Abriella made a frustrated sound under her breath before spitting out, "You know that's not what I mean! You're always throwing that at me like that's my default, Tommas. And you know it's not."

"It's sounding that way, Ella."

"It's *not*," Abriella stressed, "but does she know, Tommy? Does she understand what it means to be in the position she is? That's all I wondered. And stupid me, I thought you would have—at the very least—asked her about it."

"It's been a long fucking time since I've seen my sister, and the last time was when I put her on a plane after she barely made it through a wedding she was supposed to be in with Lea. She was a mess, Ella. A complete *mess*. She's okay right now. I don't know if that's because of him, or something else, but she is perfectly fine. I'm not going to upset that by poking around in her personal business."

"But what if she doesn't know, Tommas?"

"Know what?"

"About *him*," Abriella said, exasperated. "I've said some stuff since she's been here, just to see, you know, and it goes right over her head. It's like she doesn't know anything about him, in that regard."

"She can't *not* know."

"Really, Tommy? Because it's entirely possible, given what we know about her. She doesn't take an active role in your aunt and uncle's business, she stays out of sight of the family for good reason, and she's never had any sort of interest in being in that spotlight. She has no real reason to know. I think she might not, and *that's* why you should ask, even if it's to ... be sure."

"Abriella."

"It's not for me or you, it's for her. Don't you get that? She could be jumping head first into a deep pile of shit and not even know that's what it is, Tommas. That's not fair to her. You ask, or I will."

Tommas grumbled something under his breath that sounded a hell of a lot like, "You're awfully pushy this morning. Aren't you supposed to be picking out colors and fabrics for the wedding? Why are you bitching at me before ten? We should have an agreement about this sort of thing, Ella."

"Stop trying to be cute."

"I'm not."

"You are."

Figuring she had gotten all of their conversation that she would, Cara decided to make her presence known. She walked into the kitchen as another message buzzed on her phone. Both her brother and his fiancée, looked up at her arrival.

"Cara," Tommas said.

"Morning," Abriella said at the same time.

Cara's attention was down on her phone.

Gian had zero chill, but she knew this already.

Send another, his message demanded, *but next time, lose the panties, open your legs, and get your fingers wet for me.*

Cara swore her face was burning as she attempted to stuff the phone into her pocket, foolishly thinking that would save her any embarrassment. She was going to pretend like she didn't know her fucking cheeks matched the color of her hair.

"Something going on?" Abriella asked, a sly grin covering her pretty features.

Cara waved it off. "Nothing, so hey …" Distraction was her best friend, she decided. "Were you two talking about me just now?"

Tommas passed Abriella a look that she ignored, instead turning to grab a cup from the sink and choosing to not answer Cara's question.

Cara looked to her brother. "You were, right?"

"How would you feel about taking a drive today?" Tommas asked.

What was it with men, thinking they could change the subject of any conversation if they didn't want to talk about what was brought up?

"I was thinking we could head over to the cemetery," Tommas said when Cara didn't immediately reply.

Cara stiffened. "To see Mom and Dad, or …?"

"Lea, actually."

"Lea," Cara echoed.

"Do you not want to?"

Cara felt the old stab of pain in her chest at the thought of visiting her twin's grave, but she couldn't bear to say no. It had been too long, and in some ways, Cara had managed to put her grief aside while Gian had swept into her life like a hurricane.

Maybe she owed it to her sister.

Maybe she owed it to herself.

"Yeah, all right," Cara finally agreed.

She almost forgot about her brother changing the subject, but decided right then, it wasn't all that important, anyway.

Cara bent down to clean the shiny marble of the gravestone, stopping for a second to admire her sister's name in heavy font, chiseled into the very center of the stone below angel wings. She traced every letter with her thumb, surprised to find that the ache in her chest didn't get worse the longer she stood there.

Lea's funeral and burial had been so difficult for Cara. She barely remembered the day, but that was mostly because she had been drugged up on a mixture of antidepressants, sleeping pills, and anxiety meds. She wouldn't have gotten through it otherwise.

"It stopped for a bit—the world, I mean," Cara said to the headstone, "but it started turning again after a while. I wasn't ready for it to."

Cara went back to wiping off the stone, though she really didn't need to. Someone had been caring for the grave beyond the groundskeeper's job of mowing the grass or clearing the snow, depending on the time of year. The stone was clean of debris or dust, and fresh flowers rested along the bottom and on the top of the headstone.

She set the bouquet of tiger lilies—Lea's favorite flower—along the bottom with the rest. "You could have told me about what you were doing, Lea. I mean, I get why you didn't tell me about Frankie, but you *could* have."

"Who is Frankie?"

Cara stood from the grave, brushing off the bottom of her jeans as she faced Tommas. Her brother had been standing back on the path, far enough away that she didn't think he would overhear her conversation with her dead twin, but apparently, he had moved closer.

"You shouldn't spy," she told Tommas.

He shrugged. "Believe it or not, but spying has saved my ass more times than I care to count."

"Not this time."

"So you won't tell me who Frankie is?"

Cara pursed her lips, deciding there was no harm in giving the bare bones of the details. "Someone Lea was involved with. I didn't know about it until a while ago."

"Ah."

She turned back to the grave, pulling a string of rosary beads from her jacket pocket. They had belonged to Lea, before her death, but her sister had left the rosary behind in Toronto on that fateful trip to Chicago.

Cara wanted to return them, as it was only one thing, but it was something she could let go of. She had been able to make a quick trip to her apartment before leaving Toronto to pack a bag, and had grabbed the rosary last minute. She hung the string of beads around the stone, letting the ivory cross hang over her sister's name.

"The grave is well kept," Cara said, wanting to fill the silence.

"I come a couple of times a month to say hello, and replace the flowers."

"Do you think she hears you?"

"Do *you*?" Tommas asked right back.

Cara blinked away the tears threatening to fall. "We're the same, her and me. Even our DNA is identical, Tommas. It's like that time when we were five, and I fell off the swings at the park while she was home. I broke my wrist, and she screamed and held hers the whole way from the house to the park to find me; everyone thought she was crazy. Of course, she hears me. She's always been inside of me, listening. I was the one who wasn't talking for the longest time."

"I think there's a difference between her and you, now."

"Oh?"

"She's not alive, anymore, Cara. You are. What was cannot now *be*."

She still felt like she was living for two some days.

Sometimes, it helped.

Other times, she thought she was failing somehow.

"I still wish they had cremated her," Cara admitted. "Then I could have taken a piece of her with me."

Tommas frowned. "I think you've taken quite a lot of her with you, if you think about it."

Maybe.

Cara didn't know.

"Are you going to tell me what that whole discussion was between you and Abriella this morning?" Cara asked, keeping her back turned to her brother. "I listened to the whole thing, by the way."

Tommas snorted. "I figured you did."

"That's not an answer."

"I have another question instead, Cara."

She pivoted to face him. "Shoot."

"Are you happy?"

Cara didn't even have to think about it, not for long. "I wasn't. I was living in a black hole all the time, and I couldn't escape from it. I felt like I was drowning nonstop."

"And then you weren't," Tommas supplied.

"I guess not."

"Would that happen to be because of *someone?*"

"Do you mean Gian Guzzi?"

Tommas smiled a little. "Yeah, that's who I mean."

"I think he helped," Cara admitted, "but I think he made it possible for me to drag myself out of that black hole, too. And maybe that's the more important part."

Her brother nodded. "Then that's all that matters. It's all I need to know. The rest is details, and I've never cared for those."

Neither had Cara.

"Come sit, go through these albums with me," Abriella said from the couch, as Cara walked into the living room. "I'm sick and tired of doing wedding things, and I need a break."

From her position, Cara could see some of the albums *were* weddings.

"That kind of defeats the purpose, doesn't it?"

Abriella shrugged. "It's not mine, so not exactly."

Who was Cara to argue with the bride-to-be? She joined Abriella on the couch, curious about where Tommas was. After he had brought her back from the cemetery, he had disappeared upstairs. He hadn't come back down since.

"Maybe not this one," Abriella muttered, tossing an unopened photo album aside.

"What was that one?"

"Damian and Lily's wedding."

Oh.

The wedding that Lea was supposed to be in with Cara, but had died before she could attend. Cara did not need physical proof of how messed up she had probably looked that day, not the reminders of how it had made her feel to plaster on a smile and get shit done when she had been two seconds away from taking her own life. She opted not to open the album.

"Will you come for the wedding?" Abriella asked. "I know Tommy really wants you there."

Cara smiled. "I'll try. No promises. I have a co-op set up with a woman's shelter to do work in the summer, too, and I won't be able to take time off when it's required hours."

"Is it really that bad to be here?"

"Not as bad as I thought it would be. But it's not always easy, either."

Abriella frowned and looked away. "I get that. I guess if it was Alessa, I wouldn't want all the reminders, either."

"It's not the reminders," Cara said quietly. "It's what *isn't* here. Lea isn't here, not like she is at home. And as much as it sometimes suffocates me, I would rather her be everywhere than nowhere."

"Huh."

Cara cleared her throat, willing away the sudden emotions lodging there. "It's hard to explain."

"No, I think you did pretty well there, actually."

Cara knew all too well that Abriella Trentini was not unaccustomed to loss. In a few short months, she had lost her grandfather, both of her parents, and her brother. All that she had left now for her close family was her surviving sister. And Tommas, she had him, too.

The pain may not have been the same, but it was familiar enough. It surely stung and ached and ate away at Abriella in her quiet moments, much like it did for Cara in hers.

She didn't doubt that.

"All right, enough of this," Abriella said, blinking away the wetness gathering in her eyes. "No tears, or Tommas has a fit. Let's look at some pictures, huh?"

"Sounds good."

Although, Cara would much rather get Gian on the phone and figure out when exactly she could go back home.

She settled on the pictures, instead.

Cara found that the albums actually weren't too bad. Most were older family photos of the Trentinis, their vacations, and the kids as they'd grown up. There were other albums of weddings from other families, Christening of babies, and more. There were even some memories that Cara had forgotten, things that had brought all the Outfit families together.

It surprised her to see herself and Lea in a few of the albums, sitting off to the side in a corner, people watching as they sometimes had done together as young teens.

"Canada Vacation and Wedding," Abriella read from the front of the next album.

Cara wasn't really paying attention at that point, as she was focused on the album in her hand, and the few photos of her and Lea that were hidden inside.

She only looked away from the photos when Abriella said, "Guzzi Wedding—Gian and Elena."

"What?"

Abriella was already flipping pages, moving past decorated halls, silk-lined tables, and an ornate cake. Cara saw a familiar man in a suit standing with his father, and his younger brother. One of his mother, too, putting his boutonniere on.

No.

Cara couldn't trust what her own eyes were seeing.

She didn't believe it.

Abriella flipped the page again.

The woman was beautiful, and her white dress, modest at the top, yet covered in satin, tulle, and jewels, made her look like a proper princess.

A *Mafioso principessa*, actually.

Cara did a double take, not recognizing the woman with her perfectly done makeup and her upswept blonde hair. The ice in her brown gaze as she stared at the camera with a learned smile said she wasn't exactly happy, but her posture spoke of elegance and grace, regardless of her emotions.

Gian and Elena, Abriella had said.

Was that the woman's name?

Elena?

"When was that?" Cara asked.

Abriella turned the page, showcasing new photos, with Gian standing next to the very obvious *bride*. Both wore rings, as that too had been photographed, their hands laying one on top of the other.

"Abriella, when was that wedding?" Cara demanded, ripping the album from her.

"Whoa, relax."

Cara flipped through more photos, progressively getting more irritated as she went. "*When?*"

"Three years ago. I flew in with my grandfather. Joel came, too. The invitation was basically for everyone, but only a couple of us went. Pretty common for *famiglia* weddings."

Cara couldn't breathe.

"He was married."

It didn't even come out as a question.

Abriella cleared her throat loudly. "Is, Cara."

What?

Her inner question must have been as clear as day on her face, because Abriella shrugged and added, "Men in a position like Gian Guzzi—an heir to a Cosa Nostra family, a good Italian and Catholic, a *Mafioso*, do not get divorced. There is *no* acceptable divorce. He *is* married, Cara."

It was that moment when her brother finally decided to make his presence known again, walking into the living room as though he didn't know Cara's whole world had been tipped upside down. This was what Tommas and Abriella had been discussing, she realized. *This* was what they knew, and that she hadn't.

Cara felt dumb.

So fucking stupid.

Flashes of memories filled her mind, statements by people that she had let fly over her head, or reactions people had made when Gian took her out publically.

He had a wife.

That meant Cara ...

She was his mistress.

A *goomah*.

Whore.

"What's wrong?" Tommas asked, his gaze shooting from Cara to Abriella. "What happened?"

Abriella didn't look all too concerned. "We were going through some albums and—"

Tommas was at Cara's side before she had blinked, grabbing the album from her, only to see the last photo she had been looking at. One of Gian, and this *Elena* woman, kissing on an altar. Likely their first kiss, Cara didn't know.

She didn't care.

"Why would you do that?" Tommas asked Abriella.

"He's married," Cara said faintly.

Abriella stood from the couch, stoic and stone cold. "She deserved to know. I let her figure it out."

"*Abriella.*"

She was already walking away.

Cara wished she could be angry.

She was, but not at Abriella.

Not even at her brother.

"Tommas, he's *married*," Cara said.

How had she not known?

Tommas looked down at her, wariness filling his eyes. "I don't know much about it, just that he is, and that's all."

"I'm going home."

"I don't—"

"I'm going *home*."

It wasn't for her brother to decide.

Not on this.

Chapter 20

"Do we know who showed up?" Gian asked.

Dom looked to Stephan for an answer.

"All of them," Stephan said, the cigarette on his lips bouncing with every word.

While Gian despised Stephan for a great many reasons—including the man's attitude and ways—he had to admit that the Capo was honest and honorable when it came down to business. After carefully going through every man Gian could find, he was surprised to find out Stephan had no hand in Constantino's plots.

Given how fucking hard it was to find trustworthy people lately, Gian chose to allow Stephan into his very small circle. At least, for the time being. He didn't have to particularly like the guy, he only had to trust him.

Gian found his brother watching him, doing that damn thing that Dom always did whenever he was uneasy about a situation, and needed a steady, yet invisible support to walk him through. He didn't blame Dom for being that way at twenty-five. Shit, years ago, *Gian* had been the stupid kid, wading into the mafia with unrealistic expectations, needing guidance just the same.

He had looked to his grandfather. Who else fit the bill with his last name? Domenic only had Gian to look to, now.

"*Ça va?*" Gian asked Dom in French.

Dom shrugged one shoulder. "*Je vais bien*, Gian."

He didn't look fine.

Apparently, his attempt at using French to probe his brother's inner emotions without embarrassing him was not lost on Stephan.

"He's got to learn this shit and how to deal with it somehow," Stephan muttered, walking forward and leaving the brothers behind. "Treat him like a fragile *figa* that needs special handling, and he'll never be more than a walking, talking pussy, boss."

Dom glared at the Capo's back. "I don't like him."

Gian blew out a breath. Now or never, he supposed. Dom wanted to be *in*, he wanted his button, he wanted the title of a made man. He needed to understand what all of that meant, too.

Gian slapped his brother on the back and said, "You don't have to like him; you do have to respect him. Especially now."

"Yeah, *cazzo*."

Fuck was right.

"Let's get this over with," Gian said.

Like any good made man would do, Stephan waited for Gian to catch up with him at the entrance of the old pizzeria. Gian was careful to hold the heavy duty garbage bags out at his side, lest any residual fluids leak onto his leather shoes. Stephan held the door open, allowing Gian to go in first, but making Dom hold the door for himself before he, too, could enter.

Dom was lower on the totem pole, and so the actions of those around him would reflect his status until he earned a better title or position. Even if it was something as simple as not holding the door open for him.

It was all about the respect in Cosa Nostra.

A man had to show it long before he was ever given it.

"Look who finally showed his goddamn face," came a call from within the pizzeria as Gian strolled inside.

Gian ignored the older Capo's half-taunting tone, but only because for the moment, the man didn't know the position he was in, compared to his younger counterpart. The older generation of made men in the Guzzi family would always have some left-over feelings after this was all said and done, Gian was sure of it, but he hadn't been given much of a choice.

At the end of the day, it was *Guzzi* for a reason.

He was not willing—no matter his age, his lesser years compared to other men, or anything else he might lack—to allow his family's name to dim in the Cosa Nostra world. His grandfather would never have handed off the boss's seat, nor his status and respect, to anyone who didn't share his last name.

Gian wouldn't do it, either.

He passed a look around the old pizzeria, taking in the many faces of men he recognized, some he'd grown up alongside, others whose feet he had chased under for years. He understood far too well that his actions would have consequences, but he sincerely hoped these men didn't make it harder on him than it needed to be.

He would hate to have to kill people he considered family and friends.

He would do it, of course.

He simply wouldn't like it.

"Where's Edmond?"

"Yeah, where's the boss?" another Capo asked.

A few men shifted in their seats, ignoring the gazes of the Capos who had asked after the boss. Or rather, who they *thought* was still the boss.

Gian had figured that word would have traveled by now throughout the ranks of the family, considering how many men had witnessed him murder and take the boss's seat from Edmond. It certainly would have made part of this whole shit show easier.

No matter.

It seemed only a couple were out of the loop.

They would know soon enough.

Stephan and Dom stayed standing directly behind Gian, ready and willing to keep any man from leaving, if the need arose. Neither of them spoke as Gian tossed the extra large, heavy duty garbage bag to the checkered tiled floor a few feet in front of him.

All eyes went to the bag.

Gian didn't make a move to acknowledge it, or even to open it.

"Seems we have a lot of problems in this family lately," he said, still looking from man to man and never skipping a single one. "Seems we can't get along like proper made men."

They needed to know—all of them—that what had happened over the last several months, and the blood that had spilled throughout their streets, were all caused by their own hands. It didn't matter if they had been the ones to pull the triggers. Their culture of avoid, evade, and ignore was enough to make them guilty in Gian's eyes. Beyond that, the lines that had been drawn between the older generation and the younger made men, had not simply popped up all on its own. It was a divide that had come from unhappiness on one side, and entitlement on the other.

"*You* did this," Gian said, loud enough for each and every man to hear.

He was not going to repeat himself after today.

A boss didn't have to.

Not if he spoke properly the first time.

"Whether you looked away when things happened, or you personally held one of the weapons that took away members of this *famiglia*, you all did this," Gian said with a shake of his head. "And you never considered who would be left cleaning up the mess."

Gian pulled a pocketknife from his slacks, and bent down to slice a hole through the top of the garbage bag at his feet. Carefully, he grabbed the corner of the bag with the tips of his fingers, and used the toe of his shoe to kick it over.

The contents didn't even empty completely from the black bag before the men in the pizzeria reacted to what they were seeing.

Chairs scraped.

Shouts echoed.

He was sure he heard someone gag, too.

It wasn't a pleasant sight—bits and pieces of bodies spilling out of a garbage bag. A hand, a few fingers, a leg from the knee down, a bit of teeth, some congealed blood and gelatinous fluid, along with two battered heads.

As loud as the men's reactions had been, their silence came on as strongly, and just as quickly, as they took in the faces of the severed heads resting on the restaurant floor.

Edmond Portella, their former boss.

Constantino Rossi, a fellow Capo.

"One from each side," Gian said, drawing in the attention of the room again. He ran his fingers through his hair, knowing good and damn well, each man would be focused in on his actions, and therefore, would not miss his grandfather's ring in its rightful place. *On his fucking hand.*

Gian waved at the random pieces of corpses at his feet. "One from each side, you see? A traitor—my friend," he murmured, referring to Constantino. Then, he gestured to Edmond's head, its mouth opened grotesquely, the nose shattered. "And another traitor—my mentor. They both thought that they could manipulate me to get them, or their agenda, where they wanted it to go. This is our family because of that."

He smirked a little, adding, "None of you considered who would be the man to clean up the mess at the end of the day. Make sure each and every one of you takes a piece of this *mess* with you when you go, and dispose of it properly. You each had a hand in creating it, after all, so take equal part in cleaning it, too."

It took a second.

Then, two.

That beat of silence didn't worry Gian. He expected shock. He was *going* for shock. His men answered exactly as he expected them to.

"*Sì*, boss."

And …

"Yes, Don."

"Are you going to do it, give your brother what he wants?"

Gian stared out the window of the town car, trying to decide how to properly answer his father's question. There was no right or wrong way to answer. There was only the truth to give, and his father would not be pleased with it.

"Well?" Frederic asked pointedly.

"It's what he wants."

"He's twenty-five! He doesn't *know* what he wants, Gian!"

His father's sudden burst of anger wasn't shocking to Gian, he'd expected it. Maybe, in a way, he even felt like he deserved it, too.

"I knew what I wanted at twenty-five, and even younger than that. I always wanted to be a made man, Dad."

"Did you *really*?"

"Of course."

"He promised me," his father said quieter. "Your grandfather promised me, Gian."

Gian finally turned away from the passing streets to look at his father. "What?"

"He had two sons. He chose the older brother, not me, to bring into this life. I didn't mind—I didn't *want* it, anyway. And then my brother died, but I was already older, married, and had my own children."

He didn't like where this was going.

"You think you chose this?" Frederic demanded harshly, leaning forward in his seat, closer to Gian. A fire burned in his eyes as he stared down his oldest son. "Is that truly what you believe? You have to remember all those holidays and vacations that you would go on with your grandfather, while Dom was left behind. You have to remember all the extra gifts you were given, and the attention Corrado gave to only *you*."

Gian held his tongue, but barely.

"I don't blame you for holding him on a pedestal, Gian, because I wasn't allowed to let you see anything different than what he wanted you to see. And you loved him so much. *Mio Dio,* look how much you loved him! Right to his death, into his grave, my boy. But don't be foolish. Don't be a stupid man, still seeing things through a child's gaze. You're too old, and far too intelligent, for that now."

"I see things exactly as they are," Gian replied quietly.

"You were the bargaining chip," his father said, that bitterness never wavering. "You were the one I gave up, to spare the others. Your brother, your sister. He wouldn't bother with them in this life, when he didn't need to. He had you, like he had my brother all those years ago, and that was enough to carry on the name, Gian. He promised me—do *not* make your brother a made man."

Gian wanted to deny the things his father said, but in all honestly, he couldn't. His life had been privileged, both by the wealth of his family, and the status of his grandfather. It was *only* because of the affection his grandfather had given to him, that respect in his life came far easier than it did for the others. Corrado's attentions had always focused more on Gian. Sure, he had brushed it off as a younger man, but he was not dumb enough to pretend that his grandfather's actions had no intent behind them.

Actions always had intent.

It still didn't change a thing.

"It's Dom's choice," Gian told his father.

It would hurt him, Gian knew.

His father would be mad for a while.

It changed nothing.

"To refuse now, after everything," Gian murmured, "would mean to kill him."

It was the way of Cosa Nostra. Once a man had made his intentions clear with *la famiglia* to join their ranks and ways, there was no going back. There was no restart button, only a bullet and a grave, for those who could not follow through.

Frederic's frown grew deeper. "And what if it kills him anyway?"

Gian had a better question. "Did you consider that for me, Dad, all those years ago, when you were made to make a choice between Dom and I?"

His father didn't answer.

The silence was enough.

Gian had been the bargaining chip.

Frederic had made the sacrifice.

"And what about you, now?" his father asked gently.

Gian's brow furrowed. "What about me? I'm the boss. I did what I needed to do. I'm *fine*."

"You forget what that position means, son. Your image is now on display, and your weaknesses will become your biggest targets. This may have seemed easy standing on the outside looking in, but it becomes far harder to manage once you sit in the seat, and the only things keeping you worthy to be there for those men are your reputation, your image, and your actions. So far, you've not been doing well in that regard."

Gian's jaw ached from clenching so fiercely. "Say what you mean. Don't dance around it with pretty words."

"You know what I mean. Or rather, *who* I mean."

Cara.

Gian nodded to the doorman as the older gentleman opened the door to the building. "*Merci*, Benjamin."

"Have a good evening, Mr. Guzzi," the doorman replied as Gian walked through.

He had just entered the private elevator that would take him up to his penthouse when the cell phone in his pocket began to buzz with an incoming call. Gian almost considered not answering it, and letting it go to voicemail. After the day he had, a hot shower, food, his bed, and a phone call to get Cara back home in Toronto—at his side—sounded *perfetto*.

She wanted to come back, and he wanted nothing more than to bring her back.

Unfortunately, being a boss meant when phone calls came in, issues usually followed.

That phone call to Cara would have to wait.

Gian picked up the call on the fourth ring, his usual Italian and French greeting at the ready. "*Ciao, bonjour*."

"I have Cara booked for a flight in the morning—she'll be in Toronto by noon."

Tommas Rossi didn't fuck around with pleasantries, it seemed.

"I didn't call to ask her back, yet," Gian said, "but I was ready to do that tonight."

"You don't want to do that, Gian. Call her, I mean. Not right now."

Gian's shoulders tensed as the elevator dinged, and the doors opened to allow him entrance into the penthouse. White walls and gray marble stared back at him, but he wasn't quite ready to leave the elevator.

"She texted me this morning. She can't be that pissed off at me that I haven't called her today, can she?"

Cara was not that kind of woman. She wasn't spectacularly jealous, and she didn't demand every breathing, waking moment of Gian's days. Though if she were one of those women, and she did want those things, he would give them to her.

All of them.

Love was so messed up in that way.

He'd never understood it before.

"Listen, I tried," Tommas muttered. "She wasn't willing to stay here another minute. Seriously, don't call her tonight. Give her the evening and morning to work through some of her mood, and maybe it won't be as bad tomorrow when you see her."

"I don't understand," Gian admitted.

"She knows your secret, asshole."

Gian's hand tightened around the phone. "What?"

Shit.

No.

Gian knew he should have been the one to tell Cara about his estranged wife, a marriage that had taken place under a set of circumstances driven by his grandfather and his wife's father. He had not loved her, and even now, had very little to do with Elena.

That had always been by her choice.

Gian no longer cared.

"You heard me." Tommas sighed heavily into the phone. "She deserved to know—from *you*, though, not like this."

"I was going to—"

"*When?*"

"Soon," Gian admitted.

"Not soon enough."

Tommas hung up the phone without a goodbye.

Gian didn't blame the man a bit.

"Who is she? What's the whore's name, Gian?"

Ouch.

That one kind of stung.

Especially, to hear it as an insult to Cara, when this woman—his *wife*—had no business throwing that sort of word around at anyone, given their history.

Gian wasn't able to hide the rage. "Watch your fucking mouth, Elena."

His estranged wife stiffened across the room, her arms crossing over her chest as she frowned. "You could at least tell me something, Gian."

"Why should I?" he asked quietly. "Have I asked you about your lovers? Have I ever expected you to sit back and wait for me, when you clearly didn't want to?"

Elena glanced away. "You don't know anything about—"

"I know *enough*," Gian said, hurling the words at her. "I know we haven't lived in the same space together for two years. We haven't *fucked* in three! I know why you agreed to the marriage, because you were scared and you were young. You needed to get away from your father, and you thought to use me to do it."

Gian scrubbed a hand down his face, ready to be done with the entire conversation. He hadn't wanted to be there, sharing a conversation with Elena at all, but he didn't have much of a choice. She was, whether he liked it or not, his wife. And in their world, in Cosa Nostra, that meant something *important*.

"I gave you that, I let you lie to me, because I was trying to please my grandfather, too," Gian admitted, his anger rising to the surface all over again. "But the moment you didn't have to pretend anymore, you stopped. I've never asked you for anything—never demanded you act like my wife, unless it's absolutely needed. I've never shared your bed without you wanting me there, and when you couldn't stand to have me in the same room without throwing something at the back of my fucking head, I left! I've never asked you for more than what this has always been, Elena."

A defiant glimmer lit up her eyes as she stared him down. "You've never been so blatant with a whore before, either."

He'd never hit a woman.

Never had the urge to hurt one.

Until this goddamn moment.

Gian shoved his clenched fists into his pockets, determined to stay on the other side of the room from his wife. Elena was good at these games— too good, really. She was known for her manipulations, something she had picked up from her bastard of a father, and she used them on Gian without blinking a lash about it. He had no doubt that was exactly what she was trying to do here. If she pissed him off enough to react, then it would be to her favor, and not his, when someone came to ask for his behavior toward his wife, and he would need to answer appropriately.

"You say that," Gian murmured, "like you've known for a while that I've been seeing someone on more than a casual basis, Elena."

He saw the tightening of her jaw.

It was her one tell for when she lied.

"And?" she asked.

"If you had such a problem with it, why not call me, or send someone over, write a fucking email, or whatever. Why *today*, of all days, is it that you have the problem with this? We're not together, we don't even fuck when we do have to pretend for an evening, and I am more than happy with letting you drain my bank accounts, as long as you're content on your side of the city. Why call me and demand answers from me *now*?"

Elena tipped her chin up, looking away again. "You made me look like a fool, Gian."

"Excuse me?"

"You had her all over the city, taking her out, dressing her up, and playing pretend with your people and even some of your family. You made me look like a goddamn fool. Does she know about me, when I didn't even know about her?"

"Now she does," Gian said, offering little else in that regard.

He would deal with Cara when she arrived that afternoon.

It was none of Elena's damned business.

"The least you could have done was give me the benefit of *knowing*," Elena spat at him, that fire returning to her gaze before she had even blinked. "You couldn't even do that. My mother called, which means my father knows, too."

"I had no reason to tell you. Beyond the fact we're not even together, we haven't spoken in ten months, and the last time we did talk, it was for you to tell me to get your fucking credit card fixed because it expired and the new card didn't come to your address. I *know* you were asked to the funeral for my grandfather, and you didn't even show face for that, as a wife should do. I didn't *care*. I have never cared. We're not together. We haven't been together in—"

"Then fucking give me a divorce!"

Gian stilled on the spot, letting each one of those words stab into his skin like little daggers, tearing him apart, piece by piece.

How simple her demand was.

How much he wanted to agree.

He *should*.

He needed to.

They would both be happier, they could both put the years of shit behind them to rest, and move on to better things—better *people*.

It wasn't that easy.

"I can't," Gian said quietly.

Dio, he wished that didn't have to be his answer.

Elena let out a sound that came off broken and frustrated, all at the same time. She threw her hands high, and glared at him as she said, "I don't want to hear that anymore, not now!"

"You come from the same world as I do. You know there's no other acceptable answer. Divorce doesn't exist to made men, or their wives. It never has, it never will, and we won't be the exception. I won't give up my life as a sacrifice, simply because three years ago, you tricked me into marrying you."

"I didn't *trick* you."

"Then what would you call it?" he roared back. "What would you call the things you did and how you lied to me?"

Elena's eyes watered, but that sight didn't affect Gian like it once had. "You knew what he was like to me, the things he did to me. Don't pretend like I had a choice, Gian."

He believed that, but very little else that came from his wife's mouth.

"So be it, but here we are, because of it," Gian replied. "I have an image to maintain, rules that need to be followed, the agreement to uphold between our families, and we can continue on like we have been for the past three years—"

"You mean where it's fine and great for you to fuck any whore that glances your way, but I have to sit pretty and quiet in the corner, not bringing you any shame, right?"

"Cara is the first and only woman I have ever been in a relationship with beyond sex, not that it's any of your fucking business. And you *know* that, or you should, considering this is the first time you've ever brought it to my attention that you knew I was involved with another woman. I have always been careful as far as other women were concerned, for your sake, Elena, not mine. My status demands I remain married to the woman I spoke my vows to—'til death do us part—but it says *fuck all* about remaining faithful to you. But I would have, had you given a single shit about me. And don't pretend that you've ever held fidelity in high esteem, where I was concerned. What was his name, the last one, Matteo?"

Elena barely blinked. "Cara, that's *her* name?"

Gian cleared his throat. "You want me to confirm it, but I think you already know exactly who she is. I've never said anything to you about who you've been seen out with, or the things I know you have done. I have only asked that you be mindful of your affairs because of your father, certainly not for *me*. As long as you're careful about whoever you—"

"Go to hell, Gian."

He barked out a laugh. "Surprise, sweetheart, I've already been living in hell for years. It started with you, and I have a feeling that isn't about to change anytime soon."

He hated her for that, too.

Much like she hated him, he knew.

Chapter 21

"Early boarding for flight T1457."

Cara grabbed the carry-on bag at her feet, and readied for the regular boarding call for her flight. Tommas sat in the seat beside hers, yet he didn't speak. Likely because all someone had to do was look at Cara's face, and they would know she wasn't in the mood for any sort of conversation.

Tommas hadn't needed to do more than escort her to the airport, but he took it a step further, went through security, and decided to wait with Cara at her gate. She wanted to be thankful, at least her brother cared on some level, but she really wanted to be alone.

"You're always welcome to come home," Tommas said quietly.

Cara glanced up at the ceiling, and let out a slow breath. "Yeah, I know."

"But I don't think that's in your plans, is it?"

"Probably not."

"Even now, with … Gian and all?"

A flash of irritation settled in Cara's gut, but she pushed it away. It wasn't Tommas' fault that Gian had lied to Cara for months. Beyond that, she knew her brother thought that Cara had already known the truth about Gian and his … *wife*.

"I was getting back into a routine," Cara said, "before all this happened. I was getting better—finally—after losing Lea. I'm not going to push myself back several steps because of one man."

She had said the words so flippantly that anyone would believe them. Shit, even *she* wanted to believe them.

Cara didn't know if they were true.

"Cara."

She was lost in her thoughts, barely present as it was, and didn't hear her brother's call of her name.

Tommas reached out and placed his hand to her arm. "Cara."

"What, Tommas?"

"I'll never tell you what you can and can't do with your life. You know

216

that, right?"

Cara nodded. "You never have."

"And I'm not going to start with this. But I do want to tell you one thing, if you'll hear it."

"Shoot."

Tommas smiled, but it was measured, and not entirely genuine. "Be careful, Cara, especially in this situation. You've always been careful not to step too deep into the piles of shit left by the family, and right now, I'm worried you're knee-deep and don't even realize it."

"I'm not involved in that side of his life, Tommas."

Her brother shook his head. "You may not see it that way, but I can assure you that you are."

"Well, not for much longer."

"Maybe, maybe not. A day ago—before this came up—you said you loved him. That sort of feeling doesn't go away because bad things happen. So, today, you want to skin him alive, but maybe in a week, you won't be so angry, and you might even remember what he was like *before* you knew about his wife. I won't tell you what to do, but you do need to be careful. Whether you like it or not, you've already put yourself into a position where a label is stuck on your relationship. I get that *you* didn't know it was there, but the people around him certainly did. And if you understand what it means to be … that woman—"

Cara scowled. "The other woman. The whore. A *goomah*. Say it, Tommas."

He didn't even flinch at her truth, simply kept staring at her like it didn't change a thing about how he thought of her or saw her in his eyes. "If you understand what it means to be that woman, and you can handle it, then I'll never say a word against your choices and wishes. It is your life— live it how *you* want to, Cara. Live the way that makes you happy with the person who makes you happy. But the very second you find yourself in too deep, and you want to get out, you know where to find me. Okay?"

"*Now beginning regular boarding for flight …*"

Cara stood, slinging her bag over her shoulder.

Tommas stood with her. "Okay, Cara? Say the word, that's all you have to do."

She smiled, or as much as she could manage. "I won't need to after today, but thank you."

"That's easy to say now, sure."

"Tommas—"

"*Okay*, Cara?"

Her brother's expression hadn't changed from the moment he'd started talking. Never once had judgement shone in his eyes. He hadn't shamed her for the things that she had overlooked, or the mess she now found herself in. No, he only cared for her, and her happiness.

Wasn't that what family was supposed to do?

She forgot what that felt like, to be looked out for, and cared about, by someone who shared her last name and blood.

"Cara?" Tommas pressed again.

"Yeah, Tommas. Okay."

He nodded, and then waved a hand toward the gate where other passengers had started lining up to hand over their boarding passes. "Have a good flight, Cara. Call me when you get home and have a minute."

"All right. Thank you, Tommy."

Tommas shrugged. "It's what big brothers do, right? Or, what we're supposed to do."

Yeah, it was.

She had forgotten that little fact.

Customs was not half as bad coming back through Toronto International Airport as they had been when Cara entered through them in Chicago. The customs officer gave her passport a glance, barely opened her carry-on and purse up fully, and sent her on with a smile.

That was one damn thing to be grateful for.

While the flight from Chicago to Toronto wasn't a long one, her emotional turbulence meant that Cara wasn't in a particularly good place. She was exhausted—mentally, and physically. The only thing she wanted to do was get home to her apartment, give her brother the call she promised him, and then lie in her bed for several hours.

She needed sleep.

Cara pushed through customs, and headed toward arrivals where her luggage would be waiting, and a line of taxis outside the exit doors. She had stepped off the escalator when she spotted the guy standing at the very front of a large group of waiting people.

Several held signs with last names scrawled on them, waiting to pick up someone from their arriving flights.

Not this man.

Chris didn't need to.

Wearing all black, his hair smoothed back, and a flat smile plastered on his face, Cara let out a sigh at the sight of Chris.

She had wanted to go home. She'd hoped for a little bit of time before she would need to have an actual face-to-face meeting with Gian. Some breathing room to get her thoughts and feelings in order, so that when she did see him, her raging emotional vomit didn't spill all the way out, making a mess of everything it could reach. Surely, she wasn't asking for a lot.

Apparently, Gian was not going to give Cara that option. Well, he would have nobody to blame but himself when he faced her anger. He could have given her a day or two—anything—to let his lies sink in.

"Miss Rossi?" Chris asked as he came to stand in front of Cara.

She looked him over. "Gian sent you, Chris?"

"*Sì*, miss."

"I suppose if I said that I didn't want to go see Gian, it won't make much of a difference, huh?"

He smirked a bit. "I'm to deliver you to his penthouse, nowhere else. I only follow orders. It would be best if you didn't make a scene. Either way, the penthouse is it."

"Wonderful." Cara crossed her arms.

"I will take you home once you're done with the boss."

The boss.

Cara didn't miss the man's choice of words, in regards to Gian. Was that what had happened while she was gone? Was that what he had sent her away for, so that he could take over the new boss's seat, and get his revenge for his grandfather at the same time?

She wasn't stupid, of course, and she knew how volatile and dangerous things had started to become before Gian sent her away. Incidents that had come far too close to Cara *and* Gian. Still, he never talked *details*. He was always careful, in that sense, and only gave her the barest bones of information. Just enough to tide her over.

For good reason, her mind taunted, *you're not his wife.*

Nothing Gian ever told Cara would be safe.

Not in court.

Goomahs didn't get that sort of closeness with their men.

Whores got nothing.

It only pissed her off even more. Cara had thought she knew everything about Gian that was important, things a man who loved her *should* tell her. Even a man like him, involved in things that put a constant target on his back.

She thought he cared enough.

He clearly hadn't cared at all.

"Your brother called ahead of time and let the boss know what time your flight would be arriving this afternoon."

Cara wanted to be angry at Tommas over that fact, but she couldn't summon up the emotion. All of her anger was being saved for the one person who deserved it the most, and she knew Tommas had only been doing what was expected of him, as he'd allowed Cara to return to Toronto before Gian gave the okay.

"Am I at least allowed to grab some food on the way?"

"The boss has a lunch waiting, if you're hungry," Chris said.

Cara scowled, and walked on past the guy. "Lunch he can choke on."

"You'll be heading up alone from here," her escort said as Cara stepped into the elevator. "The boss said it would be better if no one interrupted you two for the next little while."

Cara turned to face Chris who was holding the elevator door back from closing.

"If I wasn't so pissed off, I would thank you, but ..." She let her unspoken words hang in the air, unsaid. "You know how it goes."

The man nodded once. "Given the circumstances, I understand."

Cara frowned, her embarrassment rising. "Do you know the circumstances?"

"I've known since the day he married his wife. I was invited by his grandfather to attend, since I had kept an eye on Gian for a great many years before that day. I have been around for more things that I care to mention at this moment, and you happened to be one of them."

Ouch.

Just another name to add to her list of people who'd known, while she hadn't.

"You must have thought I was foolish, then."

Chris's expression gave nothing away. "I think you were happy, and you made him happy. So, what business is it of mine, to tell my boss that he shouldn't be happy, when I've watched him simply exist for too long?"

"That's quite a black and white way of looking at it."

"Maybe so."

"Except I have the feeling that neither of us are happy now," Cara said, "and that's his fault, too."

Chris nodded again, stepped back, and let the elevator door close.

Cara grew silent as the elevator began to move upward, and she eyed the security camera in the upper left corner of the tin box, pointed right at her. She wondered if Gian was watching, knowing that the elevator was solely used for entrance and exit from his penthouse, and none of the other suites in the building. Someone had to be watching that camera.

She shot it the middle finger for good measure.

Just in case.

Childish, maybe.

Who cared?

As the elevator came to a slow stop at the top, Cara was surprised to find her inner turmoil had almost calmed completely. She didn't know what to expect from herself—more nerves, perhaps, but definitely well-deserved anger.

None of those feelings came immediately as the door opened.

White walls, a vaulted ceiling, and the huge brass and crystal chandelier caught her eye first. She stared upward, soaking in the familiarity of the penthouse, and remembering how the first time she had seen it, it had damn near taken her breath away. She almost wished that Gian had given her the decency of choosing somewhere else to have this fucking meeting. He had to know how the penthouse would affect her, how the memories would *sting* her.

Cara shook the heavy sensation off her shoulders, and walked further into the penthouse, down the entryway, and toward the main floor of the place. She didn't have to be told to know that's where Gian would be waiting for her. Not close to the elevator, where she could make a quick exit if she needed to, but deeper into the penthouse, where he might have a chance to convince her to stay.

She had news for him.

Cara wouldn't be staying.

Ever.

Gian stood in front of the floor-to-ceiling windows, staring out over the busy city streets as Cara entered the dining room. As Chris had said there would be, a lunch spread was waiting on the large table. It looked as though it hadn't been touched. Cara didn't make a move to go near the food, or Gian as he finally looked over his shoulder to acknowledge her presence.

A wariness settled in his eyes as he looked her over, and his usual grin—that sexy, confident smirk that was always in place—had vanished. He seemed older standing there staring at her, like the weight of the world had come along and sat itself down on his shoulders for the moment. His hair, the longer strands at the top, were messier than normal. A clear sign he had been running his fingers through the dark strands, speaking of his hidden stresses.

"Cara," he murmured.

She still didn't move.

Not when he spoke, or when he turned completely to face her, and certainly not when her heart ached to *go to him*.

She didn't realize how hard this was going to be.

Not being angry, or even knowing what she had to do, but actually *doing it*. Saying this would be final—the end of them, whatever they were. *That* was the hard part.

"I'm sorry," Gian said.

"I wish that made a difference, Gian."

"I know that I should have told you, *dolcezza*, there's no reason why I didn't, except that I was being selfish."

"You're right, you should have told me, and you are selfish." Cara shifted from one foot to the other, restlessness settling into her heart. "Aren't you going to ask how I found out?"

"It doesn't matter, really. You know, and that's the important part."

She was going to tell him anyway.

"Pictures," Cara said quietly, "of your wedding. She looked beautiful, like a proper bride should."

"Can I explain a few things about Elena and the marriage? Her and I, we're not together in that sort of way. We haven't been for years, we don't even speak on a regular basis. Just let me—"

Cara shook her head, cutting him off with a quick, "No."

"Cara, please." He took one step forward, and Cara moved one step back accordingly. "You might understand—or shit, maybe not, but I need you to know why and how this happened, please."

"No, Gian. I don't care, because you didn't care enough to tell me the truth from the start. You've lied to me. Maybe not in your words, but in your omissions, and the things you kept from me. You didn't let me have a choice, you made them for me. You made me look stupid—like your foolish little whore, constantly running back to your bed whenever you snapped your fingers."

He flinched. "That's not what I meant to do, *amore*."

"You didn't have to mean to, your actions did it for you!"

"I'm sorry, Cara."

"Sorry won't fix this, Gian. It's not a fucking time machine."

"I know, I just—" His words cut off as he looked away, his strong jaw working as he chewed over his next words. "I want to explain, but it won't help, will it?"

"No."

Honesty was the best policy.

He should have followed that rule, too.

Gian rubbed a hand over his lower jaw, bringing Cara's attention to the glint of jewelry on his ring finger. Never had she seen him wear the wedding band before, and in that moment, it felt like nothing more than a slap to her face.

He caught her stare, and dropped his hand when he realized that's where she was looking.

"I have to wear it, given how things have changed, for appearances and—"

"Stop," Cara whispered. "You don't have to explain. It's a little late for that, anyway, and I'm not in any position to need an explanation. Not like your wife would need one, you know?"

Pain colored Gian's brown gaze, darkening them briefly.

"That was low," he said.

Cara shrugged. "Sometimes, the truth hurts, Gian. Seems I'm not the only one who needed to learn that lesson, lately."

With that statement, Cara turned on her heel and headed back to the elevator, determined to let those words be her final goodbye. It had said much more than she could. It wasn't a proper goodbye, but it would have to do.

"Cara, wait."

His footsteps echoed behind her, but she kept walking.

The elevator came into view fast, but not fast enough.

Gian grabbed her arm, spinning her back around to face him. "Wait, I said."

Cara glared right back at him, letting her anger swell for the first time since she had entered the penthouse. "Don't manhandle me, Gian. You don't get to order me around, not now."

"Let me speak for five minutes. Let me explain, and then you can do whatever the fuck you want to do."

"What is there to explain?"

"I—"

"Are you married?" she asked.

"It's not that simple."

"Are. You. Married."

"Yes," he admitted.

"For three years."

"And a couple of months."

Cara took a deep breath. "Did you lie to me about it?"

"In a sense, yes, by omission."

"Then nothing else matters."

"It might, if you would let me explain, Cara."

She doubted it.

"Let me go, Gian, I don't belong here. You have a woman who can stand at your side, be in your bed, and whatever else you want, but I'm not her. I am not your wife. And I won't pretend to be, when you want something different for the evening. I won't be a *goomah* for a made man, and I certainly won't be your whore."

Gian released his hold on her arm, but it took a few passing seconds. "I didn't mean for this to happen."

"You should have known it would. All lies unravel, eventually, no matter how good you are at telling them. And you're so good, aren't you? You made sure no one said a single word to me, but they all knew, didn't they?"

"It wasn't like that. They had no reason to speak up, and maybe some even thought you knew. Shit, at first, I thought you might have known."

"Why would I have *known*, Gian? I knew barely anything about you!"

"I know." Gian raised his hands high and wide, as if to offer nothing but air. "I do love you, Cara. You know that's true. You *have* to know that's true."

"Do I? I don't think I know anything about you at all."

Cara blinked, and the tears she had been holding back made lines down her cheeks. She didn't make a move to wipe the wetness away, instead, letting Gian see them, so he knew. She needed him to understand how much he hurt her.

It couldn't be fixed.

He'd done this.

"I've not been in a romantic relationship with my wife from damn near the day we married, though you might not believe it, and I certainly wasn't with her when I was with you. For what it's worth, I have only loved you, ever," Gian said.

"It's not worth very much now."

More tears fell, but she didn't make a sound.

Gian didn't try to stop Cara as she took those last few steps toward the elevator. She wished that she could say it was only relief in her heart as she did what she knew was *right*.

It still hurt like hell. Her heart shattered when she stepped inside. She broke apart as the doors closed.

That was her goodbye.

Gian deserved to see every fucking second of it.

He was the entire reason why.

Every single reason.

Bio

Bethany-Kris is a Canadian author, lover of much, and mother to three very young sons, one cat, and two dogs. A small town in Eastern Canada where she was born and raised is where she has always called home. With her boys under her feet, a snuggling cat, barking dogs, and a spouse calling over his shoulder, she is nearly always writing something ... when she can find the time.

Find Bethany-Kris at:
Her website www.bethanykris.com,
or on Facebook at www.facebook.com/bethanykriswrites,
on her blog at www.bethanykris.blogspot.ca,
or on Twitter - @BethanyKris.

Sign up to Bethany-Kris's New Release Newsletter here:
http://eepurl.com/bf9lzD

Other Books

DeLuca Duet

Waste of Worth: Part One
Worth of Waste: Part Two

Standalone Titles

Inflict

Donati Bloodlines

Thin Lies
Thin Lines
Thin Lives

Filthy Marcellos

Antony
Lucian
Giovanni
Dante
Legacy
The Complete Collection

Seasons of Betrayal

Where the Sun Hides
Where the Snow Falls
Where the Wind Whispers

Gun Moll Trilogy

Gun Moll
Gangster Moll

The Chicago War

Deathless & Divided
Reckless & Ruined
Scarless & Sacred
Breathless & Bloodstained

The Russian Guns

The Arrangement
The Life
The Score
Demyan & Ana
Shattered
The Jersey Vignettes

Find more on Bethany-Kris's website at www.bethanykris.com.

www.ingramcontent.com/pod-product-compliance
Lightning Source LLC
Chambersburg PA
CBHW072354020726
47506CB00004B/1102